ALSO BY C.K. CRIGGER

Western Novels

The Woman Who Built a Bridge

Letter Of The Law

The Winning Hand

Black Crossing

Liar's Trial

The Yeggman's Apprentice

Western Short Stories

Left Behind

Double Deal

Memory of Blood

The Whereabouts of Miss Nellie Thistlewaite

Ask Parrot

Aldy Neal's Ghost

A Deal's A Deal

Other Novels

Lost Girl Lake

HOMETOWN HOMICIDE

C.K. CRIGGER

CITY LIGHTS
PRESS
~ LAS VEGAS ~

Published in the United States by City Lights Press, Las Vegas

City Lights Press
An Imprint of Wolfpack Publishing
6032 Wheat Penny Avenue
Las Vegas, NV 89122

citylightspress.com

Paperback ISBN 978-1-64119-933-9
eBook ISBN 978-1-64119-934-6

Library of Congress Control Number: 2019946346

HOMETOWN HOMICIDE

CHAPTER 1

Frankie McGill, sitting on a straight-backed chair in the Hawkesford Emergency Services building, studied the man and the woman perched near her. As the last job candidate to be interviewed, she'd had plenty of time to conduct an evaluation of the two other finalists. The first was a big guy, bluff and hearty, the other a woman, mid-thirties, self-confident, already looking the station over as if choosing her locker.

Jesselyn Pettigrew, Frankie's best friend since the first grade, had explained when she called about the EMT opening, that there were several other applicants the captain wanted to talk to. But none, she said, with Frankie's experience. And none of them had Frankie's ties to the community. "You're a shoo-in," Jesselyn said.

Watching the others now, Frankie wasn't so certain. The guy had the personality to put the wounded—no, call them the injured—at ease. A little loud and overly friendly maybe, but everything depended on whether Fire Captain Karl Mager and the head paramedic, Lew Carpenter, liked his sort of bonhomie.

As for the woman, she looked like the kind who'd always be willing to stop after work and lift a few while talking over the day. Some men really went for women like that.

Frankie fluffed her short dark hair, making sure it covered the scar on her head, and tried to ignore the headache building behind her eyes. Not now. Please, please, hold off a while longer. Surreptitiously, she pressed a certain spot on her forehead, a treatment the therapist swore would forestall the pain and the flashes of light. Sometimes it helped. More often, it didn't.

The male applicant finished his interview and left, his expression unreadable, at least to her. The woman went into the office, voice a bit overloud as she greeted Karl and Lew. Through the Plexiglas window dividing the office from the rest of the room, Frankie could see the woman talking, her hands waving.

Ten minutes later, she came out again, face flushed, and at last, it was Frankie's turn. At Karl's summons, she rose from the low bench, fighting sudden vertigo. Not now! Her limp almost imperceptible, she greeted the men with a firm handshake.

"Captain Mager," she said, "Mr. Carpenter."

Mager grinned at her. "Since when do you call me captain? You used to call me Karl way back when you were in high school and slinging hash at the café."

"That's before the army taught me to respect my superiors," she said. "I wasn't looking for a job, then, either."

Carpenter snickered into his fist. "That's a good answer, Karl. I like it."

"I do too." Mager's grin faded. "I guess I've only got two questions for you, Frankie. How're you feeling, and are you well enough to undertake a job like this?"

"I'm fine, sir," she assured him. Aside from the foot and the headaches and not being able to sleep most nights. Oh, yeah. Include a few memory problems in the roster. "The VA gave me my medical release, and I'm good to go. Looking forward to putting all that training I got in Afghanistan to work. My credentials are first-rate, and my commanders gave me excellent recommendations."

Mager's thick forefinger tapped a letter lying on his cluttered desk. "I know. Couldn't be better on all counts." He raised an eyebrow at the head paramedic. "How about you, Lew? Anything you want to ask Frankie?"

Carpenter's jaw jutted. "Yeah. I do. I wanta know if you think what happened to you in the war earned you a free pass? Because there isn't anybody here able to take up the slack if you can't or won't do your job. You'll have to prove yourself. We get a head-on out on the highway, bodies dropping left and right, we need somebody ready and willing to carry the load without falling apart. Screw up, and I'll get rid of you."

"No free passes, sir. There never are, in my experience. And I wouldn't have applied if I couldn't handle the pressure." She sat straight, mentally crossing her fingers and meeting his eyes without wavering.

The two men looked at each other, and some invisible signal passed between them. "You want to go back out and sit down for a minute, Frankie?" Mager winked at her. "Lew and I gotta talk this over. We'll be right with you."

Frankie got up. "Yes, sir. Thank you, sir."

Her back as straight as though she were on parade, she left the office, resuming her seat on the hard chair. That had been about the shortest interview on record. She had to answer more—and tougher—questions than that every time she went to the doctor. The interview seemed to have gone well, though, unless it'd been so bad Karl and Lew hadn't wanted to waste more time on her. But, she thought, fingers crossing again, they hadn't asked either of the other two applicants to wait. That must be a good sign.

The old brick building they used for emergency services in this part of Kootenai County was a laid-back place. Her grandmother, who'd been quite the historian in her day, told Frankie once the place had been a blacksmith's shop. Now a series of computer screens occupied the wide dispatch desk where Maggie Owens was on duty, ready to call out cops, fire trucks, or paramedics. People came in, did their business, visited a minute, and left.

As Frankie waited, a farmer trailing dust from his work boots hurried in to ask for a burn permit, and a kid wanted a driver's manual. Maggie efficiently supplied both requests.

A SUV bearing Sheriff's Department markings pulled in, and a man got out. Frankie guessed his age at thirty or so. He had brown hair and hazel eyes, which she saw when he took off his sunglasses as he asked Maggie a question. His gaze settled on Frankie, too, a quick, interested evaluation, and he nodded an acknowledgment.

Frankie flicked him a small smile before glancing away.

She forced herself to relax. From here she could see through the window to where her pickup sat parked under a scrawny elm tree. Banner, her dog, was lying on a patch of grass beside the truck, his pink tongue lolling as he waited for her. A skinny girl who'd emerged from the post office next door and who bore an eerie resemblance to Charlene Lindstrom, Frankie's old boss at the café Karl had spoken of, stopped to talk to the big Samoyed and scratch behind his pricked ears.

Nerves stretched tight, the scar on the back of Frankie's head began itching. She really needed this job. The Spokane or Coeur d'Alene fire departments would never accept her if she couldn't pass the physical. Which she probably couldn't. A small, rural outfit like Hawkesford, population 567 according to the sign outside town, was about the only hope she had. Oh, it wasn't a lack of qualifications holding her back. Those were good. Great, in fact. An army veteran with battlefield experience? Most places would be clamoring for her services—until they found out she had a plate in her head, shrapnel in her back, and was missing part of her right foot.

A commotion outside claimed her attention. The guys had left the door wide open to catch what was left of the morning's cool breeze, and she could see an old John Deere tractor creeping down Hawkesford's main drag, pulling a derelict Toyota Camry toward Cunningham's Auto Repair. The tractor's driver seemed oblivious to the line-up of cars following him along Highway 27. Repeated honks warned him to move over so they could pass. He ignored them.

She recognized the man at the wheel as Big Mike Pettigrew, Jesselyn's dad. Ornery old fart. Frankie smiled. He was being deliberately obstructionist, as usual. Jesselyn said her brother Russ grew more like his dad every day as he got older, his actions a bone of contention between the siblings. Meanwhile, Jesse did her best to overcome her male family member's obnoxious reputation in the community. That included helping Frankie get a job, and the Hawkesford Fire Department acquire a good paramedic.

A silence in the room behind her indicated the discussion had ended. Karl tapped on the dividing window and gestured. "Come on in," he called.

Frankie hastened to obey, managing to keep her hands loose at her sides as she awaited the verdict.

"Lew has one more question for you, Frankie," Karl said, his face sober.

Her heart sank. She should've known the interview wouldn't pan out. Live in her home town, surrounded by old friends and land a decent job at the same time? It was too good to be true.

Carpenter scowled at the captain, then at her. "Yeah. When can you start? I'm so shorthanded the whole damn crew is about to revolt and call in sick."

What had he said? For a moment, it didn't sink in. "You mean I'm hired?" she asked dumbly.

"That's the point of this rigmarole."

"I can start right now, tonight, if you need me," she burbled, momentarily forgetting about the need to find a place to live that included a place for her dog. And a change of clothes wouldn't hurt either.

"Well, hallelujah. A regular eager beaver." Lew Carpenter finally showed a grin. "You can fill out the paperwork immediately, but tomorrow is soon enough to report to work. You'll be on night shift with me for your probationary period. Twelve hours on, twelve off, work four days, and have three off. Suit you?"

Frankie would've joined forces with the devil just to have the job. Not that she thought Carpenter was the devil even if he did have a sour enough attitude. "Sounds good," she said. "Thanks. I'm looking forward to working with you."

His scowl, which she judged customary to him considering the formation of lines on his dark, leathered face, settled back in place. "We'll see how long that lasts."

"Welcome aboard," Karl Mager said. "Hope you won't get too bored in a little place like Hawkesford."

***

The cop was gone when Frankie went into the

outer office to fill in the paperwork. She'd just handed her completed forms to Karl when Jesselyn Pettigrew drove into the parking lot. Her Jeep Liberty skidded to a halt in front of the fire station/emergency services building. She entered the station in a rush, bearing a box of Rosauer's doughnuts. The greasy good aroma reminded Frankie she'd been too nervous to eat any breakfast, and it was now mid-morning.

Maggie looked up from her computer screen, nose twitching as Jesselyn walked past. "You spreading those around to all of us, Jesselyn, or are you trying to bribe Karl and Lew into hiring Frankie?"

"Am I too late?" A mock look of dismay spread across Jesselyn's pretty face. Short, a bit plump, pale-skinned to go with her strawberry blonde hair, her ready smile had always had the knack of drawing people to her.

"Afraid so." Karl's mouth drooped sadly as he lifted the lid to the doughnut box the moment she set it down. He selected a maple bar and stuffed half of it into his mouth.

"What do you mean?" Jesselyn snatched the doughnuts out of his reach and whirled to face her friend. "Frankie? You got the job, didn't you?"

Holding back a laugh, Frankie nodded. "I start tomorrow."

"See?" Jesselyn crowed. "I told you so. You're the cream of the crop."

"Watch it." Lew eyed the pastries before taking a plain glazed one. He pointed it toward Frankie. "I'm top dog around here, and I decide if you're cream or cottage cheese. And don't you forget it."

"Yes, sir," she said.

He sounded remarkably similar to a sergeant she'd had back in Kandahar. Which didn't do anything to make her more comfortable. Sergeant Pelker had died in the same explosion that killed most of their platoon and wounded Frankie.

Jesselyn grabbed Frankie's arm. "If you guys are done with your interrogation, we're going to find her a place to live. Can't have our new paramedic pitching a tent out in the boonies."

"That's interview, not interrogation, missy." Mager cast Frankie a puzzled look. "Aren't you going to live in your grandma's house? That was a point in your favor, not having to worry about housing. It's kind of hard to come by here."

"Gabe Zantos lives in the McGill house," murmured Maggie, who'd wandered over and snagged a cinnamon twist.

"Oh, yeah. That's right. Can't kick him out, I suppose."

Frankie took the comment seriously. "He's got a year's lease, captain. Don't worry. I'll find a place." She grinned. "I'll pile in with Jesselyn if I have to." Upon noticing the expression on her friend's face, she hurried to add, "Or I can always rent an apartment in Coeur d'Alene or Spokane and commute."

"Better find something close by," Carpenter said. "We can't wait for you if you're late."

She stiffened. "I'm never late," she said. "Sir."

***

"Our first step," Jesselyn told Frankie, steering her out of the station and over to the parked cars, "is to talk with my sister Victoria."

"Victoria?" Frankie remembered Jesselyn's older sister as the consummate high school fashion plate and drama queen. "Why?"

"Because she's a real estate agent now. She made beaucoup bucks until the big recession hit, and property values went to pot. Now the market is red-hot again, she's back to making tons of money. If anybody knows what's for rent around here, it's her." Jesselyn had her cell phone out. Her sister must've been on speed dial as she started talking almost immediately.

"Hey," she said, "it's me. Have you heard for sure if that duplex is empty? You did? Can Frankie and I take a look?" There was a pause and her stub nose wrinkled. "Oh, well. I can help clean it up if necessary. Where's the key? Okay. I'll ask him."

Pressing the phone's off key, she hopped into her Liberty. "Follow me," she said. "I've got a hot lead."

Taking off like a bat out of hell, gravel spewed from beneath Jesselyn's tires almost before Frankie could open her Ranger's door and get Banner inside. "Jeez," she told the dog, "I forgot she was like this, so frenetic." In fact, thinking it over as she followed her friend across the highway to the south side of town, she couldn't remember such behavior at all. Jesselyn had been the laid back one of the duo, Frankie the impatient one with lots of get up and go.

A couple minutes later, she pulled in behind the Liberty parked in the driveway of an older duplex in sad need of a fresh coat of paint. Built rancher-style, the units were side by side. A patch of weedy lawn awaited mowing—and a good watering. All in all, it wasn't what anyone would call a prepossessing place, but it was better than Frankie's current apartment in Spokane.

Jesselyn was already out of her car and pounding on one of the two front doors. As Frankie and Banner hastened to join her, the door opened a crack.

"Yeah, yeah, whatever you're sellin', I'm not buyin'," a voice growled.

"Oh, open up, Howie." Jesselyn pushed until the crack widened. "Victoria wants you to give me the key to the other apartment, so I can show it to Frankie. She's thinking about renting the empty unit."

"Why didn't you say so?" Howie St. James, whom Frankie remembered as being a basketball star a couple years ahead of her in high school, swung the door wider. His left arm was in a dirty cast that stretched from wrist to shoulder. "Hi, Frankie," he said. "Back from the wars, huh? Heard you were wounded."

"True on both counts." She forced a smile. "But I'm ready to take up life in the real world now."

"You call this the real world?" He shook his head. "Man, if it'd been me and I'd gotten out of this podunk town, I'd never have come back."

She shrugged. Every place was much of a much.

It's what you made of it that counted. But she never could tell people any different, including Jesselyn on more than one occasion. Everybody had to find out for him or herself. "Join the army, see the world."

Jesselyn was still in a hurry. "So, can we get the key, Howie, please, sometime today?"

"Sure. Wait a minute. I'll fetch it." Leaving the door open, he ambled off toward the tiny kitchen, weaving around a threadbare recliner aimed toward an old model big screen TV. A coffee table piled high with pizza boxes and beer bottles sat between the TV and the chair. A fat gray cat blinked at the visitors from the recliner's arm.

"Here ya are," he said, returning a minute later with a key strung on a length of pink yarn. "Sure is odd about Denise pulling out in the middle of the night, innit?"

Jesselyn arched an eyebrow. "Middle of the night?"

"Yeah. I'd gone to bed and figured she had too since I couldn't hear her TV or

anything. Been hard to sleep with this busted arm," he explained. "Itches to beat hell. Anyhow, I'd just dropped off when her little mutt woke me up yipping. Then the dog quit barking, and I heard her walking around, banging on stuff like she was moving furniture or something. Didn't realize she was moving out."

"I imagine that means she left the place a mess." Jesselyn sounded resigned. "C'mon, Frankie, let's take a gander. Thanks for the key, Howie."

"Sure." Although dismissed, he followed them to the other unit, scratching absently under his cast.

"A wire coat hanger will fit in there." Frankie, holding back to walk beside him, nodded toward his casted arm. "Cut and straighten the wire, wrap the end with cloth or tape or something, so you don't break the skin, and rub away. That'll help. How'd you break it, anyway?"

His mouth twisted. "I kinda got hit by a car."

"What? Kinda got hit?"

"Yeah, walkin' home from the bar one night. One minute I'm strolling along happy as a rabbit in a carrot patch, next I'm flyin' through the air and landin' in the ditch."

"Wow. Sorry about that. Did they catch the driver."

"Nope. Doubt if they looked very hard."

"Hey." Jesselyn tapped a sandaled foot, "You want to see this or not, Frankie?"

"You know, I do. Lead the way."

Howie stood back, smiling at her even as a far-away look crossed his dark face. "Sure is funny Denise didn't tell me she was leaving when I talked to her yesterday. Or say where she was going."

"Would she normally?" Frankie asked.

"Well, we were friends, kind of. Neighbors. I would've told her."

Jesselyn, ignoring Howie, worked the key and flung open the door. A stale smell wafted out, composed of cooking odors, unmoving air, and something else. Something unpleasant. "Phew. Well, this is it. What do you think, Frankie?" She waved a hand. "Been nice if she'd cleaned house before she left."

Frankie gawked around. Her friend might complain, but she herself had seen worse. A lot worse. Granted, the apartment, a twin of Howie's, was small and a little cluttered, although not really dirty. There were a couple overripe bananas and a moldy orange in a basket on the kitchen counter to account for some of the smell—all the more potent because of the heat—but nothing a good airing and some deep cleaning wouldn't cure.

She took a quick tour of the bedroom and bath,

both of which, to her surprise, looked as though they were waiting for the owner to return at any minute. An inspection of the closet space showed empty hangers, but a couple articles of clothing on the floor. An open book lay on the bedside table beside a nearly full bottle of aspirin.

"You sure this Denise is actually gone?" she asked Jesselyn. "There's an awful lot of personal stuff still here."

Her friend looked puzzled too. "Abandoned it, I guess. She really did leave, though. Victoria got an email from her."

Breathing in her ear, Howie stood tapping a bare foot. "Man, this don't seem right. Lookit. She even left her mutt's dog bed."

"At least she took the dog." Jesselyn palmed her phone, finger poised to punch in numbers. "Well, Frankie? What do you think? You going to take it?"

"Not much choice, is there?" Frankie shrugged and nodded. "Tell Vic yes.

Already regretting the necessity, a little shiver went through her as Jesselyn handed over the key. The place definitely gave her the collywobbles.

CHAPTER 2

Frankie admitted she was a little hurt at Jesselyn's hesitancy to play host for a night, even though she'd only been teasing when she mentioned it. She couldn't help thinking it might've been fun, though, jabbering about the new job with someone. A regular sleepover, like in the old days when she and Jesselyn were in grade school. What a long time ago. Did she even know how to jabber anymore? Or have fun?

Jesselyn's live-in boyfriend probably had something to do with her sidestepping of the issue. Not that acting the third wheel on a two-wheel bicycle was Frankie's idea of entertainment. She really preferred to return to town and pack up her few belongings ready to move into the duplex the next morning.

But still…

On her way back to Spokane, Frankie contented herself by gazing out at the rolling hills of the lower Palouse as she drove. In a field just before the state line, two combines were cutting great swaths of golden grain, chaff rising in a cloud behind the massive machines. Only now did she realize how much she'd missed the area when in Afghanistan's arid landscape. One more night in her crappy little Spokane apartment. Then she'd be home for good.

Home. Which meant Jesselyn and all the people she'd known way back when. Would it be anywhere near the same?

"You should've seen us when we were kids." She glanced over at Banner seated beside her, his white ruff lifting in the breeze that came in through the slightly open window. "Jesselyn and I were inseparable. Funny how time and experience changes people, isn't it? We don't have much in common anymore." Her brow puckered. "But there's no denying I got the royal brush-off. Guess it's just you and me, kid."

"You won't bother my boyfriend and me," Jesselyn had hastened to assure her, succeeding with only a half-baked job of backpedaling when she noticed Frankie's embarrassment. "It's not like we're in high school, for goodness sake."

Nevertheless, she never did get around to telling Frankie the man's name, which had the effect of raising Frankie's curiosity quotient even higher.

The thing is, Frankie wouldn't actually consider any roommate, especially an old friend. Except for Banner, of course. What if she had one of her fits during the night, crying out and carrying on? She'd probably scare Jesselyn half to death. Her friend had no clue about dealing with trauma—and Frankie knew herself traumatized, no matter how well she seemed to be dealing with pain, stress, nightmares, and a sometimes overwhelming fear of the future. Reluctant to admit these things to herself, how could she begin to explain them to anyone else?

That, she thought, reaching over and giving her present constant companion a caress as they drove a sedate five miles an hour over the speed limit, is why we have dogs.

Fifty-five minutes later, after a brief stop at the neighborhood grocery store to pick up a few banana boxes to hold her belongings, she wheeled into her apartment parking space. Packing didn't take long. All she had were a few clothes, a couple boxes of household things, and Banner's dog dishes and bedding. Oh, yes, and a stack of service and medical records stowed away in a heavy safe. That was it. Not much for a twenty-five-year-old who'd spent several years in the service of her country. Her one-room apartment didn't look a whole lot emptier after she cleared out than before. Certainly different from the clutter left in the Hawkesford duplex.

When she'd been in the service, she'd often wished for larger living quarters. Strange that when she'd first moved in, this little space had been about all she could handle. She'd split her time between the VA hospital and here, spending almost as long in one place as the other. Then later, after she rescued Banner from an abusive owner—with the help of a pistol she'd held on the worthless SOB who'd been beating him—the apartment's size had given her the motivation to take the dog out for frequent walks, then runs, during her—their—rehabilitation. After all, it isn't right to keep a big dog cooped up for hours on end in a teensy room.

At last, she was done with that.

Finished with her packing, Frankie and Banner went for a final run along the Centennial Trail. This time they both indulged their exuberance. Rehabilitation accomplished.

***

Early the next morning, belongings already stowed in the bed of the Ranger, Frankie knocked on the manager's door. She was too excited to wait any longer.

A few minutes later, she knocked again, louder this time. The bitter, middle-aged woman who ran the complex was not an early riser. Finally, the woman's wizened face appeared.

Although Frankie remained in the hall, the strong odor of cigarette smoke emitted from the room almost scratched a cough from her when the door opened.

"What do you want?" As accommodating as usual, Mrs. Lane picked a sleepy seed from the corner of her eye.

Frankie flourished the old-fashioned door key. She'd always figured she could've opened any of the apartments with it. Real security—not. "I'm moving out, Mrs. Lane. Returning the key."

"Could've given me some warning." The door

opened wider. "Did you clean up after yourself? If I find one speck of dirt, I'm keeping your deposit."

Frankie figured that was a foregone conclusion. Schooling her features to blandness, she said, knowing it wouldn't endear her to the old bag, "Looks better than I when found it. You never did knock the painting I did off my rent like you said you would." She pressed a slip of paper into the woman's hand. "Here's my new address. You can send the deposit there." Yeah. Right. Frankie nearly laughed at the idea.

"I'll be the judge of that." The door slammed with enough force to stir her hair.

Not much of a farewell considering this place had been home for better than six months. And the locals called Spokane the "friendly" city?

Apparently, the citizens suffered some kind of collective delusion.

Shrugging off her landlady's rudeness, Frankie smiled as she walked out into the rapidly warming sunlight, Banner at her side. She waited for the dog to jump into the pickup and climbed in after him, excitement bubbling inside her. A new beginning.

This time, traveling the road bisecting golden wheat fields on the cusp of harvest to Hawkesford, she remained within the speed limit, savoring the change in her life. Starting today, she planned to put aside her time in the army and all the resultant baggage. Including the personnel carrier that'd blown up beneath her and the guys in her unit.

No more bad dreams, she vowed. No more guilt for being alive. Please, God.

A heavy-metal song older than she was playing on the radio. Frankie turned up the volume, singing along with Axel Rose while Banner when he wasn't poking his nose out the half-open window, sat on the passenger seat and stared at her.

Later, as she backed into the duplex's driveway, she found Howie St. James sitting on the steps to his apartment. His legs sprawled, he was soaking in the sun and poking every now and then under his cast with a partially straightened coat hanger. His cat sat beside him, stretching out a hind leg and licking the fur with a pink tongue. The two of them looked, she thought, like they'd been waiting for her.

"Hey." She held the door for Banner to jump out of the Ranger. "What's up?"

Howie shrugged. "Couldn't sleep. This blasted arm is driving me nuts. And besides…" He stopped, glanced around like he was expecting someone to overhear, and plied the hanger again.

"Besides what?"

"Nothin'." He shook his head.

"How much longer do you have to wear the cast?"

"Three weeks or so." Making a wry face, Howie stood up. "Feels like forever."

Frankie could relate.

While Banner investigated the cat, earning himself a hearty hiss in warning, Frankie folded down the Ranger's tailgate and lifted out the first box. Household stuff. Kitchen. Like any well-organized person, she'd labeled the contents.

"Want to open the door for me?" She waggled fingers wound around in pink yarn, key dangling.

"Sure." Howie stood up and took the key, poked it in the lock and quickly stepped back.

"Thanks. Get the light?" Funny. She didn't remember either she or Jesselyn closing the blinds yesterday, but it was dark as midnight in the room.

"Sure."

Howie reached around and flipped the switch. The box in her arms, Frankie brushed past him, barely registering the wary look that came and went on Howie's face in her anxiety to set down her heavy load. She heard him suck in a quick breath and give a kind of low growl though. Even so, she was halfway across the room before what Howie had already seen struck home.

The apartment had been ransacked since she and Jesselyn's visit yesterday, and by someone who'd done a very thorough job.

"Well, shit." Owl-eyed, Howie stared around. "This is a helluva mess."

Frankie spun on him. "Who did it?"

"Huh? I don't know."

Her eyes narrowed. "You sure about that? Whoever broke in couldn't have been very sneaky. How could you not know all this was going on?" She pointed at an overturned armchair.

He reared back and looked affronted. "Hey, I went down to the bar and had a few beers last night. Not that it's any of your business. Then I came home. I didn't see anybody. Ain't nobody paying me to be a night watchman."

Maybe not, but he'd put a queer emphasis on see. Frankie pounced on it. "But you heard something, right?" Kids trying to raise money for some weed, she supposed, even as doubt raised its ugly head.

Howie scratched. "Maybe I heard somethin'. Maybe not. I thought somebody was walkin' around and figured Denise had come back for her stuff. I yelled, but nobody answered. The wind picked up about then and set her wind chimes to ringing, so then I figured that's all I heard and forgot about it. Sleepy, ya know, after the beers." He eyed the couch cushions flipped onto the dusty floor; a hole gouged in one of them exposing shredded foam, the zipper open on the other. "Guess it wasn't my imagination after all. But not Denise, that's for sure."

"No." Frankie, hands on hips, surveyed the room. "I wouldn't think so. If she'd forgotten anything, she'd come in quietly and pick it up. No need for all this." She sighed. "Well, it looks like I've got my work cut out for me. And my first shift is tonight, which means I'd better get cracking."

"Gonna call the cops?"

She gazed around and made a decision. "Nah. No real harm done, I guess, except to the couch and it's pretty ratty anyway."

Howie seemed relieved. "Might oughta get the locks changed though." On this cryptic word of advice, which Frankie took with a grain of salt,

Howie heeded her hint and went back to his side of the duplex.

With her neighbor out of the way, Frankie allowed her gimpy stride free rein, no longer feeling the need to keep up appearances. Unloading her pickup and carrying the boxes into the duplex went faster that way. Glad of the supplies she'd stopped to buy on the way to Hawkesford, it didn't take long to get the place in order. Bed made up with clean sheets over a new looking mattress pad, a shim under one leg of the elderly brass bedstead. Sinks, toilet, and floors scrubbed, the torn couch cushion, filling stuffed back inside, mended with needle and strong thread.

Most of Denise's discarded goods went out the back door to the trash. A large propane tank sat in unlovely splendor between her unit and Howie's. A barrel at the edge of the overgrown yard showed Hawkesford had yet to become environmentally conscious and ban the burning of combustibles—unless Howie and Denise had suited themselves with little fear of authority.

Following suit with a stack of ancient newspapers for kindling, Frankie trekked out to the barrel, only to find she had no matches. Something to put on her list—and soon. An odor she could smell from the back stoop emanated from the barrel, one she didn't want Banner taking it in his head to investigate.

The Samoyed, naturally, trundled after her, his curled tail waving like a flag, his nose working as he began the process of claiming his territory. Frankie, not much amused, noted the care with which he sniffed, then wet down each small pile of doggie doo littering the yard. Another chore awaited her since she didn't want him catching anything from the yard's previous resident. Denise, she remembered Howie saying, owned a small dog. Well, yeah. And carelessly left its bed and food when she left. A noteworthy oddity among the rest.

The morning passed rapidly as Frankie got her house in order; her only interruption a call from Jesselyn.

"Hi. Are you settling in all right?" Jesselyn talked so fast it took Frankie's brain a moment to catch up. Her fault, Frankie knew. Or maybe she could blame the Taliban and their roadside bombs.

"Yeah, I guess," she said. "Wish I knew what to do with Denise's stuff, though."

"Burn it." Jesselyn apparently had no doubts.

"Bunch of junk and garbage, isn't it?"

Frankie had been thinking about this. "Not all of it," she said slowly. "You remember those blouses on the closet floor? I looked them over and found they're not only expensive but the same as new. Just dirty, after somebody walked on them. But that's not all. It's weird. There's the dog's stuff, including an unopened bag of organic specialty food."

"The expensive kind?" Jesselyn spoke a little slower, too, as if she were puzzled.

"Yes. This Denise didn't stint on either her dog or herself. And there's people food left in the fridge, including a T-bone steak with today's outdate. Then there's a bunch of stuff in the cupboards, books, CDs, DVDs, and even a fully functioning iPod—although I don't care much for her taste in music. Really, Jesselyn. It looks to me like she plans on coming back."

Jesselyn made a little humming noise.

Although she hadn't meant to say anything, Frankie added, "And that's still not all."

"What else?"

"Somebody broke in here last night and pretty much trashed the place. Ripped up the couch, threw things around, tore pages out of books and smashed some CDs and DVDs. He—they—broke a window in the back door to get in." She'd found that right after Howie left.

Jesselyn's breath drew in sharply. "Did you call Gabe Zantos?"

"Who?"

"Hawkesford's district deputy. You know, the guy living in your grandmother's house. Your house. The reason you're stuck in that crappy duplex." Impatience came through.

"Oh." Had the cop who talked to Maggie yesterday at the station been this Gabe character? Despair swept over her. How could she have forgotten her own renter's name?

As though to press the question home, flashes of light blurred the vision in her right eye, an all too common phenomenon in the last several months. An eye migraine, her ophthalmologist termed it, no doubt caused by her head injury. It should get better soon, or so the doctor assured her.

Frankie pressed two fingers firmly an inch above her eye. "Too late to call him now, I guess. Everything's cleaned up. Anyway, Howie and I, we both think the trashing part was just some kids. It's the other, the things Denise left here, that bothers me. I'd hate to have her come home in the middle of the night and find me sleeping in her bed."

At this, Jesselyn laughed. "Well, yeah. A regular Goldilocks moment. But don't forget she told Vic she was leaving. I wouldn't worry about her coming back unexpectedly if I were you. And you're right. Kids probably did the trashing. Was anything taken?"

"How would I know?" Frankie paused, worry nagging at her, and decided to take Howie's advice. "Jesselyn, would you ask Vic if I can get new locks? I don't really want any surprise visitors."

"I don't blame you. I'll call her." Jesselyn's prompt agreement eased Frankie's mind.

Excitement mixed with apprehension—blast those eye migraines, anyway—built as she checked the fence around the back yard before leaving for work. The chicken wire strung around tilted posts didn't look strong enough to keep out a determined coyote, but usually, any rickety old thing would hold Banner. Bless his heart, he inclined more toward sniffing and ambling than climbing, fighting, or digging.

Besides, the weather was good. A fiberglass roof sheltered the rather shabby concrete patio, and he had easy access to his crate, which she set near the back door. He'd be fine on his own. Maybe Howie would check on him later if she asked nicely.

"Be a good boy." She stroked the dog's head and filled a big bowl of fresh water, placing it next to the back door for him. "I'll be back before you miss me."

But Banner didn't stay to watch her leave—a first in the time they'd been together. He turned, trotting across the yard toward the trees, his nose lifted into the breeze.

CHAPTER 3

We replenish our supplies at Kootenai Medical Center after every run."

They were in the station where Lew was showing Frankie around the station and explaining procedure.

"Here's the list of supplies stocked in the ambulance at all times. We keep a running tab of what we've used and what needs replaced." He pointed to a clipboard with a standard looking order form on it. Affixed to a hook super-glued inside the ambulance, a pen dangled from a string beside the clipboard.

"When you run out of something, don't forget to mark it down," he continued. "Like Chris. He's a good kid and a fair EMT, but he's forgetful as all hell."

Frankie nodded, careful to concentrate as she stowed the information in her memory banks. This kind of thing became easier with time, but she wasn't up to par yet.

Lew moved on, showing her the locked drug storage bin. "I've got a key," he said, "and if I'm not on shift, whoever is in charge will have one too. That'll be you as soon as you pass your trial month. Only the paramedic or the EMT in charge has a key."

"All right." For the first time since her shift started, the mention of drugs reminded Frankie of the break-in at her duplex. "Do you have a lot of that here? People trying to steal your drugs, I mean?"

"Nah." Lew leaped from the ambulance's open rear doors to the garage floor. "Most everybody knows we keep the drugs locked away. So far nobody's gone after any of us for the key, but you never can tell." He scowled. "Stay on your toes. Don't flash the key around or leave it in plain sight. Not ever."

"No, sir," she said stiffly. Toes, huh? Had anybody told him she only had half as many as most people?

Lew beckoned to her, so she jumped out, taking care to land on her good foot. She didn't think he noticed anything out of the way.

"You ever drive one of these buses?" He opened the ambulance driver's side door for Frankie to peer inside.

"Not this model." How much different could it be from the deuce-n-half, after all? Or even a grain truck. "I'll manage." She crossed her fingers.

Tuesday evening being one of the slower nights of the week, she spent an uninterrupted hour standing in front of a big area map nailed to the firehouse wall. Topographically correct, the terrain was familiar from when she lived in Hawkesford—mostly. The most obvious changes were the names. New residents, all strangers to her, clustered around the upscale community along the lakeshore.

"Doctors, lawyers, big money people," Lew told her. "Lording it over all us peons. They visit the casino, but don't do a lot of business in town."

The rural contingent, farmers, most of whom she knew, scattered over the rest of the county west to the state line, east to Benewah, and south to the Palouse. They did do business in the community.

Marking the duplex she'd rented, she particularly noticed how the woods behind it had thickened in the last few years. Second-growth timber, the trees had grown almost to logging size with a lot of underbrush. She'd have to keep Banner out of there—his thick white fur was prone to picking up burrs, stickers, and dirt, let alone ticks.

Their first call of the evening shift came from a frantic mother who lived down at the lake, some four miles out of town, proving the wealthy weren't above the need for help.

One of the volunteer firemen was manning the dispatch station this evening. A tall man about her own age with big hands—and sporting a big, rough gold nugget ring on one thick finger—he filled Maggie's swivel chair to overflowing. He keyed the alarm and relayed the particulars while Lew fired up the ambulance. Frankie hopped into the passenger seat, her heart racing.

Lew showed no emotion. "Tell me where I should go and what we should do when we get there," he told her.

A test.

Frankie blanked for a second then, to her relief, the information sorted through her brain. "South on Bay Road," she said, "and take the right-hand fork at the Coleburg's farm, then right again on

Shore Lane."

The medical emergency concerned a five-year-old who'd stuck a stone up her—

"Well," as Lew told the dispatcher an hour later, when they'd returned to the station, "let's just say it wasn't her nose."

The dispatcher guffawed, and even Lew's lips twitched.

Around two in the morning, another call came in, this time to the south side of Hawkesford to a shabby little house near Frankie's duplex where a man and woman had gotten into a heated... er... discussion. The man's head, laid open by a profusely bleeding gash, had a knot swollen to the size of a turkey egg.

"Whaddya think?" Lew yelled over the woman's wails of, "I didn't mean to hit him so hard."

Funny, since she'd used a cast iron skillet, which still lay on the cracked vinyl floor beside the man's head.

Frankie didn't think Lew's question referred to the weapon, however.

"Stitches." Frankie probed the swelling, her fingers light and gentle. The guy, dark like Howie St. James, opened bleary eyes. She checked his pupil size.

"Pretty sure he has a concussion. An X-ray might be a good idea," she added. "And I guess we'd better let the tribal police know."

Lew grunted, his lips taking a faint upturn. "Let's load him up."

By three-thirty a.m. they were back at the station. At four-thirty they made a run for a kid with a fractured leg, having been kicked by a cow at the morning milking. A high school sophomore and determined to show toughness, the upcoming football season fretted him more than the pain of his leg.

At six, Frankie went home, exhausted beyond belief.

***

The duplex was surrounded by early morning peace. Birds stirred in the woods behind the building, somewhere a diesel engine grumbled awake. A dog barked a few houses over. At Howie's place, the window shades were drawn down tight.

After a short, though effusive greeting, Banner took off on a quick circuit around the yard out back of the duplex. He raced along the wire fence with his tail straight out behind him and his ears laid back.

"What's up, lovey?" Frankie called the dog, a little impatient with his antics. "Come on in. I'm tired. I want to go to bed." When he ignored her, she went inside, washed her face, and donned sleep shorts and a tee before going after him again. She had to physically lead him in.

"What in the world is the matter with you? Strange place getting to you?"

Banner emitted a soft whine.

"Yeah." She sat on the side of the bed and checked the clock. "Me, too. I don't blame you. Feels weird here, doesn't it? Like a premonition—" She stopped, thinking, don't go there. Too much like a couple times in Afghanistan when visions of tragedy had visited her—and then come true. Including the one that cost her part of a foot and a plate in the head.

"Kind of stinks in here, too, doesn't it? I'll get some air fresheners this afternoon and open up all the windows."

She removed the prosthesis doing duty for her missing toes and patted the side of the bed, inviting Banner up. He launched himself, all right, but instead of snuggling against her like he usually did, he sniffed, circled, scratched an ear, lay down, got up, and jumped back to the floor.

"All right, I get it," she said, disappointed. "But be quiet."

The command held for all of four and a half hours.

***

A snuffling noise accompanied by a cold, wet nose in her ear snapped Frankie awake, her heart pounding.

"What're you doing?"

Banner had deigned to join her on the bed at some point as she slept. At the sound of her voice, he bounded over and straddled her recumbent form, peering down with concerned black eyes.

Groggy with sleep, she pushed him off her chest. "Go away."

Squinting, she peered at the digital clock's glowing red numerals and groaned. Eleven-thirty a.m. Too early by far.

Banner, stepping over her as he lurched from the bed, managed to poke his toenails through the thin blanket into her belly.

"Ouch." Determined to ignore the dog, she

closed her eyes. A moment later, the sound of those same toenails on the uncarpeted floor brought them open again. "Will you kindly stop your damn pacing?"

Flipping over, she attempted to shut out his click, click, infernal clicking. Adding to her aggravation, sunlight crept around the edges of the ill-fitting mini-blinds, brightening the bedroom beyond tolerance. She drew the blanket over her head. The relief lasted approximately one full minute before she couldn't stand it anymore. The apartment was already hot inside, bringing out the unpleasant odor.

She sat up, her nose wrinkling. "Phew. Gross. This whole bed stinks like—"

Dammit. Blood. The smell reminded her of blood.

Banner's insistent whine demanded attention. Ever mindful of his comfort, she got up to let him out, fully intending to return to bed. She needed to be sharp for her shift at work tonight, not so tired her abused brain refused to function. It already had too many problems.

The dog's behavior thwarted this plan. Frankie frowned as he pushed her aside and dashed out the back door. Far from simply lifting his leg, he raced to the rickety chicken-wire fence separating the yard from the woods directly behind it. The trees grew so close a few Ponderosa pine branches, their needles smelling of resin in the noon heat, overlapped the neglected lawn.

Banner jumped against the chicken wire and set to barking. Loudly. Uncharacteristically. Persistently.

The fence swayed under his weight.

Wide awake now, as well as puzzled, Frankie watched him paw at the dirt under the bottom wire. "Stop that."

Ignoring her, he lifted his head and sniffed the hot breeze, then went back to digging, soil, weeds, and tufts of grass flying out behind him.

"What is it, Banner? What's gotten into you?"

She started across the yard, hardly aware of her jerky gait compensating for her missing toes. From the corner of her eye, she saw Howie open his back door and peer out before walking onto the patio.

"Somethin' the matter with your dog?" he called.

"I don't know. I've never seen him act like this before." She stopped, reluctant for Howie to watch her moving or maybe see her mangled foot. Then she decided it didn't matter because Banner swiftly excavated a hole big enough to squeeze himself through. Which he did, again ignoring her command of "Banner, come."

Frankie kept going, barefoot or no, hoofing it after the dog who'd slithered under the fence and with a flash of his waving white tail, disappeared into the woods.

What in the world was wrong with him?

At the fence, she stopped, telling herself, "Damned if I'm crawling under that thing." No, but with only a few scratches from broken wires, including a bloody scrape along her shin, she succeeded in forcing the dilapidated thing down far enough to scramble over. Banner's frantic barks led her into the trees, following the sound. Running and stumbling over uneven ground, prickly dry pine needles and the occasional pinecone stabbed her feet.

About a hundred feet into the woods, she spied the dog. He'd quit running, even quit barking and seemed to be intent on nosing a pile of white rags mottled with rusty brown streaks.

The pile, to her disgust, was moving.

"Banner!" Frankie huffed toward him. "You leave that alone. If you get sprayed by a skunk, so help me God I'll—"

Only it wasn't a skunk. Or an albino rat. Or a pile of rags infested with wiggly maggots.

It was a dog. A small white dog. It had been shot.

CHAPTER 4

Frankie grabbed Banner's ruff, dragging him away from where he nosed the quivering heap of wounded dog. "Okay," she told him. "I've got it. Stand back. I'll take it from here."

Banner cocked his head to one side and, as though understanding her words, allowed her to push in front of him. He sat down a couple feet away, whining now and again deep in his throat as though asking a question.

Frankie knelt beside the small dog, a cobby munchin with curly white hair. White, except, of course, for the blood-soaked parts, dried now and stiff. With gentle fingers, she pushed up the animal's lip to see its gums. Gray. Not a good sign if she remembered correctly. It, a female, she noted with one part of her mind, whimpered, a whisper of sound. Hazy brown eyes slitted open.

"Poor baby." She ran her hands over its body. Blood had spilled over much of its head and chest and turned one floppy ear rust colored.

She separated the dog's hair where most of the blood had gathered. Her stomach lurched as she spied the wound, a raw gash between shoulder and neck and a hole in the ear leather where a cluster of maggots wriggled.

Her earlier guess hadn't been so far off.

Pure rage flared through her. "Some dirty sonofa—"

The animal's condition was no accident. A deliberate shot, the bullet had passed through muscle and skin and, although Frankie felt no broken bones, the dog had bled profusely. Too much, leaving the dog near death, even though the bleeding had stopped some time ago.

From over her head, a voice said in a revolted tone, "Hey! That's Denise's dog. That's her bitchin."

Frankie went sprawling, catching herself on one hand. In her anger, she hadn't heard Howie's approach.

"Denise's dog?" She turned to him, noting the worried expression that settled over his face.

"Yeah. Who would do such a thing? A nice little dog like this?" He sounded horrified, sad, appalled.

"Not Denise?"

"Oh, God, no. Not Denise. She's gaga over this dog."

The dog's legs twitched. Her tongue, dry-looking, poked between black lips, and she made a weak snuffling sound. Banner stood up, the fur on his back on end.

"Okay." Frankie laid a calming hand on his head. "I'm on it." She looked up. "Denise's dog or not, I'm taking it to a vet."

"Can't you do anything for it? You know, being a paramedic an' all?"

"She. The dog is a she. And no, I can't. She needs a transfusion, something for shock, something for infection, surgery to close her wounds."

Howie nodded. "Think it—she'll—live?"

Frankie shrugged. "Maybe, if she can hold on just a bit longer." Two, no three, days since Denise left. "She must be a tough little cookie."

As they talked, she'd been inching her hands beneath the dog's body. Spread fingers provided as much support as possible as she rose, lifting the dog with her. Howie's sudden intake of breath indicated he'd seen her foot, although he didn't say anything. Good of him.

Conscious of every stick, stone, and pinecone just waiting to prod sensitive bare feet, Frankie stumbled toward the yard to the duplex, carrying the dog. "Hold this fence down so I can get across, will you please, Howie?"

"Sure." Howie, who wore a pair of cheap rubber flip-flops, stepped on the wire. One of the rotting fence posts bent and cracked, snapping off level with the ground.

Sighing, Frankie mentally noted the major fence repair awaiting her when she got home. She didn't want Banner out by himself with only this between him and the woods. As though in proof, he scrambled easily over the mashed wire in front of Howie.

She found easier going as they crossed the weedy back yard. With Howie getting the doors, she paused in the kitchen for her car keys and took the dog straight out to the pickup. A blanket already padded the floor behind the driver's seat. She set the dog, barely moving and with only a weak whimper, on it.

"Shotgun," she said, upon which Banner jumped onto the passenger seat up front.

Howie stood at the door as Frankie started to climb in.

"Hey." He gazed at her with a quizzical expression. "Ain't you going to put on some clothes and shoes before you take off?"

***

Dressed in yesterday's jeans and T-shirt, Frankie put the pedal down, reaching the nearest veterinary clinic in thirty minutes flat. Seeing the sign, she turned into the lot. Pioneer Animal Clinic, Dr. Violet Kelly, she read. She'd never heard of this vet, although she'd often gone past it. The place was clean and well kept, the patch of green lawn mowed, a set of corrals out back in good repair. Two horses and a longhorn steer lounged in the shade of a massive crimson maple.

The decision to go with the first animal hospital she came to seemed a good choice when the receptionist took one look at the limp bundle in Frankie's arms and rushed the little group into a treatment room. Banner, not about to stay behind, walked with them, bold as brass.

Fortunately, only one other patient occupied the waiting room, an elderly gentleman with a fat golden retriever, and he waved them in ahead of him. "Bowser just needs his bordatella," he said, eyeing Frankie's burden. "And we're in no hurry."

"Put her there." The receptionist pointed to a stainless steel tub topped by a flat rack before hurrying off down the corridor. "I'll get the doc."

Frankie laid the little dog, still wrapped in the old blanket from the pickup, where indicated. The bichon didn't stir, although Frankie knew she was still alive. She could feel a heartbeat, slowly, gamely thudding along.

The man with the bordatella dog followed them and stood in the doorway looking in. "Your dog get hit by a car?" Sympathy oozed from his soft-spoken query.

"Shot." Frankie wasted no words. She'd save her explanation for the doc.

The old fellow's eyes popped. "My goodness. Who'd do an awful thing like that? You been making enemies, young lady?"

"Not me." And yet, Frankie had been thinking along those same lines, only picturing Denise Rider as the one with enemies. Just then, the receptionist and a girl wearing an electric blue lab coat strode into the room. The girl, who looked about twenty, turned out to be the veterinarian, Dr. Kelly.

Murmuring an apology, the doc closed the door in the old gent's face and nodded to Frankie. "What happened?"

"I have no idea. My dog," she nodded toward Banner, sitting at heel beside her as he watched the proceedings, "found her in the woods behind my apartment. We just moved in yesterday."

The doctor held a stethoscope to the dog's chest and listened, shaking her head. Moving on to inspect the wound, she murmured, "Ummm," in a disapproving manner, and pried up an eyelid, closed now. "Ummm," she said again. And a few seconds later, "This dog has been shot."

Frankie imagined for a moment she heard the doctor growling just like one of her patients.

"Yes. I know. About three days ago, from what I can tell."

Dr. Kelly straightened, eyeing Frankie as if wondering how she came by such knowledge. "Are you willing to take financial responsibility for her care?" She aimed a fierce glare at Frankie. "She's fading, but I believe I can save her."

Inwardly, Frankie winced. Guess where her first paycheck was going? And maybe the second, too. But she'd seen too much of death and lost causes to back out. Banner—she laid her hand on his head and felt him look up—would never forgive her.

"So who needs to eat?" She sighed. "I guess I'm good for the bill. For her to have survived this long proves she's a real fighter. I can't give up on her now."

"Good for you." Smiling approval, Dr. Kelly opened a pocket door leading farther into the clinic and called, "Bernie, bring an IV setup STAT. And do we have any universal donor blood in the freezer?"

From down the corridor, a man's voice answered, "Used every drop on that Newfoundland last night. I've ordered more in. Should be here late this afternoon."

"That won't do. We need it now." The vet cast a speculative glance at Banner sitting unmoving at Frankie's side.

"I don't suppose you know anything about her history," she said to Frankie as she peered in the dog's mouth. "Or the owner's name? She looks familiar to me. See, she's got this pronounced underbite and this whorl of hair on her shoulder that grows longer and straighter than the rest."

Yes, Frankie had noticed the flaws, but she answered the real questions. "Sorry, no. I have no clue about her history. All I know is her owner, Denise Somebody, who lived in the apartment before me moved out and I—or rather Banner—found the dog in the woods behind the place. But my neighbor told me the woman loved the dog. Gaga over her, he said. Insists she wouldn't harm a hair on the dog's head."

"Did you say Denise?" The vet's eyes narrowed.

Frankie nodded. Fresh worry crept over her now she had a chance to think, and it showed.

"Well, somebody shot her, and I'll be reporting it to the proper authorities." Dr. Kelly opened a drawer and withdrew an object that resembled a high tech TV remote. "I'll try this. There's something I want to check."

She pressed a button and wafted the instrument over the dog's neck and back. "Aha," she said as the instrument beeped. "Got a hit."

"A microchip?" Frankie asked. "Great."

"Yes." The vet sounded grim.

It occurred to Frankie she'd been thinking of Denise in the past tense.

Man, she hated it when she got premonitions like this, an impression out of nowhere telling her that Denise What's'er-Name was in trouble.

Big, big trouble.

***

Frankie soon discovered what Dr. Kelly's cock-eyed look at Banner had meant. Evaluation of a potential blood donor, the clinic having depleted their donor blood as well as their frozen supply on the Newfie. Banner met the criteria of age, being about three years old, the right weight, his being seventy-five pounds—although Frankie attributed some of that to hair—patient, obedient, perfect temperament.

With her permission, the Samoyed sat unflinching through a test blood draw and then, after Dr. Kelly's assistant ran the labs and found him both healthy and compatible, allowed the vet to take a couple cups of his blood.

"Your little rescue friend is in luck today." Dr. Kelly quickly and efficiently removed the needle from Banner's jugular and capped the insertion point. "Banner is DEA 1.1 negative. Do you know what that means?"

"No, but you say it like it's good."

"Very good for this little one. Banner is a universal donor." Dr. Kelly began detaching the bag of blood from the collection equipment. When the IV tubing tangled, Frankie automatically moved to help, drawing a strange look.

"Most people would've left the room as soon as I went into his neck," the vet said. "You didn't."

"No." Frankie helped Banner from the table where he'd lain during the blood draw, offering him the water and treats the assistant had ready. "You're such a good boy," she murmured, caressing his pricked ears. "Brave and good."

Banner's tail swished a response.

Dr. Kelly's smooth forehead creased in a slight frown before she shrugged. "He is, indeed. I'll start the bichon's transfusion and treat her wound now. You can either wait in reception or go home. I can call you when I know more."

"I'll wait." Muffling a yawn, Frankie thought longingly about sleep. Even so, rest would be impossible without knowing if the little dog would live.

***

Forty-five minutes later, Dr. Kelly called Frankie into a utilitarian office at the rear of the clinic and invited her to sit in the stiff leather visitor's chair. Her assistant Bernie, a reedy guy who looked only a little older the doc, puttered around a bank of filing cabinets.

"How's the pooch?" Frankie waved Banner, unaffected by his blood donating experience, down beside the chair. From the doc's serious demeanor, Frankie half expected her to say the dog had died while at the same time presenting her with a six or seven hundred dollar bill to pay.

"With proper care, she'll be fine." Dr. Kelly clasped her hands and narrowed her blue eyes. "I'd like you to tell me again how you acquired the dog, Ms. McGill."

A wary thought flicked across Frankie's mind. Acquired? Found, rescued, helped—all better ways to put it. She knows something she isn't telling me.

Tamping down a flicker of temper, she repeated the story. Banner, her, Howie. All parts played. She noticed how the vet's gaze jumped from her face to her hands to her legs and back again. With an effort, Frankie stilled her right leg from bouncing with nervous energy. "And that's it," she finished. "Your clinic is the first animal hospital between Hawkesford and Spokane, so I turned in."

Dr. Kelly tapped her teeth with the tip of her forefinger. "Fortuitous."

Fortuitous? Who says that? Frankie stirred in her seat, causing Banner to look up at her out of almond-shaped black eyes. "Is it? Why?"

The vet and Bernie exchanged a look. "You saw me scan for the microchip." Dr. Kelly picked up a pen and gripped it until her fingers turned white. "From it, I discovered a few things about the dog, including her name."

"Did you? Good. What is it?"

"Shine."

"Shine?" Frankie grinned. "As in sun, do you suppose, or moon?"

Evidently, the vet didn't find the quip as bright as Frankie did. "The chip also gives me information that I find disturbing on several levels."

"Oh? Like what?"

"Like the owner's name."

Frankie sat dumb. She distinctly remembered saying she didn't actually know the owner and that she'd found the dog. And yet Dr. Kelly's words sounded quite a lot like an accusation.

"Denise Something or Other, right? I can't remember her last name."

"No," the vet said. "Not Denise Something or Other. Denise Rider. The microchip proves it." Her chair creaked as she sat back, still holding the pen.

Frankie couldn't wrap her head around why

the name thing disturbed the doc so much. "That's right, I remember now. The woman who dumped her dog in the woods."

"Never," the vet said, so positively that Frankie actually recoiled.

"How do you know? Because the woods is sure enough where we found her."

"If so, Denise didn't put her there. Because Shine is my patient—I told you I thought she looked familiar. So I know Denise, too, and I'm positive she wouldn't abandon Shine."

"I don't understand." Frankie didn't try to hide her surprise at the doc's sudden attitude. No. Nor her own aggravation, either. See what you get? she thought. Try to be a good Samaritan and as reward, receive a big ole kick in the be-hind. "Are you accusing me of stealing the dog? Because I assure you I did not. I found the poor little thing and brought her here for treatment, trying to save her life. That is all the connection I have. If you know the owner, fine." She stood up and brought Banner to heel. "Better than fine, in fact. Maybe you can contact Ms. Denise Rider and collect your fee from her, although I've gotta warn you, she left Hawkesford like a thief in the night. C'mon, Banner." She spun on her heel, her balance turning precarious.

"Wait." Dr. Kelly rose from her seat, too, placing the pen in a cat-faced cup holder. "I'm sorry. That came out wrong. Honestly, I'm not accusing you of anything."

Frankie, clinging to the edge of the desk as she regained her balance, didn't quite buy the apology. "Not the impression I got." Letting go, she took a step.

"Wait," Dr. Kelly said again, adding in a rush, "I tried to call Denise using the number listed on the chip. It's a cell phone, going straight to voice mail at present. Then I searched our records here and found the same number for her. She has an Idaho area code."

"Yes. So? I told you I just came from Hawkesford." Frankie stopped to hear the vet out, her anger fading. Dr. Kelly's concern for the dog and the woman struck Frankie as genuine.

"The thing is, I saw her just last week when they were in to renew Shine's rabies shot, so they were together then. It's just so odd when you tell me how you found the dog. This isn't like the Denise I know at all. It doesn't make any sense."

Frankie, a frisson of something... another of those apprehensive feelings? ...slithering through her brain, sat back down. Banner sank onto his haunches close to her side. "Howie—my neighbor now, Denise's before—did say Denise adored this dog, whom he called 'bitchin'."

Dr. Kelly's lips twitched ever so slightly. "He may have meant her breed. Bichon. Bichon frise."

"Oh." Frankie felt foolish. "Of course."

The two women stared at each other, Dr. Kelly frowning, Frankie feeling blank. That premonition had taken firm hold by now, and she didn't like it one bit.

"Does this Howie have any idea where Denise has gone?" The vet was still frowning.

Frankie shrugged. "He seems as baffled as anybody." She thought a moment. "Maybe we should ask him when he last saw them." Not just heard. She remembered him saying—

"Good idea. Do you have a phone number where we can reach him?" Dr. Kelly pushed her phone across the desk.

Ignoring the dial phone, Frankie dug out her cell, in which she'd programmed Howie's number, and keyed it in. What had she gotten herself into, anyway? This doing the right thing was for the birds.

On the fifth ring, Howie answered. "Oh, hey,

Frankie. So, is that dog, okay?"

"Looks like she will be. Doc says I got her here just in time. Umm, Howie, do you happen to remember the last time you saw Denise and the dog together?"

"Sure." Howie's answer came without hesitation. "Monday. Denise had just got back from one of her little trips, her and Shinola."

"Trips? Shy Nola?"

Howie chuckled. "Yeah. Or Shine, or Shiny. Depends on Denise's attitude at any given time what she calls it. The dog don't care. She answers to any of them. Anyway, it was about suppertime when I saw 'em."

"Did she say where she'd been?"

"Nope. And she always tells me when she's gonna be gone. Pays me a few bucks to keep an eye on her place."

"Did she—"

But Frankie didn't get to finish her question because Howie broke in sounding both puzzled and hurt. "Then a few hours later, she moves out and doesn't even tell me adios? It don't make sense."

"Strange." It was all Frankie could think to say.

"Hey, why you want to know?" Howie asked

before she could end the call. "What's going on?"

"I don't know. That's what I'm trying to find out. Thanks." She disconnected and sat a moment, looking down at her phone.

"Well?' Dr. Kelly hovered. Bernie, behind her, had stopped his pretense of looking through the files and stood leaning against them, waiting to hear Frankie's report.

"He last saw her three days ago," she said finally, "when he says Denise and Shine got back from a trip."

"Oh, but—" The worried expression on Dr. Kelly's face grew.

"Howie can't figure it out either." Frankie grimaced, flashing on all the stuff left in the apartment. Good stuff. Stuff a normal person would never abandon. And Shine. Shine most of all. "Why do you suppose she left in such a hurry? And where has she gone?"

The women stared at each other. An idea popped into Frankie's head that wouldn't turn loose, even though she tried her best to force it out.

What if Denise hadn't gone anywhere of her own volition? What if she, like her dog, lay somewhere out in the woods? Shot.

CHAPTER 5

Heading for Hawkesford as fast as the law allowed, Frankie pushed the Ranger along at a good clip—or maybe just a little faster. Outside the air-conditioned cab, a storm threatened, the weather turning muggy. While she'd been inside the veterinary clinic, black clouds had gathered on the northern horizon, swooping down out of Canada. They fit right in with her mood.

She cast another glance at the copy of a snapshot laying on the seat between her and Banner. The photo dated from a couple months ago, according to Dr. Kelly, when Denise Rider had brought Shine into the clinic. All Spokane veterinarians had taken their patrons pictures that day, selling them copies to raise money for the local animal shelters. They also intended publishing the photos in a special fundraiser sponsored by the newspaper.

"Denise didn't like her picture and asked not to be included," Dr. Kelly had said, "although she gave us a generous donation. The word didn't get passed along, though. The photo appeared in the paper's special section along with everyone else's."

The snapshot showed a woman in her late twenties, of medium height and medium build, as dark haired and dark eyed as Frankie herself. Ms. Rider was a good-looking woman, smiling for the camera. Nothing not to like.

Unless—Why would a woman be that public-ity shy? Frankie's imagination worked overtime, conjuring scenarios.

She and Dr. Kelly hoped Howie could dredge up a few more facts about the woman. He proba-bly knew more than he thought he did, consider-ing Denise had trusted him to look after her place when she was away. They were friends, he'd said. So why had Denise not told him she was leaving?

"I hope I'm wrong," Frankie said aloud, caus-ing Banner to shift his attention away from the wheat fields passing in a blur.

He may as well have been saying, "Huh?"

"Wrong about Shine's owner being in trouble, I mean." Reaching across the seat, she ruffled the Samoyed's pricked ears. "But I don't think I am."

No, and Dr. Kelly shared her foreboding. Well, and why not? Evidence of some kind of nefarious goings-on stood out clearly, once they'd opened their eyes. The worst part appeared to be in convincing the law of their suspicions and for them to take action. Notoriously short of people and funds, the Kootenai County Sheriff's Office had pretty much blown the veterinarian off when she called to report an act of animal cruelty in the matter of Shine's injuries. They even refused to file a missing person report. The deputy taking her call hadn't laughed at her—quite—but he hadn't said they'd investigate, either. Not without something more concrete than a wounded dog and an apartment with personal stuff left behind when the occupant moved out.

"Are you insinuating Ms. Rider shot her own dog?" Dr. Kelly's fair skin turned red. Her phone was on speaker, so Frankie heard every word.

"It's been done," the officer replied and added wearily, "nothing new about that."

Dr. Kelly and Frankie could rail against the shortsightedness all they wanted. The police needed more to go on before they'd stir a muscle.

***

Howie's side of the duplex appeared deserted when Frankie pulled onto her half of the driveway. Probably out for his afternoon libation, she thought. His help in discovering more about Shine's owner would have to wait.

No matter. As she jumped into and out of the shower in under five minutes flat, it occurred to her to ask Jesselyn's sister if she knew anything else about Denise Rider. Anything at all. Before renting to her, Vic had asked Frankie about a source of income, along with a bunch of other stuff. Denise must've filled out the same form.

But questioning Vic would have gone on a to-do list because Frankie didn't have time to pursue the matter anymore today. Already in danger of being late on her second day of work, and with her short hair still damp from the shower, she grabbed up her car keys from where they sat atop Denise and Shine's picture. At the same time, her belly rumbled, reminding her she'd had nothing to eat today.

Hunger gnawed at her stomach in surprising

intensity.

How in God's name could she neglect eating? A kind of despair claimed her. Stupid, crappy hole in the head! What else might she ignore to her own detriment?

A quick glance at her watch told her she had only a few minutes to spare. Too late for food now. Snatching up a pencil, Frankie scrawled instructions to herself across the bottom of the plain paper photocopy. Info about Denise Rider? Ask Howie or Victoria tomorrow.

Frankie started for the door just as the first deep roll of thunder reverberated overhead. The lights flickered. Banner, a dumbfounded expression on his face, let out a little howl. The next clap of thunder sent him dashing past her, paws sliding across the vinyl floor. Zipping out of the kitchen and down the hall to the bedroom, he forced his head and shoulders into the not-quite-large-enough space under the bed. His tail quivered, swishing the floor outside the draped bedspread at a new peal of thunder.

"Banner, my darling boy," Frankie said, following him, "you are such a puss. We don't have time for this." Not that she liked the racket either. The closest reverberation reminded her too much of bombs and explosions. It was all she could do not to duck and join him.

Still, she couldn't resist reaching over and tweaking the dog's tail where it stuck out from under the bed. He made a kind of hiccup low in his throat and jumped, whacking his head on the bed springs.

Frankie snickered. "Come out of there, you big baby. Listen—the thunder is dying away already."

A lie.

Unconvinced, Banner shuffled around until his black nose peeked out. Still, with a little encouragement and a lot of promises, at her command, he fought his way from under bed until he sat close to her—on her foot, to be precise. Sheepish now, his head hung, and his tongue lolled as she gave him a hug. "There's just no explaining to you, is there, that you don't need to be afraid of the thunder? It's the lightning that'll get you."

Banner whimpered as he followed her to the door. At the last minute, Frankie decided to take him with her to work, hurrying him through a downpour out to the pickup. No way would she leave the terrified dog on his own in a strange house. No way. Lew, Karl, and the crew would just have to put up with him.

What Karl or anyone else thought turned out to be a nonstarter. Maggie Owens, staying overtime to run the dispatch desk was the only person at the station. "They're all at a traffic accident a couple miles south of here," she informed Frankie even as she bustled into the restroom and came back with a handful of paper towels. She put them to use rubbing the rain from Banner's glistening white coat, apparently not noticing Frankie suffered from a like degree of wetness. "Marc and Chris have the new ambulance out on that one. Report said the car caught fire, so Karl took the pumper truck, too, with Darryl Holland and a couple other boys."

With no change of expression, she added, "This dog is shaking like a leaf. What have you been doing to him?"

Frankie snorted as a particularly close roll of thunder made Banner flinch.

"Oh." Maggie nodded. "I see. He doesn't like storms."

An understatement.

"No, he doesn't." Frankie, smelling the rich aroma of fresh coffee, brushed past Maggie, and went into the lunch room. The pot was still gurgling as she reached down a clean pottery cup from a collection beside the coffee maker. "Do I ever need this." She poured a cup and took a scalding sip.

An open package of Oreos sat on the counter. Frankie crammed one into her mouth and took an extra to munch.

Maggie finished her self-imposed dog-drying task. "You look tired, Frankie. Couldn't sleep last night? Pretty common when you start a new job. My husband always says..."

Frankie lost the rest of Maggie's rambling dissertation on adjusting to employment as she watched Lew pull into the parking lot and run through the rain into the station. He looked distinctly sour and out of sorts. This shift might not turn out as warm and fuzzy as the previous night's.

"Damnedest thing," he said. "Almost had to call the ambulance out for me. Some dumbass kid pulling out of a driveway came within an inch of broadsiding me."

Just as Maggie opened her mouth—to ask for particulars, Frankie supposed—the computer switchboard lit up. Maggie slid into her chair as the report came in, fingers on the keys and typing at breakneck speed. At the same time, their siren blared a summons. The call, it turned out, was for them, Frankie and Lew. A wreck on Highway 95, a half-mile south of Cecil B. Harmon Road.

Lew screwed his ball cap down and jerked on a pair of yellow coveralls hanging from a rack by the garage. "Saddle up," he snapped at Frankie. "Move it."

In less than thirty seconds, Banner left in Maggie's tender care, they were underway, Lew complaining about being stuck with the back-up bus.

"Lousy weather brings out every idiot on the road," he muttered. "Need new wiper blades for this rig, Frankie. Put them on the list."

Lacking note paper, Frankie tried to embed the words in her brain. "Got it." She crossed her fingers.

Face a little tense Lew peered through the wall of rain streaming in heavy rivers down the windshield. The wind still howled with crop-flattening force, shaking the heavy ambulance and blowing the faulty wipers askew.

Dispatch reported sketchy information about the accident. Word had come in from a good Samaritan with a cell phone saying he'd seen a car overturned in the ditch. The state police had a unit enroute to the scene with an ETA only a minute or two less than their own. Their own resident deputy, Gabe Zantos, came on and reported he was available if they needed him. Lew replied he'd get back with him.

Frankie held onto the edge of the seat as Lew made the turn onto the highway and sped north. She was sweating inside her own yellow breakout gear, not only because they were horribly hot in the oppressive atmosphere, but because she hated these road conditions. The rain and wind reminded her too much of the dust and wind prevalent in Afghanistan. Better Lew at the wheel than her.

She peered out into an afternoon as dark as most nights. "How much farther?"

"Couple miles." Lew's gaze never strayed from the road. The emergency lights flashing on top of the ambulance glared off the rain-wet highway. Their siren warned an old beater of a pickup creeping along at thirty-miles-an-hour to get out of their way.

Were they never going to get to the scene? Frankie squinted through the rain and steady beat of the windshield wipers. Consciously, she knew only a few minutes had passed since the call, even though it seemed much longer. Wind buffeted the ambulance.

***

Ed Bennett, the ISP officer, had flares out when they arrived, glowing beacons warning motorists of the accident. He stood on the road above the ditched car with rain dripping from his hat brim and smoking a cigarette he held inside his hand.

Frankie sprang from the ambulance as soon as Lew stopped, ran around to the back, and grabbed the medical bag.

Rain splattered on her uncovered head, the drops striking like ice pellets.

"How many victims?" she asked Bennett.

"Just one." He grimaced. "But he's a humdinger. Bleeding like a stuck hog. Squealing like one, too. You'd better double-glove and put on ear muffs."

"Ear muffs?"

"You'll see," he said.

Lew, grunting, said, "Hand me the bag," and taking it from her, slid down the embankment to lead the way.

As far as wrecks went, Frankie supposed this

one could've been far worse. The first report had been a little erroneous, for the car, a late-model Cadillac Escalade, wasn't completely overturned. Judging by the crunched front-end and the passenger's side quarter-panels, it had gone over the shoulder and hit the ditch pretty hard.

As long as his seatbelt had been fastened and the airbags worked, the victim should've been okay. Of course, Frankie reminded herself, you never can tell for sure until you take a look. Sometimes—

She cut off the memory before it could take hold.

In the slash/slash of the lights atop the patrol car and ambulance, she could see the lone occupant. To her relief, he was sitting up, wiping his face.

Also yammering a blue-streak and cussing up a storm.

Dribbles of blood had splashed onto the beige leather and suede upholstery inside the Cadillac. The deflated airbag flopped dismally over the top of the steering wheel. Lew swung open the driver's door and held it against the wind.

"Damn well time some of you people got here," the patient grumbled, snuffling through a profusely bloodied nose. "Thought maybe you were waiting for the Saudis to start selling snow cones instead of oil."

"Take it easy, sir," Frankie said. As Lew stood back, allowing her to take point, she bent into the car, using her most soothing, professional voice. She pulled on gloves—a single pair, not double. "You'll be all right. We'll have you out of here in a jiffy."

Opening the medical bag, she found a splint and fitted it around the man's neck as a precaution against spinal injury. A blood pressure cuff velcroed onto his left arm took a reading that was a bit high, though not outrageously so, considering. She counted his pulse, rapid, strong. Her flashlight flicked a couple of times in each of his eyes. Pupils normal and reactive to the glare.

"Do you hurt anywhere, sir? Legs, arms, back?"

"Christ on a crutch! Of course, I hurt. All over. What do you think? Take a look at this car. Take a look at my nose. I could've had my eyes put out with all the glass flying around in here."

She ducked in time to avoid a waving fist, which he used to punctuate his words. His legs and arms must be all right, considering they moved just fine. Out of the corner of her eye, she saw another police vehicle—this one a four-wheel drive SUV—pull up, lights flashing. A man got out.

"The glass is tempered safety glass, sir." Frankie broke open a package of sterile gauze pads and swabbed at the blood coating the lower half of his face. "You'll be glad to know it fragments into beebees instead of shards. Did you hit your nose on the steering wheel?"

"What? Yeah, I guess. I don't know. No. Must've been the airbag exploding. Good God Almighty, look at this mess! Blood and glass all over everywhere. What's a goddamn airbag good for, anyway? Made the car cost more, and still busted my nose."

In Frankie's humble opinion, it was too bad he hadn't hit his mouth instead of his nose. Not to be unsympathetic, but she'd just as soon he shut up and quit hollering in her ear—or at least say something helpful. In Afghanistan—

Her mind shied away from memories of the wounded there. Agonized cries for help. Cursing. Silence.

The only apparent injury this man had was the broken nose. That much had been obvious even to him. He may have had previous experience with such an injury because before she could prevent him, he reached up and wrenched at the offending appendage. Cartilage grated, making her wince with annoyed sympathy.

"Sir," she protested, "please don't do that. You may do yourself more harm."

Not to mention getting the whole emergency services team in trouble if something went wrong and he filed suit against them.

He moaned aloud, permitting her to pull his hands down. Fresh blood rolled down his face. She made a clicking sound with tongue against teeth and tried to pack his nose with gauze, standard practice, only to have him brush her off.

"Leave it," he said. "It's all right. I don't want that stuff stuck in my head."

"It'll help stop the bleeding."

"No."

"Your eyes are already turning black." Frankie derived a little satisfaction in the warning. Give the obnoxious devil something real to complain about, she thought.

"Jesus H. Christ," he said and then mercifully fell silent. He looked pallid and ghostly under the car's dome light. She dabbed at his face with more of the gauze, applying light pressure to a couple small cuts.

Outside, she heard Lew talking to somebody before he poked his head in the door beside her. "How is he, Frankie? Think he can answer a few questions? Bennett's directing traffic past us, but Deputy Zantos is here."

The injured man answered for himself. "Hell, yes, I can answer questions. My goddamn nose is broke, not my vocal cords."

She couldn't help murmuring a little something under her breath that caused him to give her a sharp look.

"What?" he asked.

Frankie gave herself a mental slap. "Sorry. Talking to myself," she said.

A man in a tan uniform hunkered down beside the car, his knees burrowing into the sopping wet weed patch beside the Cadillac's doorframe. He ignored the discomfort, pulling a pen and an accident report form from under his uniform jacket where he'd been keeping them dry.

"Now then, Mr. Pettigrew," he said, "I'm going to take the accident report. I'll need your driver's license, address, and phone number if you don't mind. And then you can tell me what happened."

It wasn't until he said, "Mr. Pettigrew," that the penny dropped, and Frankie recognized her patient as Jesselyn's older brother. At one time, she'd had a huge crush on him, but he'd changed a lot with the passing years. When she lived in Hawkesford as a girl, he'd often been around. Not so now. Jesselyn said he lived in Spokane and drove between his home in the city and the old family homestead to do the farming. He spent spring, summer and fall working the Pettigrew land belonging to his elderly father, Big Mike Pettigrew.

That had been his destination tonight, Pettigrew said. "I saw the storm brewing early this afternoon. The old man's had a lot of trouble getting around the last couple of years, taken some bad falls lately. Most of the neighbors blame me for his trouble, God only knows why seeing as how he has two frigging daughters living right here in Hawkesford. You'd think they could look in on him once in a while, but no. It always falls to me.

"Anyway, I got worried about him, and it's a damn good thing I did. The old man hadn't so much as latched the barn doors, let alone put away his patio furniture. If I hadn't come, stuff would've been blown from here to hell and back. He'd have been on the horn starting about four a.m. yelling at me to come gather his junk for him."

It took a puzzled moment for Frankie to catch up, Russ Pettigrew's complaint putting a new twist on things. She could have sworn Jesselyn had said she spent a lot of time at the farm helping her dad out. It seemed strange for Russ to say he was the one old Mr. Pettigrew depended on to take care of the odd chore or two.

Sibling rivalry, she supposed. Or just Russ's bad mood.

A fresh flow of blood spurted from his nose, heavy enough to cause Frankie extra concern. "Can't this wait?" she asked the cop. "He should take it easy."

The cop glanced at her. "Quicker if we do it now."

His hazel eyes were black-lashed and beautiful, she noted, her attention caught. Also, he was young to be a district deputy.

Russ snuffled through his swollen nose. "Right. Get it over with, Zantos. Where was I? Oh yeah, what with one thing and another, I took off too late to beat the weather home. Guess I should have sat out the storm, kept the old poop company."

He fell silent, then swiveled his eyes toward

Frankie. "Sonofabitch. You got anything for pain?"

Frankie shook her head. "I'm so sorry. You may have a head injury. I can't administer drugs without first consulting a physician."

"Well, consult then. Jesus Christ!" His leaned against the seat and took a couple of deep shuddering breaths.

She peered over the deputy's shoulder. "Lew?"

He nodded and clambered up the embankment to the ambulance.

Rain drummed on the Cadillac's roof. Some entered through the broken windshield. Wind shook the open door. The nutty aroma of ripe wheat blew in from the surrounding fields, the scent all the more intense for being wet. Underlying that was a faint odor of spilled gasoline and hot oil. She hoped Ed was being careful, smoking up there on the road. Didn't want him blowing them all up. She shivered, reminded again of Afghanistan.

"What caused you to go in the ditch?" the cop asked. "Or did a deer run out in front of you?"

"Nah," Russ said. "Deer don't come out in weather like this. They're too smart. Some asshole sideswiped me, is what happened." His grumbling voice was strong and angry. "The idiot crossed the center line over to my side of the road and damn near hit me head-on. My windshield shattered when I hit the ditch, showered me with broken glass. Scared the holy living shit right out of me, I can tell you. Thought I was going to get my throat cut." He added as an afterthought, "Bastard trashed my car."

"I think your car can be repaired," Frankie said. She couldn't help thinking the accident could've turned out a whole lot worse.

"What do you mean—repair my car?" Pettigrew snorted. "I wouldn't keep a car that's been wrecked for five frigging minutes. I'd be scared to drive the thing out to the mailbox and back. Who knows what'll turn up after you've signed off on your insurance. If it's later, you're shit out of luck."

The deputy cleared his throat with a rough, dry cough that made Frankie glance toward him and smile.

"Maybe I could just take the accident report in plain English, Mr. Pettigrew," Deputy Zantos said. "I know you're upset, but there's no need to yell or swear at either of us. We're trying to help you."

In the midst of reading Pettigrew's blood pressure for the third time, she saw the needle quiver, then steady.

After a moment, he said, "You're right, deputy. I apologize Ms....You're little Frankie McGill, aren't you? Jesselyn's friend, home from the war. I'm sorry. Forgot myself.

"I've heard worse." She sensed, more than saw, the deputy's quick glance.

"Anyhow," Pettigrew said, leaning back against the headrest, grumbled, "this is what happened." He hacked a globule of blood from the back of his throat, spat past both the cop and her out the open door, and took up his story. "Wind drove the rain hard enough my wipers couldn't keep up. I suppose the other guy had the same problem. The car seemed to come out of a regular wall of rain. I saw a flash of headlights. Next thing I know, bam! He scraped the side of the Caddy. I swerved enough to avoid a head-on but landed in the ditch before my brakes even cut in. That's all. I didn't even see what kinda car it was."

The deputy finished taking down Russ' report and closed the book with a sharp snap. "Unfortunately, it's unlikely we'll find the other driver. Our best chance is if he brings his car into a body shop and claims damages on his insurance. Maybe we'll be lucky enough to match a paint sample and make an arrest."

Pettigrew's eyes drifted closed, the black spreading beneath them like a slow-moving oil slick even as Frankie watched. "Oh, hell, yes. My guess is it'll be just like when somebody stole ten thousand dollars' worth of tools out of the old man's shop. Then a few weeks ago, we lost a chain saw, a roll of fencing wire, and a slew of other tools. A deputy took the report then, too, and that was the last we ever heard. We don't even bother reporting the petty stuff anymore, like emptied gas tanks. We finally figured out as long as nobody gets killed, the law doesn't give a shit. Maybe not even then. Depends on who it is, I suppose."

Now that, Frankie thought, sneaking a wary look at the cop, was voicing an opinion with a vengeance.

Although the officer's face remained oddly expressionless, a flush painted his cheekbones red. "Then be grateful you're alive to complain."

"We're done here," Lew broke in, having slogged back to the car with authorization to administer a pain injection—which Frankie promptly did.

"Let's get Mr. Pettigrew transported."

The storm had rolled east by the time they finished loading their patient. Frankie climbed into the ambulance alongside Russ Pettigrew for the ride into Coeur d'Alene. The rain tapered off to a sprinkle, then stopped as Lew urged the four-wheel drive out of the slick stubble and onto the highway.

"Look at this," Russ said, sitting up against Frankie's protest and gesturing at the rolling hills on either side of the road. "Crops flattened. Grain sopping wet, what the wind has left in the head. It'll be three days before we can get in the fields again, and that's supposing another gully-washer doesn't blow through. Some harvest weather!"

Frankie remembered hearing the same kind of talk all her life. She was looking for more of the same when he abruptly changed direction.

"So what do you think about your tenant?" he asked.

"My tenant?" Frankie blinked.

"Yeah. The cop. District Deputy Gabe Zantos. The guy living in your grandma's house. Your house now, so Jesselyn says."

"I don't think anything about him. We haven't even formally met." Well, maybe she thought a little about him. But telling her patient, she admired the cop's eyes wasn't exactly kosher. Guess she could say she'd expected someone older, someone... different.

"Not much formal about meeting a cop—or a tenant." Russ lay back with a sigh. "Wonder when he's gonna get off his duff and go after the criminal element around here."

Like who'd shot poor little Shine and why, for instance, Frankie agreed internally. And maybe investigate where Denise Rider had gone in such a hurry.

She'd broach the subject when she saw the deputy again. After all, he was the guy who rented her grandmother's house. He couldn't blow her off.

CHAPTER 6

The neighborhood was quiet around Howie's place when Frankie got home in the early morning. No real surprise since she doubted he was an "up with the birds" kind of guy.

Just as well, too. Yawning, she let herself into the duplex. Discussion regarding his friend Denise would have to wait another few hours. Howie was going to be surprised when she started questioning him about his neighbor.

Unfortunately, plunging right into bed didn't come up big on Banner's screen. The moment Frankie opened the door to let him in, he gave a sharp bark and dashed through the living room with his nose to the floor. Next came the bedroom, where he sniffed long and hard around the bed before going on to the bath. His final stop was the kitchen.

"Oh, please, not again." Frankie, sighing, dragged after him wearily. "Now what's the matter with you? I swear—" She broke off, standing immobile in the doorway.

"Crap," she said. "Crap, crap, crap."

The back door hung open, swinging in the gentle breeze wafting through. Papers lay scattered on the floor. Chairs at the table sat at an angle, items on the counter had been knocked over and moved around. The bottom drawer in the bank of cabinets left of the fridge sagged open several inches.

Banner growled; a first in Frankie's recollection during the whole six months they'd been together.

"Banner, my boy, I don't like this any better than you do." Speaking out loud, her voice echoed in a silence so deep she jumped when the refrigerator's motor kicked on.

Had Howie been in her apartment, by any chance? No surprise if his key worked in her lock as well as his own. But why would he do such a thing?

Or, and here a sinking feeling gripped her, had she forgotten and left the door open when she went to work? Remembering her hurry in shooing Banner out the front, was it possible?

No. The storm, going strong by then, denied that. Besides, she distinctly remembered buttoning the place up. Verification came a moment later when her gaze touched upon several large, muddy footprints tracking across her clean kitchen floor. They alone were enough to confirm a prowler had paid a call—correction—another call. The chairs and the open drawer were added evidence.

It hadn't been Howie. The feet were much too big.

"Come here, Banner." Banner's actions reminded her all too much of the bomb-sniffing war dogs. As if expecting one to go off in her kitchen, she called the dog away from his business of sniffing every surface the intruder had touched.

Frankie breathed a sigh of relief when he made it back to her unscathed. Her hand on his neck, she led him outside again, to the pickup.

They got in, Banner staring at her with questions in his eyes when they sat there without starting the engine.

"I've got to do it," she told him. But she didn't

want to. Especially not on only her second day in Hawkesford. Flipping open her cell phone, the cheapest pay-by-the-month model available, she gritted her teeth and punched in nine-one-one. Dispatch answered. She stated her problem.

"No," she said. "No one is in there now."

"Don't go back inside the building," the day shift dispatcher, a guy named Benton, instructed. "But remain available. Someone will be around as soon as possible."

"I'll be out front." Frankie reached for the handle that tilted back the seat and closed her eyes. A minute later, they popped open again.

"Damn." Righting the seat, she sighed and got out of the truck, telling Banner, "Stay here." A cautious look around showed no lurkers hiding nearby. Any activity came from the sound of traffic on the highway three blocks over. Walking swiftly the few steps to Howie's door, she gave it a good series of thumps.

Nothing.

Another round with her closed fist. Waited. Nothing. Either Howie hadn't come home the night before, or— Forget that. He was probably just sleeping off the rigors of the night. Having done what she considered her neighborly duty,

Frankie returned to the pickup. Howie was all right. He must be.

**

Two hours later, Gabe Zantos woke her up, tapping on the half-open pickup window. Heart playing leapfrog in her chest, she squinted out at him.

It was a damn good thing she wasn't carrying a gun because—between the deputy pounding on her car and Banner, who'd been sleeping too, yelping in surprise—she just might have shot him. Meaning the deputy, not the dog.

More moments than she liked to think of ticked past as, heart pounding, she stared into his eyes. Hazel, verging on green in this light, like deep lake water.

Finally, he blinked and crooked a smile. "You all right?" he asked.

Frankie sat up. Even with the windows rolled down and the building still shading the driveway, the pickup's interior was stifling. Banner panted, tongue hanging out, as he tromped onto her lap to check on the intruder. Frankie pushed the dog aside.

"Tired," she answered, the deputy's question finally sinking in. "I've been up all night." Not to mention most of the day and all the night before.

"Yeah, I'm aware," he said. "Night shift. We met yesterday evening. You had a break-in?"

"Yes." Wits slowly coming back to her, Frankie opened the pickup's door and stepped out. Banner jumped down beside her. "Somebody broke into my apartment during the night. Whoever it was came in through the back."

Zantos, making a come along gesture, led the way to the duplex. "Anything taken?"

"I have no idea." Frankie felt stupid. She hadn't even looked, not really.

The deputy pushed open the front door, stopped and peered inside. "Doesn't look bad. Nothing broken that I can see, in this room at least."

"No, I know. I didn't even realize anyone had been in here at first."

Banner squeezed into the house in front of Frankie. As he had earlier, he put his nose to the floor, sniffing out traces of the prowler.

"He did that when we came home, too. I didn't pay much attention until he kicked up a fuss in the kitchen. I followed him in there, which is when I found the back door open and stuff—" Frankie hesitated. "Stuff out of place. Poked through, disturbed, tossed around. And then I saw he'd gone through all the rooms."

"He?" Zantos held the door for her, and they followed the dog into the duplex.

"Yes. A guy with big feet. Maybe even size twelves."

"Huh. And you know that how?"

"Thanks to the storm, he left muddy footprints all over my kitchen."

"Careless of him. I hope you didn't wipe them up."

"Of course not. I'm not stupid." Wounded maybe, she added silently. A bit forgetful. And she couldn't deny information often took a few clicks longer to process than before Afghanistan happened. But not stupid.

Her tart reply brought his full attention back to her. "I didn't mean to imply you are. I've had people do things like that. Destroy evidence without thinking."

"Oh." Frankie shrugged. "It never occurred to me to clean up. I'm not that good a housekeeper, I guess, especially not at six in the morning after working all night." Although, it did sound like something her grandmother might have done.

The deputy smiled back. "I can relate to that. Busy night considering it's mid-week." A friendly statement, not a question.

"Yes, pretty much non-stop until three. Then it tapered off."

He nodded. "Russ Pettigrew okay?"

"As far as I know. His nose is the worst of his injuries. Treated and released."

"Good." He sounded preoccupied. "That's good." Taking a small digital camera out of his pocket, he clicked off a few shots of the kitchen—the door askew, the littered floor, the most outstanding set of footprints.

"Hiking boots," Frankie said helpfully. "Cabela's house brand."

"Yep." Zantos didn't seem much impressed by her observation. "But if you're thinking we can trace the perp through them, I'll remind you Cabelas has probably sold several hundred pairs out of their State Line store alone."

"But maybe not hundreds of size twelves. And the tread looks new."

Frankie refused to let him put her down, and to her surprise, he grinned and replied, "Good point."

The next item out of his pocket was a little notebook in which he wrote a few lines. When finished, he looked up and said, "You want to see if you're missing anything?"

A quick walkthrough showed her drawers had been pawed through, providing an almost overwhelming "ick" factor to the break-in. Curiously, her small store of DVDs, no more than a half dozen, had each been broken into quarters. In the kitchen, she found the garbage can under the sink, almost empty since she hadn't fixed even one meal here as yet, had been dumped on the cupboard floor. The drawer intended to store her few bills and papers looked like it had been stirred with an electric mixer.

The deputy leaned against the kitchen counter, watching her. Banner, smiling his Samoyed smile, stayed right with him, enticed by the way Zantos chose just the right spot under his ear to scratch.

"Nothing is gone that I can see," she said, at last, gnawed by the idea there was something. She just couldn't put her finger on it. "Except I guess he didn't care for my taste in movies since he broke all my DVDs. No great loss, I suppose."

"But curious."

"Yes." She thought a moment. "Are you going to take fingerprints?"

His hesitation was palpable. "You say nothing is missing?"

Frankie, frowning, shook her head. "I don't think so."

"Then I'd recommend changing your locks and getting a dead-bolt for your doors, Ms. McGill."

"Forget it happened, in other words." Just like Russ Pettigrew had said.

"Not forget. Take reasonable precautions, so it doesn't happen again."

"I'd rather you caught whoever did it." The challenge sprang from Frankie's mouth before conscious thought. "This is twice somebody has ransacked this place. You'd think he would've figured out by now that whatever he's looking for isn't here."

Gabe Zantos snapped erect. "Did you just say this isn't the first time? Did you report the previous incident?"

"No." Frankie felt uncomfortable, aware now that she'd committed a blunder. "It happened the night before I moved in."

"So how do you know—"

Frankie cut him off. "This place came up for

rent suddenly. Jesselyn Pettigrew—you know Jesselyn?"

He nodded.

Of course. Everyone in town knew Jesselyn and the rest of the Pettigrew family.

"Well, Jesselyn's sister Victoria is the realtor who handles the property, and she told Jesselyn the previous tenant had just moved out. So we dashed over here after I landed the EMS job to take a look. It's funny—not haha funny, strange funny—but the woman had left a bunch of her stuff here, good stuff. Weird. Anyhow, the next morning when I moved in, Howie St. James from next door was helping me open up, and we discovered the couch cushions ripped open and some other damage that hadn't been present the night before."

"Sounds like Howie and I had better have a talk." Gabe clicked his ballpoint pen and made a note.

"It wasn't Howie," Frankie said. "He has a broken arm. And, for a guy, he's got really little feet."

The deputy cocked an eyebrow.

"He wears flip flops. Besides, I notice feet." Women's feet mostly, especially if they wore heels, but anybody wearing sandals. Both fashion statements barred to her forevermore.

"I'll talk to St. James," Gabe said again and put his notebook in his pocket.

Frankie guessed he'd decided he was done here.

Wrong guess.

"That's not all." She planted herself in his path before he could get around her.

His brow lifted. "What else?"

Frankie took a deep breath. She was pretty certain Dr. Kelly's animal abuse and missing person report hadn't been passed on because Deputy Zantos didn't seem the type to just blow it off. Not in view of his prompt—well, fairly prompt—attention to her break-in.

"Yesterday morning Banner—my dog—dug his way out of the back yard."

At his name, the dog came over and sat beside her. The deputy's shoulders twitched, a sure sign of impatience.

Frankie hurried her words. "He found a little dog behind the duplex, out in the woods. She'd been shot and was barely hanging onto life. I rushed her to a veterinarian, and, between all of our efforts, we managed to save her. Turns out she is the previous tenant's dog."

Zantos shook his head. "Sad. Sometimes a person will kill an animal rather than take it with them. Despicable truth."

Frankie gulped. Yeah. She knew that. "But it's not likely this person did."

"What makes you so sure?"

"Because it so happens the vet I chanced upon is the same one who has been treating this particular dog. This perfectly healthy, purebred bichon frise, microchipped and current on all vaccinations whose most recent check-up was less than a week ago. Does it sound reasonable to you the owner would just up and kill it? Quixotic, wouldn't you say?"

"Yeah, I would." Gabe's deep hazel gaze sharpened as he thought over the information. "It doesn't mesh. I'll—"

"There's more," Frankie cut in.

"I'm probably not going to like it, am I?"

"Probably not." Frankie's lips turned up in a tiny smile. "Turns out Denise Rider, the woman who lived this place, seems to be out-of-touch. Dr. Kelly, the veterinarian, tried all the contacts and couldn't reach her. Her phones rings and rings." She took a breath. "Does this tickle your curiosity in any way? Because the person Dr.

Kelly spoke with in the sheriff's department in Coeur d'Alene couldn't have cared less."

Gabe dragged a chair away from the table and sat down. "Consider my curiosity tickled. You have my attention." He pointed at the chair opposite, which Frankie took to mean she also should sit. When she was perched on the edge of the chair, he folded his hands in front of him and eyed her appraisingly. "What are you getting at, Ms. McGill? Are you saying the woman hurt the dog and did a bunk, or are you implying something has happened to the woman? Something related to what happened to the dog? And if so, what makes you think so?"

Frankie was glad they were sitting in the kitchen where the open door helped air some of the peculiar odors from the place. She wished she'd combed her hair after work, though. Made sure the thin spot over the plate in her head was covered. And maybe washed her face. Gabe Zantos, with his warm, soft voice and compelling hazel eyes, had a peculiar effect on her. She brushed it aside and collected her thoughts.

'Report,' she heard her commanding officer, a certain lieutenant named Jay Woodson saying as clearly as though he stood over her. 'Short and to the point. What did you see with your own eyes? That's all I want to know.'

So Frankie reported. Reiterated about the torn-up apartment, the wounded dog, the repeated break-ins and, most of all, the peculiar actions Denise Rider seemed to have taken.

At first, the deputy kept his eyes on her as he listened, intent on the story. Then his attention, caught by Banner's odd behavior, wandered. He wasn't alone. Frankie stopped in mid-sentence to watch the dog, and neither of them seemed to notice when she stopped talking.

"Is your dog typically so nervous?" Zantos asked apologetically. "Or have I got him upset?"

Frankie caught Banner by the scruff of the neck and held him the next time he paced past her chair. Her hand caressed, trying to soothe. "I don't think it's you. And he's not normally a hyper dog. I've gotten him over his aversion to men."

The deputy's dark eyebrows took a jump. "Aversion to men?"

"A man abused him rather badly before we adopted each other. Kicked him. Yelled. Starved him."

"Bastard." Gabe shook his head, disgust on his

face. "But he didn't seem to mind me petting him earlier."

She nodded. "I saw. He's good now." Mostly. But even as she spoke, Banner pulled away and took off toward the bedroom, his toenails clattering on the floor. Once there, he let out a pitiful little cry followed by a short, sharp bark.

Frowning, Frankie lurched to her feet. "Excuse me. I've got to see why Banner is so upset. Dammit! I think it's this place. He's hated it here from the second we moved in. I can't say as I blame him. I do too."

The deputy trailed them both into the bedroom.

They found Banner sniffing and scratching at the mattress Frankie had found so smelly and disgusting the first time—the only time—she'd slept on it.

Good grief. Had he scented bedbugs? Puzzled, she told Banner to stand back. When he did, she bent to peel away the sheet and lift the mattress corner at the foot of the bed where the dog had pointed.

"Shit." She dropped the mattress and jerked erect.

Gabe started forward at the alarm she failed to

hide. "What is it?"

"Oh, shit," she said again, although, it wasn't feces, actually, but blood, which once disturbed, released an acrid metallic stench—one you didn't need to be a dog to smell—into the hot room.

CHAPTER 7

Frankie's stomach twisted, knotting into a leaden ball. No mistaking the bloodstain for anything other than what it was. She was all too familiar with spilled blood to be mistaken.

She dropped the corner of the mattress like she'd latched onto a fire-roasted potato.

"Well," Gabe Zantos said from over her shoulder, "that's interesting."

"Is that what you call it?" Interesting wasn't the word racing through Frankie's mind. Scary? Yeah. That worked. So did disgusting and unnerving. She rubbed her hands on her jeans.

"I wonder if this is where the dog was shot." The deputy shouldered her—gently, to be sure—out of the way and did his own mattress lifting to take a look. He flipped the whole thing, bedding and all, off the springs, revealing more blood-stains at the head of the bed. The mattress had not only been switched over but also end to end. Someone had taken time to try and cover up the deed. At least for the short term.

"No bullet hole. A lot of blood." She kept her voice level, unwilling to reveal that while blood, even in amounts more than this didn't ordinarily bother her, finding any in the bed where she intended to sleep—had slept—freaked her out big time.

"True." Zantos eyed the mattress again. "Not enough for a person to have bled out, but too much for anything simple, like a cut. I suppose you could tell if the bullet went through the dog."

"Yes. It did. Her ear first, then cutting through her shoulder muscle."

The deputy scratched the back of his neck.

"You'd think Howie would've heard a gunshot." Even to herself, Frankie sounded accusatory.

"Provided he was home and sober enough to hear anything."

The deputy, Frankie thought, must be well acquainted with her neighbor. "There is that."

Zantos didn't look happy. "You got someplace to go for the next few hours?"

"Go?" What did he mean? Her head felt thick as the mattress, brain slowed by sleep deprivation and worry.

He had his phone open. "This place will need to be processed. You need to clear out while that's going on. Pack a bag, take your dog and find a place to stay."

She stared at him. "But—"

"Pretty obvious somebody flipped this mattress to hide the blood," he explained, not even sounding impatient. "Probably didn't have any way to get rid of it without being seen. We need to know what we're dealing with. If this is dog blood, it's one thing. If it's human blood, something else."

She had to ask. "Do you think someone has murdered Ms. Rider?"

"Do you?"

Frankie winced. "I hope not."

"So do I, but that's what we need to find out. When you combine this—" His gesture took in not only the bed but the whole apartment. "—with everything else going on, I don't think we can just wait and see." The phone connection he was trying to make went through. Turning his back, he set cogs in motion. When he turned again, she was still standing there. "Bag?" he urged.

Not being a high maintenance woman, five minutes was enough for Frankie to scout out a fresh set of clothing, a few toiletries and some minimal makeup, all under the deputy's watchful eye.

It took practically as long to grab Banner's food, sheepskin bed, and grooming tools. He was due for a good brushing.

Gabe stopped her as she started out the door. "Leave me a phone number. I'll need to get in touch with you when the crime scene people get here."

Frankie's head tilted, asking a question.

"They'll need a sample of your blood, among other things," he said. "Let me know where you'll be."

Aware that her gaze back at him was as blank as pure white paper, she fought a yawn. "I don't know, right now. Coeur d'Alene, probably, until I go to work. I've gotta find a motel that'll allow a dog."

He cocked his head. "Don't—" He stopped, seemed to make up his mind about something. Reaching into his pants pocket, he drew out a key ring. As she stared at him, puzzled, he worked one loose. "Take this."

She didn't move. "What is it?"

"Front door key to my house." A faint smile quirked. "Your house. Use one of the upstairs bedrooms."

"I can't do that." Even to her, the protest sounded weak.

"Why not? It's a big place, and I'm not using it all right now." Grimacing wryly, he added, "And probably won't be for a while. Go get some rest."

***

Frankie's grandparents' house, where they'd raised their daughter's child, was on the other side of town. Backed by a ten-acre field filled with grazing alpacas, the two-story farmhouse—genuine to the era, not one of the pseudo styles built in the 1980s—sheltered under a mixed scattering of trees, some deciduous, some evergreen. A row of tall poplars made a windbreak along one side.

The house was still the finest place in town, she thought loyally as she pulled into the driveway and parked in front of the detached garage. The pickup fit there like it belonged. As it should. The Ranger had belonged to her grandfather. Close to twenty years old, it still looked great and ran well.

Either Gabe Zantos had a green thumb, or he hired a yard service. The lawn had been cut within the last twenty-four hours. Wide flowerbeds on either side of the walkway burst with spicy smelling red and white petunias and the huge peony bushes spaced under the front windows had been dead-headed after blooming and trimmed back. Gramps and Grandma would've been pleased.

Mr. Furnough, who'd lived next door to the McGills since the 1940s or before, was outside watering his roses. He waved to Frankie.

She waved back. It was as if she were in high school, coming home for lunch. As if her six years in the service of her country had never happened. The nerve behind her eye twitched.

The McGill house may have looked like it just stepped out of the nineteenth century, but the locks were new. Frankie, weary near to dropping, keyed the smooth-working mechanism gratefully and pushed open the door. She hadn't been inside since the year before her grandmother died, being overseas at the time. Once stateside and out of the hospital, she'd dropped by and, under the trust lawyer's aegis, taken possession of the pickup, but hadn't entered the house. Zantos had already been living here by then, his lease handled by an agency.

Victoria Pettigrew's agency. The thought clunked in Frankie's brain, along with the memory of something else to do with Jesselyn's sister. Talk to her—ask her something. But what?

Dammit!

Like any thrifty homeowner, Deputy Zantos had pulled the blinds before he left for work this morning, shutting the sun out of the house to keep it cool. Frankie passed through the foyer into the dim living room—parlor, so Gram always called it—stumbling a little as Banner brushed against her leg.

"Mmmm." A small sound came from deep in her throat as if from far away. Memories rose up in waves, and she felt like crying.

Banner cocked his head at her, swiping her hand with his tongue.

Zantos rented the place furnished, so everything looked pretty much as always. Except for the big UHD LED TV, taking the place of her grandma's twenty-seven-incher, and a modern leather chair with a separate ottoman that sat in front of it. Those must belong to the deputy. One of Grandma's walnut tables stood next to the chair, its surface filled by a reading lamp and a stack of books and magazines. An empty plate held a few crumbs of what looked like carrot cake.

The deputy didn't seem the baking type. A good-looking guy with a well-paid job in a small town like Hawkesford, he probably had a slew of girlfriends. Frankie could easily imagine them beating a path to his door, armed with, among other enticements, carrot cake.

Shrugging, she led Banner into the kitchen and found it almost as tidy as in an earlier day. The fridge's motor kicked in with a hum as she fished a familiar old bowl from the cupboard, filled it with water, and set it on the linoleum floor. Banner surged forward, lapping as if he were dying of thirst.

By the time she'd climbed the steep stairs, which took a ninety-degree turn about halfway up, it felt as though she'd never been gone. The place even smelled the same—old, with a slight fragrance of wood from the cedar-lined clos-ets—especially the second story. Downstairs, the tiny scent of eau de man had floated through the living room. Not at all unpleasant.

In her old room, Frankie removed her shoes and her prosthesis, donned her sleep shorts and tee shirt, and slid between the sheets. Comfort slid over her, and she slept.

***

She awoke five hours later. Yelling. And with her cell phone ringing. Hard telling which had interrupted her nightmare first. A toss-up.

Banner's front paws were braced on the bed as he stared at her, worry in his almond-shaped eyes. He gruffed when he saw her eyes open.

"I'm okay," she muttered to him. She swallowed, her throat dry, and flipped the phone open. "Hello."

"Frankie!" Jesselyn's voice boomed from the receiver.

Wincing, Frankie distanced the phone from her ear. "What's wrong?"

"What in the world have you been telling Gabe Zantos about Russ?"

Frankie pondered for a moment. Came up blank. "Your brother?"

"Yes, my brother. Of course, my brother." Jesselyn didn't sound the least bit happy. "Why did you tell Gabe that Russ broke into your apartment?"

"I never told the deputy any such thing." Frankie pressed on her forehead, hoping to quell the lights already sparkling around her vision. "Why would I?"

"I'm asking you. And it'd better be good." Real anger colored Jesselyn's voice.

Frankie stood up and twisted, trying to work a kink out of her back. A vertebrae crackled. Better. And she was awake now. "Jesselyn, I swear, I don't know what you're talking about. You tell me. Are you saying the deputy has arrested your brother for breaking into my apartment?"

"Well..." Jesselyn's voice quieted, "not arrested him. I guess. Yet. But Russ said he—Gabe—drove out to the field where he was greasing the combine and shut him down long enough to ask a bunch of very strange questions."

"What questions? Why would the deputy do that?"

"Well..." This time Jesselyn paused before speaking. "Is it true your apartment was broken into?"

"Yes. Last night. For the second time."

"Good Lord." Jesselyn took a sharp breath.

"Are you all right?"

Her concern came a little late, but better, in Frankie's opinion, than never coming at all. "Sure. I was at work and discovered the door busted open when I got home. Whoever did it was long gone. But I don't understand. What led the deputy to Russ? Why did his name even come up?"

Jesselyn's silence allowed Frankie to picture her friend chewing the inside of her cheek, an involuntary indication of tension familiar from tiny tot days. Finally, she said, "Maybe because Russ has dated Denise a few times and Gabe was asking about her. Russ didn't even know she was gone and now he's mad at Vic and me for not telling him."

"Oh."

"Yeah. And mad at Denise for not telling him she was leaving. He thinks she should have said something. He takes getting dumped kind of personal."

"Doesn't everyone?" Frankie's face hardened. "But I expect Deputy Zantos is just trying to get a handle on who broke into my apartment. He's probably questioning everyone who knew Denise."

"Knew her? That's a funny way of putting it. Don't you mean, knows her?"

"Yeah, sure," Frankie agreed far too quickly. "That's what I mean."

"So he thinks the break-ins are aimed at Denise and not you?"

Closing her eyes, Frankie pressed harder against her temple. "I think it's pretty certain they are. I'm not the one who skipped out overnight without notice. What's more, I doubt I've been here long enough for anyone to hate me."

"Hate you? Wait a minute. What part of this conversation am I missing?" Now Jesselyn really sounded pissy. "Why her? Are you and Gabe implying something awful has happened to Denise? And you think Russ is involved?"

Frankie's mind raced. What was she supposed to say? Evidently, word hadn't gotten around yet that Gabe was investigating whether Denise's abrupt departure and Frankie's discoveries meant the woman was a missing person, a dead person, or the instigator of a horrible hoax. And if Jesselyn didn't know any more than what she just mentioned, it must mean Frankie's apartment had yet to see the crime scene people. Once they showed up, none of this was apt to remain quiet.

But she didn't intend to shoot off her mouth any more than she already had. So—

"No, ma'am," she said, her denial firm. "I'm not implying anything. Not jumping to any conclusions, either. Deputy Zantos speaks for himself."

Jesselyn remained on the other end of the phone, silent, except for the sound of hurried breathing. Frankie maintained her quiet and waited.

"Is this because of all the stuff Denise left in the apartment?" Jesselyn asked at last. "I know you were worried. Is that it? But Vic got that email saying Denise was leaving. The message came from her phone. Doesn't that prove anything?"

"Pretty easy to send a text from a phone," Frankie said before she could stop herself. "Anyone's phone. All you have to do is hold it in your hand."

"Frankie, just what is going on?" Jesselyn's tone indicated she meant business, but Frankie wasn't about to fall for the added pressure.

"I don't know what you mean." She wriggled uncomfortably at the lie. "The deputy is looking into the break-in. That's all I know." It just wasn't all she suspected. And what about Howie? Tension nagged at her.

"Where are you?" Jesselyn demanded. "I know you're not at the apartment. I just drove past and didn't see your pickup. But Rudy Swallowtail's rig is parked out front."

"Rudy Swallowtail?"

"The tribal cop. Frankie, we need to meet and talk."

Frankie glanced at her watch. "Sorry. No time, today, Jesselyn. I've got to get to work."

"You have an hour. Where are you?" Jesse asked again.

The question dragged an answer from her. "I'm at home. Grandma's house," she clarified.

Jesselyn gasped. "With Gabe? That was fast."

"What was fast? The deputy wanted me out of the duplex and offered me a bed." That didn't sound quite right either. "He's not here! He's working. He knew I needed to crash somewhere that would accept Banner. That's all. Simple."

"Hah! You're simple." Jesselyn abruptly hung up, her final sentence puzzling Frankie no end.

She doubted she'd heard Jesselyn's last word on the subject.

CHAPTER 8

Providence must have been on Frankie's side for once. On her way to the station, she met Howie headed toward the apartment, trudging along the verge of the road. His flip-flops slapped through dry, yellowed weeds, stirring grasshoppers into motion.

Relief flowing over her, she stopped beside him, reached across and rolled down the window. "Howie! Are you all right?"

He raised his head, squinting bloodshot eyes against the sun's glare. "Kind of sick, Frankie. Got a little drunk last night." He raised his arm, the one in the dirty cast. "Kept this damn thing from itching. Anyhow, lost my coat hanger. Think somebody stole it."

Frankie fought back a relieved giggle. "Have

you seen Gabe Zantos today?"

"Nah. Not for several days. He pretty much leaves me alone since I ain't got a car anymore. The only one I gotta look out for is Rudy Swallowtail." He noticed Frankie's puzzled expression. "Tribal police. But," he added hastily, "I ain't done anything wrong in a coon's age. Ask anybody. They'll tell you."

"I believe you." She glanced at her watch. "Get in, Howie. I'll give you a ride home."

He lit up. "Heh, thanks, Frankie. I appreciate it."

With her neighbor belted in—under protest—she turned the pickup around and drove slowly toward the duplex. "You know those noises you told you've been hearing at night? Well, my apartment was broken into again last night."

"Wasn't me. I wasn't home." His reply came quickly.

"I know. I told the deputy so. But we found something—" Frankie couldn't bring herself to tell him the details. Gabe would probably frown on her for spilling the beans.

Howie's face lit up. "Heh. Yeah. How's the dog. Shine gonna be okay? She looked pretty beat up."

She gave him a succinct synopsis of Shine's

ordeal and Banner's heroism. "The thing of it is," she continued, "we—Deputy Zantos and I—think whoever keeps entering my apartment is looking for something."

"What?"

"We don't know." She waited until he looked at her again. "Do you have any idea? See, Denise... well, she may not have been the person you think she was. She may have hidden something in the apartment. Something the burglar badly wants." A beat later, she realized she'd use the past tense again. Howie, fortunately, didn't pick up on her slip the way Jesselyn had done.

"Whadaya mean?"

"I mean because she seems to have disappeared, and she's not answering her phone, and because someone keeps breaking into my duplex."

"Disappeared?" Howie fixated on the word. "I thought you said—" He stopped, his expression hangdog.

"What?"

He gave a little jump.

Frankie took her eyes off the road long enough to give him a good stare. "I hoped you might know why she'd leave like that. Or if you think she left of her own volition."

"Her own what?"

"Because she wanted to leave."

"I don't know. Why ask me?" he answered. Fast, like he couldn't wait to get the words out.

"Because you said you were friends. Friends sometimes tell each other things."

"Yeah," he admitted, "we're friends."

Excitement quickened. "And does she tell you things?" It was almost a disappointment to wheel into the duplex's driveway. Apparently, nothing much had changed since early morning except for the tribal police cruiser parked out front. That, and the yellow crime scene tape blocking off the door to her unit.

"Crap. What's he doing here?" Howie glared at the cop.

"I told you. The break-in. I think it's just procedure. Never mind. They're not after you. Anyway, you're not a Coeur d' Alene tribal member, are you? So he can't hassle you.

"Says you."

She flapped a hand. "Please, Howie. Tell me what you know about Denise."

"She didn't tell me anything much." His voice was muffled as he looked out the window instead of at her. "But there was this box of old DVDs and computer stuff. It was just junk waiting to go in the garbage, or so she said when I asked her about it. But she had a funny look on her face when she was talkin'."

"And?"

"And nothin'. Then yesterday. You know, after you took Shine to the vet, I found the box shoved under the porch. My side of the porch. It was almost hidden under an old piece of canvas. Seemed strange to me." He rattled off the last so fast Frankie had to wonder.

"Very strange. Just junk, huh?" Frankie pondered. "What did you do with this junk?"

"Nothin'. I threw it out again, of course. What do I want with a bunch of—" He broke off then said, "—old computer programs. I ain't got a computer."

A flash of movement made her glance in her side mirror. It showed Gabe's SUV turning the corner and proceeding toward them. A police cruiser followed the SUV and an unmarked van. Looked like the crime scene unit had arrived at last. Her talk with Howie had come to an abrupt end.

And if she didn't hurry to work, Lew would have a fit.

"Thanks, Howie," she said. "I want you to tell Deputy Zantos everything about Denise that you just told me, okay? It might be important."

"Okay." In a hurry now, he got out of the pick-up. "Thanks for the ride. Appreciate it."

"Anytime."

Gabe waited to pull in, allowing Frankie to back out of the driveway. She stopped beside his SUV. "I hope it's all right, but I left Banner in the back yard. I didn't know what else to do with him. I can't keep taking him to work with me and this place—" She made a helpless gesture.

"Fine by me." He jerked a thumb toward Howie who was fumbling, trying to fit his key in the lock, and making slow work of it. "St. James is not the most reliable of witnesses, you know. He has a few bad habits that skew his thinking."

Frankie felt her face flushing. "I wasn't trying to preempt you, deputy. I just saw him walking along the road and gave him a ride home, that's all."

He grinned. "Yeah?"

"And I told him to tell you everything he told me." Virtue oozed from her every pore.

"Good of you." His voice was so dry it crackled. "I'll do a cross check with you later." He drove on, the cruiser and van parking behind him.

***

Howie, Frankie came to realize, had been lying to her. He either knew something or had suspicions about Denise and her sudden departure, and for some reason was keeping mum about it. Judging by the bold manner in which Mr. Size Twelve had tracked mud across her floor, as if he didn't care who knew he'd been there, Howie may have been wise. Wise to stay out all night, too, away from harm. With a broken arm, defending himself, if necessary, became an issue.

She drew into the station's parking lot dead on time, which, according to her, meant five minutes before the hour. Heat shimmered off the pavement, a stench of old motor oil rose from a stain beneath one of the firemen's cars. Garbage in the dumpster behind the station exuded an alcoholic pungency. Frankie hurried into the building, away from the smells.

Maggie, seated at the computer station, called a greeting when she entered. Chris Adkins, about to go off shift, grinned a welcome as he slammed his locker and keyed a two-inch padlock closed.

Beyond him, in the glassed-in office, she saw Lew talking to Captain Karl Mager.

"Thought you were gonna be late." Chris made heavy business of winking at her. "A word to the wise, Lew doesn't like that."

"So he told me," Frankie said. "Good thing I'm never late. Busy day?"

He flapped his hand in a teetering motion. "So, so."

"Dull," Maggie said, then, as her screen lit up, added, "Looks like the calls were waiting for you to get here." She hit a key and spoke into her headset. "Nine-one-one. What is your emergency?"

A scant sixty seconds found Frankie and Lew speeding down a gravel road toward the lake. Frankie was at the wheel, Lew in the passenger seat. Rocks spurted from beneath the ambulance's tires. The siren wailed. Lights flashed. A bulk semi-truck, its racks filled to the brim with a load of wheat bound for the elevator in town, swayed out of the road's middle as they crested a hill.

Lew leaned past Frankie and sketched the driver a salute. "Dry enough for Wright to resume cutting wheat, I see. Guess the storm didn't do too awful much damage the other night."

Frankie answered, absently. "The rain didn't last long, even it was a gully-washer. And it's been hot. The fields dried pretty fast."

"Yep."

From there, another mile took them off the main road onto a narrower private one leading down to Breezy Bay. The road stopped at a dock, a neat affair formed of Trex decking with a thirty-foot SeaRay tied to it, fenders bumping lightly. Looming above the water was a stone and timber house sporting turrets and a copper roof. Like something out of the Middle Ages, Frankie thought, eyeing the edifice, only more expensive.

Where the dock ended a hundred feet out on the water, they found two women and a kid in his late teens hovering around a bikini-clad girl lying on a hot pink beach towel. A lean, well-preserved man of about fifty was leaning over her performing CPR. The girl wasn't moving.

Lew carrying the medical kit, he and Frankie trotted onto the dock. Pushing through the bystanders, they knelt beside the woman. Frankie eased the man doing CPR aside and took over. Lew applied a blood pressure cuff and felt for a pulse.

"Thank God you're here," the man said. "Finally. It's been ten minutes." He was panting, sweat dripping down his face and onto his hands. No surprise, A fine summer day, the temperature had hit ninety degrees at last report. Sunlight glared off the water that sparkled as though strewn with diamonds.

Besides, CPR was always hard work.

"We've got it now, doc," Lew said, which was when Frankie realized the CPR guy looked familiar because she'd seen him in the hospital during the run with Russ Pettigrew. This doctor had looked in on a patient in the next cubicle, an elderly man with breathing problems.

"How long was she in the water?" Lew asked as he shook his head and made another try for a blood pressure.

The doctor arched an eyebrow at the three bystanders.

"Maybe four or five minutes." A tall, skinny kid wearing wet swim trunks answered. "We were going over to the resort in Coeur d'Alene to get a hamburger. I was almost out of the bay when I noticed she wasn't behind me. I turned around, saw her machine bobbing close to Dr. Muncie's dock, and heard a woman yelling. It wasn't my fault."

"Nobody said it was." One of the women, an almost emaciated blonde, patted the kid's shoulder. "I saw it happen. Looked to me like she was going too fast, lost control and ran her jet ski head-on into the dock. It bounced. She held on long enough to head back out, but then she just fell off. Went under like a rock."

Frankie noticed the woman's bikini was dry. Evidently, she wasn't the one who'd pulled the girl in.

"Will Chandra be all right?" The young guy still sounded scared.

Frankie, bending over the girl and breathing into her mouth, raised her sights above the pair of big bare feet to the kid's concerned face. She left the answering to Lew who gave a nod that could've meant anything.

"Got a pulse, Frankie. You can stop chest compressions now."

In affirmation, the girl suddenly turned her head and choked out a mixture of lake water and vomit. Frankie helped her onto her side, waited until the spasm was over, and cleared her mouth. In the background, she heard someone say faintly, "Eww."

"Keep it up, Frankie. I'll get a blanket and the oxygen."

She started the breathing part again. Back before she missed him, Lew had made the roundtrip to the ambulance with a stride almost as fast as a flat out run.

They worked in quiet tandem until the girl stirred and pushed weakly at Frankie, who rocked back on her heels. Her foot hurt, toes pressed—hah, a joke—too hard against the dock. Lew snapped an oxygen mask onto the girl's face, and they wrapped her in a couple layers of blanket.

"Why a blanket?" one of the women demanded. "It's already so hot. She'll suffocate."

"They know what they're doing." The doctor, whose name Frankie had already forgotten, snapped an answer.

Lew, monitoring the girl's pulse, exchanged a worried glance with Frankie when Chandra started coughing. Pink froth formed around her mouth.

In another five minutes, they had the girl stabilized and on a stretcher. Lew at the head, Frankie at the foot, they carried her up to the ambulance and soon had her out to the main road and on the way to Kootenai Medical Center. Lew drove, leaving Frankie in charge of the girl. He pushed the ambulance to the limit on the straight stretches of highway.

***

"Was that the doctor's place? You know, where we picked up the girl?" Frankie yawned, tired to the bone as, the run completed, the ambulance rumbled toward Hawkesford.

"Yep. His summer place. Pretty palatial, huh?" A note of amusement tinged Lew's voice.

Frankie looked at him. "I'll say. I wouldn't have recognized Breezy Bay. Seven years ago, we had our senior high school keg party down there. Lit a fire of driftwood, sat around on stumps, and drank beer. Now the whole area is bought up, and million dollar vacation homes have taken over the whole shoreline."

"And not a one belong to locals." Lew scowled. "And don't ever overlook the No Trespassing signs. I understand the doc's place owes something to his wife. She's a high powered lawyer with an outfit that has about a dozen names in the title. Works mostly over in Seattle and is only here a couple weekends a month. Or so I hear."

"You're kidding."

"Nope. And the happy couple's nearest neighbor is Bugs Swisher." Lew noticed Frankie's blank expression. "Football player. Retired to beautiful North Idaho with a boatload of money."

"Oh. Well, I liked it the way it was before. It looks like Breezy Bay is about to become another Tahoe."

"Wouldn't know." Lew shrugged. "Never been there."

In another fifteen minutes, they were back at the station, ready for their next run. Frankie was still bummed about the local changes, almost enough to take her mind off the duplex break-ins, spilled blood, and the missing Denise Rider. Almost, but not quite.

When Dr. Kelly called Frankie at the end of office hours to tell her Shine was ready to be released from the veterinary hospital, yet another problem presented itself.

"She'll need antibiotics, pain meds, and the dressings changed periodically over the wound for the next few days," the vet warned. "In other words, someone who knows how to care for her. If you're serious about taking her on, that is. You're about her best bet right now."

Frankie couldn't help sighing. "I guess I let

myself in for it when I brought her to you, didn't I?"

This time, she heard a smile in Dr. Kelly's voice.

"That's what I wanted to hear, Ms. McGill."

"Frankie," she corrected.

"Frankie. Has anyone heard from Denise? Or found any trace of her?"

Doubting the deputy would want the news of their discovery noised about, Frankie didn't know what to say. Finally, she settled for, "Not that I know of. I'll pick Shine up around noon or so tomorrow if that's all right."

"Fine. I'll have her ready to go. You won't be sorry, Frankie. She's a loving little thing."

Yes. And so was Banner. She hoped he wouldn't get his nose out of joint.

What in the world was she going to do with two dogs, one of them hurt? With her duplex out of commission, where was she going to find a place for them to stay, let alone find a bed for herself when she got off shift?

Turns out Gabe Zantos came through for her again. Sort of.

CHAPTER 9

Frankie, busy checking supplies and cleaning the ambulance an hour before day shift came on, looked up when Gabe Zantos strode into the station just before daylight. He greeted Lew and the dispatcher and, ignoring the glance the other two exchanged, ambled into the garage where she was working.

Deputy Zantos looked tired. As I no doubt do myself, she thought ruefully. Gabe's britches had stains on one knee, and a splotch of something that looked like blood on the sleeve of his shirt. Giving her a little salute, he peered into the bus's depths, watching as she tossed a stray syringe wrapper into a bag of garbage.

"I'm going off duty for a few hours' sleep," he said quietly, so the others wouldn't hear, "but first, I wanted to let you know Victoria Pettigrew is arranging a new mattress for your duplex. It should be delivered late this morning."

Internally, Frankie groaned. Great. Another day without sleep. "Does this mean the crime scene people came up empty?"

"Not exactly. We're waiting on results of the blood profile. And I put somebody to checking with Cabela's on the boots, although I wouldn't hold my breath on that being a hot lead. Anyway, the duplex has been freed up."

"Oh. Dang."

"Dang?" He sounded amused.

Her head fuzzed for a second. "I mean, dang, the boots aren't a hot lead. It's good, and the apartment is okay." Good lord, he'd think she was a blathering fool.

He grinned like already he thought so. "Yeah. Another thing, Frankie."

When did we become Frankie and Gabe? Did she like it? Maybe.

"What?" she asked.

"Victoria Pettigrew said to tell you she'll be there to accept the new mattress since she has to sign for it. You might want to crash at my place again."

His eyes were bleary from lack of sleep, but that didn't mean he lacked wit. She suspected the expression on her face showed him her doubts on that score. Like maybe, staying at his place was not quite kosher—especially if he was there too.

"Another 'another' thing," he added. "About that old fence around the duplex. One of my guys accidentally broke down a big section when they went out to see where you found Ms. Rider's dog. Howie showed us. Anyway, you better let me keep your guy until it's fixed."

"Oh, thanks. What a relief." Frankie's brain worked overtime, trying to process everything he'd said. Her brow puckered. Was she forgetting something? Yes. Dammit! "Uh, oh."

"Uh, oh, what?"

"I told the veterinarian I'd keep Denise's dog. Until the poor little thing recovers, at least. She needs nursing."

For a moment, he looked nonplussed, then he shrugged. "Lots of room, I guess. Just don't wake me up when you get there."

He strode out again, pausing only to warn the dispatcher coming on shift that if they awakened him for anything less than a typhoon in the next six hours, they were in trouble. The dispatcher, a chubby college-age summer volunteer named Gina, fell all over herself with repeated, "Yes, sirs."

Gabe was that kind of guy. And judging by the dreamy look on the girl's face as she watched him leave, she had other ideas about him as well.

Maybe some of the same ones Frankie had been having.

***

Yellow crime scene tape, loosened now, fluttered in the breeze around the duplex's front door when Frankie pulled into the driveway. Tearing down the tape and wadding it into a ball to throw away gave a sense of satisfaction.

She might not be able to sleep here without a bed, but she sure could take a shower, put on clean clothing, and eat a meal, in that order. As on previous mornings, the street was quiet, somnolent as the day heated up. A sprinkler whirled in a neighbor's yard a few hundred feet away, spray beating rhythmically against a cedar fence that stood in need of staining. A quail perched on the corner post called out for "tobacco." The smell of weeds and wheat and a faraway forest fire drifted over all.

There was no sign of Howie, not that she expected anything else. He'd been keeping out of sight lately.

Wondering if the presence of cops, or if Denise Rider's disappearance had him freaked, Frankie let herself into the apartment. Lacking Banner and his feeling for trouble, she did her own walk-through, peeking into the kitchen, bathroom, and finally the bedroom, giving a huge sigh of relief upon finding the old mattress gone.

Her nose twitched. Although stuffy, the room already smelled better. Having the blood source removed, the apartment opened up, and police milling around had done wonders.

Signs of the search for evidence were all around. Her clothes in the closet pushed to one side, stuff in the dresser appearing to have been stirred, items in the bathroom jumbled, the kitchen a mess. Somebody had left several take-out coffee cups on the counter, complete with brown-colored drips and spills.

Trying her best to ignore the disorder, Frankie grabbed a clean bra and panties from the drawer to don after her shower. Warm water, as she'd been taught would conserve body temperature, beat down on her head, tingling against her skin. Her body wash, a pretty floral scent, came from one of the specialty stores, and she sniffed appreciatively. Lord, how she'd missed such luxuries in Afghanistan.

Pushing the thought away, she enveloped her hair in a turban of lather. It was a special shampoo she bought from a ritzy salon. Her hairdresser assured her it encouraged hair growth to fill in over the scars. If so, Frankie reflected wryly, it worked pretty damn slow.

Clean enough and still in her underwear, she nuked bacon, fried an egg, burned a couple slices of toast and ate standing up. By then, almost asleep on her feet, she'd about decided to curl up on the couch when from next door, Howie's stereo started in with an unholy din.

"Oh, Gawd. Not rap."

But it was, the thunderous beat nearly shaking the building. Her fists pounding on the wall between the two apartments went ignored.

Giving up on trying staying in her own place, Frankie scrawled a quick note to Jesselyn's sister and left it on the counter. Thanks, Victoria! the note said.

Dressing quickly in shorts and a T-shirt, she

shoved a fresh set of work clothes into a plastic grocery bag with an Albertson's logo and set off for Gabe's place.

Which worked out fine. Silent as a shadow, she let herself into the old house where she found Banner curled up on a clean rug laid out for him on the back porch. Her eyelids nearly glued together, she played with him a few minutes before calling him in. Together, they climbed the stairs and fell into bed.

Banner, to her satisfaction, stretch out at her side with a huge sigh. She flopped an arm across him and slept.

***

Gabe was gone when Frankie got up five hours later. No surprise there. In some far reach of consciousness, she'd heard a shower running and later, a door slamming on a muttered curse. Somehow comforted by the small sounds, she'd rolled over and gone back to sleep. Downstairs, a note on the table welcomed her and invited the use of a French press coffee maker.

Who'd ever have guessed Gabe'd be such a connoisseur? Anyhow, she took advantage of his generosity while Banner did his thing outside, and she got ready to go pick up Shine.

***

Dr. Kelly, rushing against time-constraints with what appeared to be a sudden influx of sick animals, greeted her with open arms—so to speak. Out back of the clinic, as it happened, where she found the vet stitching a barbed wire cut in a horse's shoulder.

The receptionist, visibly shaken, stood at the horse's head.

"Oh, good, a helper," Dr. Kelly greeted Frankie. "Hold him. Mary needs to get back to the desk."

Wordless, Frankie took the lead shank Mary thrust into her hands.

"One of my assistants called in sick today." Dr. Kelly smiled at her receptionist's retreating back. "And I'm afraid soothing sick horses isn't Mary's forte."

Frankie snugged the horse's head to her chest to keep him from tossing it and moving around. She blew once into his nostrils and talked soft nonsense to him. Bernie, the assistant she'd met the other day, kept the thoroughbred's hindquarters pinned against a sturdy wall while he handed Doc necessary items.

The animal's skin rippled as the doctor's needle flashed in and out. "I've numbed him," the vet assured Frankie. "But he knows what's going on and doesn't like it."

"I can't say as I blame him." She peered around. "That's an awfully big needle."

The vet grimaced. "I've heard that one before. Though not from the horse, you understand."

Frankie smiled.

Banner, who as always accompanied Frankie, touched his nose to the horse, providing an instantly calming effect on the larger animal.

Dr. Kelly brushed back a lock of her brown hair. "I think I need to offer Banner a job around here."

The Samoyed's tail waved at the sound of his name.

"He wants to know if you pay in money or in rawhide chews," Frankie spoke for him.

Laughing, the vet finished her handiwork, daubed antiseptic over the neat row of stitches, and affixed a dressing to keep the flies away. "Looks good," she told her paid assistant as she stripped off latex gloves. "You can put him in the back stall, Bernie. Check him every half hour, please, but I'm sure he'll be fine. Come with me."

Aiming the last sentence at Frankie, Dr. Kelly was several steps ahead before it sank in and Frankie hurried to catch up.

"You'll be amazed at how quickly Shine's recovering," the vet said over her shoulder. "Another debt we owe Banner. Anyway, I don't think you'll have any trouble with her. Like I said yesterday, you'll need to administer some meds, change the dressing as necessary, and give her lots of love. I can tell she's missing Denise. Has anyone heard from her?"

They'd reached the clinic's rear entrance. The vet keyed open the door and held it for Frankie and Banner to enter, allowing Frankie enough time to formulate an answer to Dr. Kelly's rapid-fire dialogue.

Deciding to keep it simple, she said, "Not that I know of. But at least the police are on the case now."

"They are?" Dr. Kelly's eyes rounded as if surprised. "Huh! What changed? You must know someone with clout. When I spoke to them the other day, they could've cared less." She led the way between crates, dogs on one side, cats on the other. The room was noisy, as barks and meows greeted their intrusion. Several animals, sedated, no doubt, slept right through the din.

"I know." Frankie raised her voice. "There've been other developments in the last couple days. But—"

Just then Dr. Kelly stopped in front of a crate where a bedraggled looking little dog lay, one of the quiet ones. Big dark eyes dull, it sat up with some effort and uttered a tiny whine.

With all the hair around the wound shaved down to the skin, and quite a lot of what remained discolored with blood stains, Shine looked about as woebegone as possible.

"Oh," Frankie crooned, instantly melting. "You poor baby."

***

Her cell phone, tossed onto the dashboard to be handy in case of emergency, pealed as Frankie passed the cut-off to the tribal casino.

"Frankie, here," she said, expecting a demand to report to the station early. The call wasn't from work, though, thank God. Victoria Pettigrew was on the line.

"Hi, Frankie," Vic spoke quickly as if she had no time to waste. "I wanted to let you know the new mattress has been delivered."

A sudden flash of how the other had sagged and smelled, intolerable even for the few hours she'd slept on it, almost made her ill. "I hope it's a good one." She tried for a cheerful effect.

"Well, it's not a Tempur-Pedic or a Davenport Hotel special." Victoria's voice held a trace of amusement. "But it's better than the owner wanted to spring for. Anyway, you can sleep in your own bed tonight—if you like." Her pause seemed fraught with sexual suggestion. "I understand you've been staying with Deputy Zantos at your grandmother's house."

Frankie knew innuendo when she heard it. Instantly, she flashed on Gabe Zantos and his hazel eyes. Damn! It was crazy since she hadn't as much as seen Gabe at any time while staying at his house. That, in turn, caused her temper, somewhat unreliable anyway, which she liked to blame on the plate in her head, to turn up the heat.

"Deputy Zantos has been very generous, taking me and my dog in," she said, aware she sounded like she had a corncob up her butt. Well... too bad.

"He sure didn't have to. He has no obligation to me, not even as a co-worker."

Had that been clear enough? She didn't want to spoil Gabe's reputation in the community. Or her own, for that matter. Not so soon, anyway.

Victoria snorted. "Huh! Well then, lucky you. Gabe's a good-looking guy. Anyway, the bed is delivered. Whether you sleep in it or not is up to you."

The turn off to the casino with its garish neon sign in her rearview mirror, Frankie sped up for the long winding hill leading to Hawkesford. "Thank you, Victoria." She said it sweetly, meanwhile gritting her teeth. "That was quick service. I appreciate your efforts."

"You'd better."

Sensing Victoria was ready to hang up, Frankie hastened to hold her just a moment more. "By the way, did Gabe talk to you about the previous tenant?"

"Not yet. We've missed connections twice now, but we have an appointment for this evening when I get home from work. He said he had questions about Denise. Why?"

Opening her mouth to tell Victoria about Denise and the other stuff going on at the duplex,

Frankie as quickly closed it again. She'd meant to pump Victoria about the missing woman, but that seemed an awful lot like infringing on Gabe's territory.

"There's been some odd things going on around the apartment is all, stuff you should know about," she said instead. "I'm happy to leave all that to Deputy Zantos."

Victoria's normal staccato speech slowed. "That sounds very mysterious."

"Yes. I guess it does." And then, as Shine whimpered from her bed behind the driver's seat, she added, "But there's more than you can guess. Gotta go. Thanks again, Victoria. I owe you."

"You bet you do. Count on me collecting."

The phone went dead.

Rats, Frankie thought, if Victoria is making something of Gabe's generosity to Banner and me, what about the rest of Hawkesford? She had a pretty good guess, and while it didn't bother her especially, having no one she needed to impress, Gabe's reputation was another matter. Any hint of fraternization could mean slower promotion. Or wait. Was that only relevant in the military? Or in business? Or...

Without warning, lights flashed behind

Frankie's eyes, megavolts of unrestrained energy. Anvils clanged inside her head.

"Oh, no." Fighting a blaze of pain, she took her foot off the gas and pulled off the highway into a field where shorn stubble showed the wheat had been harvested. Grasshoppers flew up around the pickup cab, banging into the windows.

She got the truck stopped and threw the shifter into park before pressing two fingers against her temple, hoping to quell the situation or wait it out. Banner barked his annoyance.

"Sorry, lovey," she told him faintly, a second before the world went black.

CHAPTER 10

Frankie's eyes blinked open, her face, fiercely hot in a couple places, pressed against the steering wheel. Sunlight glared through the side window. Groaning, she straightened. She had no idea how long the blackout had lasted this time. Probably no more than a minute or two.

A nerve in her temple spasmed, the sharp ping doing more to awaken her than Banner's tongue lapping her cheek, his nose stuck in her eye.

"Good boy." She raised a hand to defend herself. "I'm all right. Stand down."

The dog backed off, watching her anxiously with sharp dark eyes.

After her time in the hot, dry mountains of Afghanistan, Frankie never went anywhere without a bottle of water. Thank God. She slopped some over a tissue and wiped dog slobbers off her face before guzzling down a couple long swallows. Gradually, her head stopped spinning and, with a little help from the therapist's pressure technique, the flashes behind her eye quieted.

"A real zinger," she told the dog, squinting against the afternoon light. "I thought we were through with them. Let's hope this one was an anomaly."

Banner looked like he hoped so too—whatever anomaly might mean.

"Good thing I got off the road before I blanked."

This time he definitely agreed. He barked. Shine stirred in her bed behind the seat.

"Yeah. Okay. We'll go in a minute." She took another gulp of water and a few deep breaths before nerving herself to put the pickup in gear and reverse out onto the highway. The dashboard clock showed an hour before her shift started.

"Looks like we're cutting it pretty fine, doesn't it?" Not quite trusting her reaction times, Frankie drove a little slower than usual as she dropped off the hill leading into town. Her hands shook on the steering wheel. Maybe she'd better ask Lew if he'd drive tonight if they had any calls. What kind of excuse could she use? Hah. Best scenario was that they'd get lucky and there'd be zero calls. Maybe they could spend the night studying protocols and memorizing maps instead of attending accident victims.

Yeah, right. Memorizing.

Crossing her fingers, she steered for the duplex, bypassing her grandmother's house. Hearing Victoria's comments helped strengthen her determination to avoid Gabe just now. Besides, Frankie knew how she looked. If Gabe was home, she didn't want him to see her like this, eyes like dark holes, skin pale as a fish belly, trembling like a Parkinson's victim.

Small towns. So many busybodies with his or her eye aimed toward his neighbor, each eager to pick and choose from facts and think the worst.

Too bad the busybodies hadn't checked out Denise Rider more closely.

Howie's door stood open at the duplex, flies busy swooping in and out. No sign of the man himself.

Wrinkling her nose, Frankie gestured Banner out of the pickup before sliding the driver's seat forward and scooping Shine into her arms. The bichon recognized her home territory. She wiggled until Frankie set her down, allowing the dog to limp toward her accustomed unit where she sat waiting until Frankie got the door open.

Frankie's heart almost broke when Shine paced a slow way through all the rooms, most assuredly looking for Denise.

"I'm sorry, sweetie. She isn't here. I hope you'll learn to make do with Banner and me." Whatever else about Denise, she had her dog's love.

With Banner as a protective escort, Shine headed for the kitchen door. Frankie hastened ahead to open it and let both dogs out. She found Howie sitting in a lawn chair on the communal back porch. He was drinking a beer. Not, according to the empties at his feet, the first.

"Hey." He waved a Keystone can at her.

"Hey yourself."

His bleary eyes focused on the dog. "Hey, Shine. Glad to see you up and at 'em."

Shine waddled over to him and nosed his bare toe. Smiling, Howie reached down and gingerly patted her over the hips, as far away as possible from the wound.

"Kinda scared to touch her," he told Frankie. "Afraid I might hurt her. Man, they sure shaved her down, didn't they? Denise ain't gonna like her looks, that's for sure. She takes Shiny to the groomer about once a month." He scowled. "Denise says this kinda dog gets sunburned just like people. Have to make sure she has shade. Or smear on sunblock."

She thought the last might be a joke. Or maybe not. "I think we'll skip the sunblock, but keeping her inside and out of the sun is a good idea. Maybe I can find a lightweight T-shirt in her size."

"A T-shirt. Huh. Might still be one around the apartment somewhere. Denise dresses the pooch up sometimes. Dog has more clothes than I do." Howie's dark face turned serious. "Seeing as the cops broke down that crappy fence, we'll have to keep an eye on her. And on this one, too." A gesture took in Banner who hovered near the bichon as she maneuvered off the porch steps on three legs and found a patch of grass to water. "Looks like he's taken a shine to Shine."

Definitely a joke this time. Something, a sort of unnamed fear Frankie had been harboring about her neighbor, got up and flew away. Howie hadn't been the one to hurt Shine. She knew for certain, now.

"Howie, do you know any of Denise's friends? Anybody who might know where she is? Or did Deputy Zantos already ask you?"

Howie's face reddened a little. "I ain't got around to him yet. But I can tell you women don't seem to like Denise much. None of the women around here, anyhow. She talked to me about them sometimes. Said they must be jealous of her, but she just laughed about them."

"Oh? Why should they be jealous?"

"'Cause Denise don't even have a job, but has nicer clothes than anybody, even some of the ladies at the lake. Expensive and lots of them. She takes a lot of trips. And her car—"

A car hadn't even occurred to Frankie. "What about her car?"

"A Beamer convertible." His face grew wistful. "She used to give me rides sometimes. You know, like you did."

"Guess I'm a disappointment with my old pickup."

"Nah. It's all good."

Gabe must be looking for the car. But Frankie didn't get it. If Denise had the money for a BMW convertible, trips, lots of expensive clothes, and for Shine's needs—all without needing to work—what the dickens was she doing living in this crappy duplex next door to Howie St. James? Frankie's head whirled.

"Anyway," Howie said, "I never saw a woman come around, but men did sometimes. She dated a bunch of guys, you know."

"I didn't know."

"Well, she did." Howie fell silent.

"So, did anybody come around here last night or today?" Frankie changed the subject. "I worried about you."

"You did?" Looking pleased, he tilted the beer can to his mouth and drained it, dropping the empty beside three others.

"I did."

"Nah, didn't see anybody." Then he changed his mind. "Except the real estate agent, of course, and the mattress delivery guys. Wish they'd brought me a new bed. Can't sleep on the worn out piece of crap in my unit."

Hadn't he heard about the blood on Denise's mattress? she wondered. Or seen the police take it away? Maybe not. Even if he'd been home, it didn't mean he was awake enough to see what went on. Or aware enough, considering the rapidly growing pile of empty beer cans. If he had, he wouldn't have been so blithe about the need.

But then he surprised her. "Oh yeah. Seen somebody else, too. One of the guys from the fire department was here looking around."

"Who? Captain Mager? Or Lew?"

"Nah," he said, "not Captain Karl or Lew. One of those new dudes. Don't know his name."

Puzzling. "Did he say what he wanted?"

"Nope. He came around back and saw me here. I told him you wasn't home, and he left. That's all."

"When was this?"

"Noon, maybe. Or one." He shrugged the cast on his arm, hampering the movement and making him wince. "He didn't ask where you was, but hell, I didn't know anyway."

He looked anywhere, but at her, Frankie noticed. A habit of his she found a little disconcerting. Finally, he came up with something else to say. "Hey, Frankie. You remember I told you about them CDs and DVDs of Denise's I found?"

She nodded.

"Well, I took a DVD over to my buddy's house a while ago. His sister has a computer, and she let me plug in the disc. It ain't a movie, even though Denise labeled it Smoke Signals. You know, that movie they filmed here on the Rez back before I was even born?"

Frankie's breath caught, the pain in her head

overridden. "I remember. I watched it with my grandma. But if the movie wasn't on the disc, what was?"

Reaching behind his lawn chair, Howie fished around in a Styrofoam cooler until he found a fresh beer. He popped the tab. "An Excel document with a bunch of names and addresses and dollar amounts."

She thought a moment. "Does the document have a title? Does it say who created it?"

Howie chugged a couple deep swallows. "Sure. Denise created it. No title. Just columns with the names." Now he did meet her eyes. "Kind of odd, though, 'cause it don't look like anybody's Christmas list. What do you think it means?"

Heart in mouth, Frankie watched Shine hobble up the single step onto the porch and safely collapse in front of the door. "I don't know." Truthful, but not an answer that kept her from having suspicions. "May I see the disc?"

He shot her a quick look, gave a shrug, and sipped his beer.

She judged she'd been blown-off. "Have you shown it to Gabe? Or Rudy Something or another, the tribal policeman?"

"Rudy Swallowtail. Nah. Not him. Nor Zantos

either. Them guys, I don't trust 'em."

"Why not?"

He shrugged, another non-answer.

"They're trying to figure out what happened to Shine, you know," she urged him. "And they want to find Denise."

"Yeah. I guess." He pondered. "Okay. Maybe next time I see Zantos, I'll tell him I got it."

"Good." And if he doesn't, I will. Frankie looked at her watch. Barely enough time for a quick shower and a sandwich, as long as the bread hadn't become a penicillin farm. She stood up. "Or better yet, call Deputy Zantos and give the disc to him right away. Those noises you've been hearing, Howie, and the people breaking into the duplex? That's not happening for nothing. I'll bet that file means something to them. I'll bet they're looking for the DVD. If you want, I can take it and see the deputy gets it tonight."

Howie tilted the beer can to his mouth and took a long quaff. "Nah, I'll do it," he said. "As soon as I finish my beer."

He was still sitting on the porch staring blankly into the trees behind the property when Frankie, showered and fed—no mold, thank goodness— brought Banner and Shine out for a final pit stop before she left for the station.

"You gonna call Gabe about the DVD?" She hated to pressure him, but he showed no signs of moving from his comfortable spot. Howie struck her as the kind of man who needed reminders every five minutes. She'd served with a few guys like that in Afghanistan, the ones who hung back and let others take the lead.

He waved a lackadaisical hand. "Yeah. Pretty quick, I guess."

"Make it sooner. Oh, if the dogs start a ruckus, call me on my cell, and I'll dash home, all right? I want to keep a close eye on Shine."

"Sure. Be glad to."

She wrote her number down for him on a scrap of newspaper from a rain-soaked stack by his back door. "Thanks."

"Welcome." He tucked the paper in his shirt pocket and closed his eyes.

Filled with a sense of unease, Frankie took her leave.

***

The egg sandwich and fruit did wonders for Frankie—her shakiness gone, flashes cleared, brain fog dissipated. Driving the ambulance, she decided, was nothing to fear.

When she walked into the station at precisely five minutes before her shift began, she spied Lew in the office talking to Karl. Maggie hovered in the corner poking paperwork into the bank of metal drawers. Chris Adkins and Darryl Holland, one of the volunteer firemen, were hanging around the lockers, laughing and sharing a joke. Quitting time and they couldn't wait for their shift to end.

She stuck her own small bag in the locker next to Chris's and slammed the door shut. That was it.

"Busy day?" she asked the burly young volunteer medic and nodded to Darryl.

"Not bad. Long is all. I'll be glad when we all get our regular shifts back." Chris glanced at the big round wall clock as though wishing away the next four minutes, his cheeks turning red as he saw her notice.

"Got a date?" Not that Frankie cared, but she wanted to be friendly.

Laughing, Darryl elbowed him. "Yeah, Chris, got a date?"

His heightened color ebbed as quickly as it'd

come. "No. Heck no. Why— Well, yeah. Kind of a date."

"Hang in there," she said. "The shifts will go back to normal when Lew says I'm ready to handle the bus by myself. Not so awful much longer." No way she'd mention today's blackout—not to anyone, and especially Lew. He'd be sure to set the schedule back if he had any inkling of her... um... weak spells.

No. That's not what he'd do. He'd fire her.

Taking pity on both guys, she added, "If the alarm goes off in the next few seconds, don't worry. I'll take the call."

Chris smirked as if he'd forced a confession out of her. He was such a clock-watcher. The sort of bumbler most people ended up covering for, although she sometimes doubted he'd do the same for anybody else unless maybe Darryl.

Still, twelve hours was a long shift when scheduled for several days in a row. When she was fully trained, they'd be back to regular shifts, each with a fully accredited paramedic or EMT, and their three days off.

"What are Karl and Lew talking about?" She seized the moment to change the subject. Whatever the two men were saying, she saw them nodding their heads as though some sort of agreement had occurred.

"No clue." Chris sounded petulant again. "They don't tell me anything. I'm just a peon around here."

"You and me both," Darryl agreed. He rubbed the gold nugget of his ring on the front of his shirt.

Frankie shook her head.

"Oh, wah. Hush your complaining." Maggie, fetching her purse from her own locker, had approached without any of them noticing. "You know Lew or Karl will let you off whenever you ask for the time."

Chris's face, which had gone back to tan, reddened again. "That's not very often."

Darryl backed him up. "Or never."

"Nobody said it was. But they'd still do it." Maggie, seeing the evening dispatch person seat himself at the computer, went over to speak to him and share the news of the day before leaving.

"Maggie," Darryl muttered. "Wish she'd butt out."

Surprised, Frankie blinked at him. "What did Maggie do?"

He turned away without answering, tromping

on heavy feet out the station door without saying goodbye.

With a grimace, Chris strode after him. "Hey, Darryl, what's up?"

Shaking her head, Frankie, went to chat with the dispatcher, an older man named Benton who worked three days a week in Coeur d'Alene. She still hadn't figured out what he did, some kind of consulting work from the sound of it, but he was certainly efficient at this job. Benton, a Hawkesford old-timer, lived one cove over from Dr. Muncie in a house about a quarter of the size of the doctor's. Or so he said, smiling.

Wandering over to the ambulance to check supplies, Frankie discovered Chris, or maybe Marc, the other paramedic, had neglected to replace two bags of saline solution used during a run with a hemorrhaging mother-to-be. She made a note on the checklist. Everything else was in order.

Before boredom could set in, Benton answered a call and sounded the alarm. A car/farm truck accident between Hawkesford and the cut-off to Highway 27, injuries reported. Without a second thought, Frankie climbed into the ambulance's driver's seat. Lew bolted out of the office to join her.

The evening rush had begun.

Before they could park the rig from returning from the first call, another came in. Tractor
accident—a bad one. An amputation. Frankie
clenched her hands, trying to still their trembling.

God, how she hated amputations!

Lew, being Lew, took immediate notice of her
reaction. Concern deepened the set of frown lines
between his brows. "You all right with this?"

Damn. He knows all about my foot. She wanted to say "No." How could she be all right? But she
didn't. With only a tiny hesitation, she clamped
her jaw. "Sure. Don't worry. I'll do my job."

Lew touched her shoulder. "I know you will."

And she did.

A lull struck around ten thirty. The bus was
back at the station, Lew at his desk reading a
newspaper, Frankie working on a paperback
copy of a Craig Johnson mystery someone had
left on the lunchroom table. In the novel, the hero
was battling a snowstorm—a contrast between
her real-time Idaho summer and the story's Wy-
oming winter that had her riveted.

At one a.m., the book finished, she started
worrying about her dogs. Banner she could trust

to hold his water, but Shine? The poor little thing shouldn't have more stress put on her.

Lew, waking from an hour's nap, opened his eyes to find Frankie staring at him. "What?" he growled.

"Do you know you snore?" Actually, she'd been in firefights barely any louder.

"So I've been told." He stood up and stretched. "Slow night."

"Yes."

"And you're worried about that orphan dog."

She'd told him about Shine when he asked where Banner was. Apparently, her Samoyed had already wormed his way into her co-worker's hearts.

"I am."

He glanced at his watch. "Go home and check on her. I'll hold down the fort."

She shook her head. "Against regulations."

He gave her a questioning look.

"Did you think I wouldn't read them? Well, I did. And they say there has to be at least two people on shift twenty-four hours a day, or we'll lose our accreditation and funding for the station."

Lew huffed out a short laugh. "I suppose you think we were running according to Hoyle before we hired you. Think again, girlie. And the sky didn't fall."

She gaped at him.

"Go ahead. It'll take you what? Ten minutes? Fifteen? If the alarm sounds, Benton will call you. You can follow the ambulance and be wherever you need to be as soon as I can get there. Hell, that's basically how we cover days off. Didn't you read that in the regulations guidelines?"

If so, she didn't remember. "Thanks, Lew." She patted her pocket and found her keys. "Ten minutes tops."

He made that growling sound again, but his mouth turned up at the corners.

***

The streets of Hawkesford were deserted. Not a surprise for a farming community that rolled up the sidewalks, figuratively speaking, at dark. Only a few neon lights advertising Coors and Budweiser still gleamed in the window of the local pub as Frankie drove past.

Well, except for a white cat that ran in front of her pickup. A quick swerve avoided tragedy. Up on the hill above the duplex, she saw car lights come on, then blink off. Twice.

She forgot the oddity as she pulled into the driveway and got out. Immediately, alarm touched her.

Inside the duplex, the dogs were barking. Howling, really. Banner with a deep, heavy sound, Shine sharp and piercing.

Not good. Definitely not good.

Why hadn't Howie called?

Frankie ran. Keyed the door. Ducked down and slipped through the narrowest possible opening in case an unwelcome visitor was inside. Wished she had her M9A1 Beretta sidearm. Her heart thudded as though anticipating combat.

Banner, his howls shutting off the second he recognized his mistress, edged up against her. Though the room was quite dark, Frankie could see Shine standing back on three legs, holding her ground and still barking.

"Shh," Frankie whispered. "Hush." Oddly enough, Shine obeyed, inching closer to her and Banner.

Frankie heard it then—noises coming from Howie's side of the duplex. Thuds, moans. A shot. Deadened as though muffled, but still unmistakable.

Her heart lurched.

Howie's back door slammed. A fist or a boot or something hammered against hers. Shine began caterwauling again.

Frankie froze. Weapon. Weapon.

Then running footsteps faded into the night, going south, toward the woods.

A dread silence fell beyond Howie's wall.

Oh, shit, Frankie thought. Oh, shit.

CHAPTER 11

Frankie knelt on the floor, her arms around Banner. Shine came forward and claimed protection too. Somehow, her reach expanded to encompass both dogs.

The silence from next door continued. Shine's whole body quivered. Both dogs' agitated panting filled Frankie's ears, even over the pounding of her heart. Damn it. Damn it! Unless the pounding on her door had been a ruse, whoever had invaded Howie's house had gone. But Howie was there. Dead. She knew it sure as she knew her own name.

Except hope remains in the face of doubt. Frankie had lots of experience with the concept.

Gently, she set the dogs aside.

"Stay here." Her voice whispered and shook in

the quiet dark. Banner nosed Shine and sat.

She went to Howie's front door, tapping first, and then trying the knob. The door was locked, and although she figured her key with the pink yarn string would've opened it, she couldn't bring herself to do so. Tampering with the evidence. That's what Gabe would say.

"Cart, horse. Horse, cart." The inane words drifted through her mind as she returned to her own apartment and went out the rear. Banner construed her passage as a release from stay. He followed her and, glad of the company, she didn't reprimand him. Shine, on three legs, hobbled after them.

She found Howie's back door gaping open; the screen ripped from its hinges. Light flickered beyond the dark kitchen, coming from the living room where a movie played on the television, its audio muted.

Frankie took a couple steps inside and stopped, scenes straight out of Afghanistan flashing through her mind.

She shook her head. No one was in there waiting to shoot her. She knew that, didn't she?

Forcing herself forward, a few more steps allowed a glimpse into Howie's messy living room where his old recliner lay on its side. A flash of bright eyes showed the gray cat huddled under a table, its fur bristling.

The unmistakable smell of blood and feces rose up and caught in her nose.

Oh, God. Her worst fears confirmed. But she had to see, had to be sure.

Craning her neck, she made out the figure of a man sprawled on the dirty carpet. He was facing her, as though he'd been trying to run. Blood pooled beneath him. An arm wearing a dirty cast had splashed drops in a bow-tie pattern.

Howie.

She went just far enough into the room to touch his wrist below the cast. No pulse. She'd known, of course, there wouldn't be. Not with the way—

Frankie backed out of the room, fumbling her phone from her pocket. Dialed nine-one-one, in a steady voice, told Benton enough to get things rolling. There'd been a murder.

Not, she felt certain, the first.

***

Before help arrived, Frankie gathered the dogs

and put them in her pickup. She put herself in the pickup, too, and locked the doors and started the engine, just in case the murderer came back for a whack at her and she had to peel out fast.

Only then did she notice her shaking hands and heard the funny catch in the in-and-out expulsion of breath coming from her mouth.

She was left alone with her fear until Lew drove up with the siren silenced. Caught in the glow of the ambulance's headlights, Frankie killed the Ranger's engine and, leaving the animals inside the cab, got out to meet him.

"You okay?" Lew strode toward her.

"Yes. No. But Howie—"

Gabe, also sans flashing lights and siren, wheeled up only seconds behind Lew, brakes squealing as he ground his Tahoe to a halt.

Frankie made a mental note, meaning to suggest he get his rig in for maintenance.

He'd been roused from bed and was out of uniform, his dark hair mussed, but with hazel eyes sharp and alert.

He asked the same question as Lew. "You okay?"

She nodded.

"Benton said there'd been a murder. He said

Howie St. James is dead."

"Yes."

"You found him?"

"I...yes. I guess so."

"You guess so?" Gabe was in full deputy mode, forceful, stern.

Frankie, with her mind still whirling, felt as if she should be apologizing for doing something wrong.

Well, she had. She'd been in the wrong place at the wrong time.

Shuddering, she drew herself tighter. She was not some puling little civvie, after all, but a combat veteran who'd seen about every kind of havoc humans can wreak upon each other. Trouble is, she'd thought she left all that behind in Afghanistan. Hawkesford was no war zone. Violent death here was out of place. It didn't belong.

"I wouldn't say 'found' is the exact word," she retorted. "I came home on my break to check on the dogs. When I got here, they were having a fit—barking and crying. They quieted right down when I got inside, which is when I heard a bunch of thuds and bumps coming from Howie's side of the duplex. Then I heard a shot, and someone ran out the back. He slugged my door as he went past.

On foot, by the way. I didn't hear a car."

"Good observation." Gabe's approval encouraged her.

She took a breath. "A little later, I got up my nerve to see about Howie."

"How much later?"

Her brain fuzzed, then cleared. "I don't know. A minute maybe. I didn't look at my watch. The dogs," she added, "were pretty freaked."

As if guessing they hadn't been the only ones, Gabe's expression softened. "Did you see who it was?"

Frankie shook her head. "Just heard him. I wasn't about to confront him, you know. He had a gun, and I didn't."

"Wise of you." He looked like he meant it. "You said him. Tell me why."

"Why?"

"Impressions, Frankie. Anything you can remember."

From down on the main road running through town, a siren began wailing. Gabe winced as, answering the siren's call, dogs around the neighborhood began howling. A minute later, Rudy Swallowtail's cruiser screeched—literally—to a halt behind Gabe's SUV.

Rudy, a stocky man more than three-quarters Coeur d'Alene Indian, strode quickly toward them. "Heard the news over the scanner. Murder?"

"Afraid so," Gabe answered.

From the closest house, a door slammed. A man called out, "What the hell's going on over there?"

Gabe sighed. "Somebody'll have to quiet him down."

"I'll go," Lew said. "That's Jerry Honicker's place. He's a nosy bastard."

Frankie couldn't help thinking any normal person would be curious if the cops and an ambulance showed up in their neighborhood in the middle of the night, especially one with a klaxon blaring.

Gabe nodded his thanks and turned back to Frankie. "Did you go inside St. James's unit?"

"Yes. Just far enough to see if there was anything I could do for him." She shuddered. "There wasn't. The only thing I touched was his wrist."

"All right." Gabe jerked his head at Rudy Swallowtail. "C'mon. Let's see what we've got."

The two policemen, big flashlights throwing a bright beam ahead of them, started off toward the front.

"That's locked," Frankie said. "You need to go around back. Through my unit is closest."

But Gabe nixed that suggestion. Taking the lead, he and Swallowtail slowly circled the duplex, examining the ground with minute care before they stepped ahead, through the gate, and skirting the propane tank. Frankie followed, not because she wanted to revisit the crime scene, but because she didn't want to be left alone.

Gabe stopped. "Walk where we walk. In case our perp left any sign, I don't want it disturbed."

Her nod went unseen as the men pressed on.

Lew, running up behind them to join the group, made her jump.

Eagle-eyed, Rudy Swallowtail spied a partial footprint on the porch steps. Blood still glistened in the heavy tread. Grunting, he pointed it out, shining his light straight down.

Gabe used his phone camera to shoot a picture. "Watch that," he said to no one in particular.

Lew and Frankie shied away like wild horses from a lasso, although she squinted at the print on her way past.

"Cabela's," she said. "Just like the one we found in my house."

"Looks like." Gabe unsnapped the latch over his Beretta. "We'll see if it's a match."

At the door, the screen creaking eerily on ruined hinges, he held up his hand, indicating Frankie and Lew should stay back. Drawing his weapon, Rudy Swallowtail led the way into the kitchen, his shoes squeaking on the dirty vinyl floor.

Frankie, with Lew peering over her shoulder, watched the flashlight beam bounce off the living room walls, back and forth, slowly working its way to the floor. The beam touched on Howie's body. Leaped crazily. Sank again.

The two police officers murmured. Gabe's voice became louder as he opened his phone and called for back-up, the M.E., the CS techs, detectives.

"You got it." Voice hushed, he spoke into the phone. "Same address as yesterday. And get Boyd Holliday and Freak out here. We've got a blood trail."

"Freak?" Swallowtail sounded pale.

Frankie cocked an eyebrow at Lew. Sure he'd know what Gabe meant.

Sure enough, Lew nodded. "Bloodhound and his handler."

"Good plan." Swallowtail, given a minute, gained confidence. "I'll get Sam McAllister over to guard that print until the dog gets here, make sure nobody wanders over the top of it. Sam's in Plummer. Take maybe fifteen minutes to get here."

"That'll help."

That's when Gabe—or it might've been Swallowtail—flipped the overhead light on. Behind her, Lew sucked in a sharp breath. "Jesus, Frankie, you could've warned me. Let's get out of here and let these guys work."

He—they—had finally seen what Frankie hadn't wanted to mention. What her brain wanted to deny. Howie's head, thanks to a high caliber bullet slamming through the base of his throat, had pretty much been separated from his body.

***

Gabe escorted Frankie and Lew back to her side of the duplex. "I'll want to talk to you," he told her before he left them with a warning to stay inside. "Why don't you make a pot of coffee? Make it strong. We'll all need some before this night is over."

"I'd sooner have a straight shot of Maker's Mark." Lew plopped heavily onto a kitchen chair. "Or three or four."

Mute, Frankie nodded, even though booze of any kind didn't agree with her nowadays. The meds she was on, one of which helped anxiety, the other for headaches, were bad enough by themselves, let alone mixed with alcohol.

She was running water into the coffeemaker when Rudy Swallowtail rushed in, asking to use her bathroom. Permission granted. She and Lew exchanged a glance as they heard him vomiting as though to wring his stomach into a knot. The toilet flushed, flushed again. Water ran in the sink.

After a while, he came out, looking pale as an Indian possibly can. "Something I ate," he said, refusing to meet their eyes. She and Lew nodded as though they knew a bad food virus had been going around and affecting lots of people's stomachs, not just his. Frankie hoped he was properly grateful for the fallacy.

She waited until he went back to join Gabe in the other apartment, out of earshot. "How long has he been a cop? I don't remember him from when I lived here."

"He's been around a couple years. College boy. Graduate of the police academy. This is his first murder if I'm not mistaken. Been a while since the last around here." He inspected a torn fingernail. "There's always a different slant on death when it's murder."

"As opposed to plain old dying?"

"That's the way it looks to me."

Yeah. It did to her, too. And it was true. There was something different about murder.

Ten minutes later, twelve cups of coffee had dripped through the filter and filled the carafe. She and Lew had both downed a cup and poured a second before they heard a car drive up. Well, they heard tires crunch on the gravel. The engine had that quiet hum that, in Frankie's book, meant the car was expensive. Lew went to the door, standing open to the night air, to see who it was.

Inside the pickup, Banner was standing in the driver's seat and baying at the newcomers.

A few seconds later a short, thin Asian woman who looked a lot like Vera Wang, the clothing designer—only Frankie doubted Ms. Wang would be caught dead wearing those baggy navy coveralls—stalked past. An identically dressed young blond guy followed a few feet behind, trying to keep up under his burden of a large black bag. The blond guy hammered on Howie's front door. It opened, and they went inside.

"Dr. Beth Huong, the medical examiner," Lew informed Frankie over his shoulder. "Detectives should be here soon."

With the words no more than out of his mouth, both his and Frankie's pagers went off, making Frankie jump yet again.

"Accident north on Highway 95," Benton reported from the station. "Deer versus car. Multiple injuries."

"That's us." Lew headed for the ambulance. "Saddle up."

***

A deer lying half-on, half-off the road, appeared in the ambulance headlights. No question it was dead. Lew braked, dodging a scattering of broken glass.

The wrecked car, an anonymous gray sedan, had rolled a couple times, coming to rest nose-first in a deep ditch a hundred feet beyond the deer carcass. The pair of twenty-somethings who'd stopped and called in the accident were waiting for them, standing by the wrecked car fidgeting like they had bugs up their butts. An old Honda Civic sat on the verge, its stereo playing a bass heart-pounder, its emergency flashers blinking.

Lew pulled the bus in behind the wreck's rear-end, which stuck out on the highway.

"Jeez, guys!" One of the guys took the role of spokesman, greeting Lew and Frankie with undisguised relief as they climbed out of the rig. "What took you so long? I was beginning to think you'd piled up somewhere."

It had been seven minutes, thirty seconds since they'd slammed the doors shut at Frankie's house. She'd clocked their time.

"Not us." Lew made a chopping motion toward their old car. "Kill that noise."

One of the guys leaped to obey. The resulting quiet allowed Frankie to hear a series of soft moans. At least one man was alive in the wreckage.

Lew slid down the side of the ditch on his heels. She followed, grabbing the branch of a slippery-leaved bush as her bad foot slid on dry grass. The other men stayed on the road—a wise decision.

The aroma of beer and pizza coming from the young guy's car couldn't quite overpower the smell of hot metal, blood, and a field full of ripe wheat on the other side of the ditch.

Lew turned his powerful flashlight into the sedan's interior. "This isn't good."

The comment, especially coming from Lew, as hard-bitten and emotionless as they come, struck Frankie as being out of character, even if the people in the wreck were fatalities. "What's up?"

He reached into the car, felt for the driver's pulse. "These men are the sheriff's department's detectives. I expect they were on the way to Howie's." He huffed out a breath. "This is sure as hell going to put a damper on the investigation. And you know what they say."

"What?" Frankie opened the medical bag and handed Lew a pair of latex gloves before donning her own.

"That every hour after the first twenty-four, chances of catching a killer start to fade."

The good news was that the detectives weren't dead.

CHAPTER 12

The more Frankie thought about Lew's comment regarding the time factor in a murder investigation, the more disturbed she became. What if he was right in his guess about the effect two injured detectives would have on solving Howie's murder?

One of the detectives, his name already forgotten—which was beginning to seem normal for her nowadays—had a concussion and internal injuries. The other, Detective Armbuster, whose name she remembered solely because it struck her as appropriate in the circumstances, suffered cracked ribs and a shattered ulna. Neither would be on the job for a few weeks, leaving the police department shorthanded.

Or so went the less than optimistic diagnosis

by an emergency room doctor when they arrived at Kootenai Medical Center. In Frankie's opinion, he came across as positively macabre with his hearty bedside manner.

His exact words to the detectives were, "Looks like you guys won't be chasing crooks for a month or two."

"How many detectives does Kootenai County have?" she asked Lew in a whisper as they helped transfer Armbuster to a hospital bed.

Apparently, this wasn't far from the detective's own thoughts. He, the one with the concussion answered. "Not enough. Damn all budget cuts." He groaned as an orderly wheeled him away to the operating room.

This met Frankie's worst expectations. Great. More delays with Lew's twenty-four-hour time frame ticking away. And it meant Gabe would be in charge.

She couldn't help fretting. "I wonder if Gabe and Officer Swallowtail have heard about the detectives' accident?"

"If they haven't by now, they soon will. Don't worry. Gabe is an able cop." Lew was more prosaic and not as anxious as she was. But then, he hadn't been a thin wall away when Howie's murder took place. He hadn't slept in a bloodstained bed. "You take care of the paperwork for this run, Frankie, and I'll restock the ambulance. Let's get this show on the road."

Lew went off to replenish their supply of splints and IV solutions, among other items, leaving Frankie at the counter to fill in the necessary computer forms. As she prepared to sign off, a vaguely familiar voice caught her attention. Looking up, she spied the physician from the dock accident escorting an elderly gentleman into the emergency room. The old fellow wore an oxygen tube in his nose and sat hunched in a wheelchair. He looked stunned and sick, and, although rail thin, the slippered feet poking from beneath a lap robe were grossly swollen.

"Mr. Shenker is here for his dialysis treatment," Dr. Muncie told the receptionist. "I'll wheel him back myself." Without waiting for the receptionist's go ahead, he pushed off with an impatient jerk, causing his patient to grunt with the effort of staying upright in his chair.

Frankie wondered if the old fella was the doctor's friend? Nobody else got personal service from a physician. She never had, that's for sure. But then, army doctors were constantly in rotation, so she never had the same one more than twice, never got to know one well. Many had been brusque to the point she dreaded facing them.

Kind of like Dr. Muncie just now. If the patient were a friend, Frankie thought, concentrating on dating the paperwork correctly, you'd think he'd be a tad more considerate.

The dialysis room must've been just around the corner because less than a minute later the doctor strode out alone, brushing past Frankie so closely they touched.

She cleared her throat. "Dr. Muncie."

"Yes?" He turned to her, forehead creased in a frown. Maybe it was her imagination, but she thought his frown faded a little as he eyed her from top to bottom and back up.

"I just wanted to ask—how is the girl my partner and I treated at the lake the other day?"

He looked perfectly blank for a moment. "What? Who?"

After a pause long enough Frankie began to think his memory shorted out even worse than her own, recall apparently flooded in. "Oh, right. You're one of the local EMTs, aren't you? I suppose you mean the young woman who ran into my dock with her Jet Ski. I really can't say how she is. She's not my patient."

She blinked. That sounded pretty cold. "Even so—" she began, but he cut her off.

"I'm sorry if I sound crass, but in my position, I don't dare show too much concern. There's a certain element that would take that as an admission of some sort." He looked at his watch, a platinum Omega, and sighed.

"Admission of what?" Frankie drew a blank. What was he talking about?

"In this case, of supplying the dock the girl rammed, thereby causing injury."

Enlightenment dawned. "Oh. You mean a lawsuit."

"Exactly. If you're curious about her condition, ask at the front desk. I'm sure they can give you an update." He strode out through the ER's automatic doors without pausing, supremely confident they'd open in time to keep him from running head first into them.

Open they did, whooshing apart just in the nick of time.

Lew, his arms full of supplies, showed up while she was still staring after the doctor.

"Ready to go?" His elbow in the ribs brought

her attention back to business.

"Yep." She hit enter, sending the paperwork into the system.

Once outside, they stacked the supplies in the rear of the ambulance and headed back to Hawkesford with all due speed. Neither wanted to be away from town any longer than necessary, in case... just in case.

Dawn stabbed pink fingers of light into the milky sky as they climbed the hill south of Coeur d'Alene. Below them, Cougar Bay glimmered darkly.

"Was that Doc Muncie you were talking to?" Lew dimmed his headlights for an oncoming semi.

"Trying to, yes." Frankie made a face. "Do you know him well?"

Lew cracked one of his rare grins. "Me? Know him well? Frankie, I'm a paramedic, he's a doctor. What do you think?"

"Oh. One of them." She grinned too. "He's a study in contrasts, isn't he? Do you know he hasn't even bothered to see whether that girl we treated on his dock lived or died?"

"Not surprised. Under his wife's advice, I'm sure."

"His wife? What's she got to do with anything?"

"She's someone big in the legal profession. Keeps an eye on her husband's malpractice insurance claims, from what I hear."

"Does he have many?" Frankie's mouth twisted.

"Don't they all?"

"Hmm. But on the other hand, he's up early helping some poor old guy make his dialysis appointment."

Lew blew a raspberry. "I wouldn't give him angel wings, Frankie. Doubt if his time goes unbilled."

She looked over at him, a little surprised by his mockery. "What do you mean?"

"I mean Dr. Muncie has a large practice. Really large. And many of his patients are elderly, just like you saw. The doc makes sure the old geezers get in for checkups early and often. Word is, he has Medicare on speed dial."

"Oh."

"Yeah."

Disillusioned by Lew's comments, Frankie was unable to stop worrying about—among other things—her dogs, locked in the Ranger. She needed to get them out of there. Banner could be depended on not to pee on or tear up the seats, but Shine was an unknown factor. More worrisome, she could feel the rapidly rising sun shining through the ambulance's side window, already gathering warmth. And her pickup was sitting right in the sun's full blaze without a trace of shade. Everybody knew the statistics when it came to animals—and small children—left any length of time in a closed vehicle.

Lew noticed her agitation as she glanced at her watch—a big old Timex with an indispensable sweep hand—for the umpteenth time. "We don't pay overtime, in case you wondered."

"Huh?"

"I said—"

Realization of his meaning struck. "It's not that. I don't care about the time. Or I do, but it's because the dogs are shut in the cab of my pickup. Do you think I can call Gabe and have him let them out? Maybe put them in the duplex's bedroom."

Lew's foot came down on the accelerator. "I wouldn't recommend it. He's the officer in charge now. He'll be working his butt off to bag this murderer ASAP. Be my guess he's got enough to worry about without babysitting a couple dogs."

The cosmic universe must've been listening because no sooner did he close his mouth than Frankie's phone rang. She picked up.

"Frankie!" Jesselyn squeaked. "What the heck is going on at your place? I heard cops are swarming around like flies on poop over there."

If Jesselyn hadn't heard about Howie's murder, it must mean either the grapevine had crop failure, or the sheriff's office—meaning Gabe—was keeping a tight lid on things. But now people would be getting up. Word would spread. The murder wouldn't stay hidden long.

"It's Howie," she said. "He's been... killed."

"What?" Jesselyn's voice went shrill with shock. "Killed? How? What happened? Don't tell me someone ran over him as he was staggering home from the bar!"

"Good guess, after what happened to his arm, but no. Not that." Frankie knew no other way to say it. "He was at home. Somebody murdered him."

"Are you serious?" Jesselyn's question rose into a high-pitched mini-scream.

Holding the phone away from her ear, Frankie nodded as if Jesselyn could see her. "I'm afraid so."

"Who did it?"

"Don't know yet. Turns out the detectives assigned to the case had a collision with a deer. Now it depends on whether Gabe and Rudy have caught anyone or not. Lew and I had to go on a run, so we've been out of the loop."

Jesselyn was silent a few moments, then said, "Wow. I'm glad you were working. What if you'd been there? You might've been murdered, too."

As if the idea hadn't been tumbling over and over through Frankie's brain since it happened. "I was there," she admitted. "I'd gone home to check on the dogs when I heard a shot."

"Jeez, he was shot?"

"Yes." Now Frankie was the one who sounded stark. She didn't want the vision of how Howie had looked, lying there with—Didn't want the picture in her memory, didn't want a reminder of the smell. Didn't want the sound of gunfire reminding her... Reminding her.

"Did you see the killer?" Jesselyn whispered.

"No. Wish I had. Gabe would have this all wrapped up by now."

But Jesselyn just had to put a name to Frankie's fears. "But, Frankie, what if the killer saw you? What if he knows you were there?"

In Frankie's opinion, her friend could've gone

all day—or forever—without bringing up that point. Anyway, what difference did it make if Howie's killer had seen her? He'd known she was there. That was enough.

"Oh, he knows."

"He does? Frankie, you didn't try to—"

Her mouth tightened. "Try to what?"

A silence. Jesselyn said, "Play hero."

"No."

Gritting her teeth, Frankie shifted the conversation, asking Jesselyn if she'd mind checking on Banner and Shine. But by the time she finished explaining how she'd acquired Denise Rider's dog and answered at least fifty more excited questions with monosyllables, they were cresting the hill into Hawkesford, and it was no longer necessary. Relieved, she hung up.

"Jesselyn should've hired on as a detective." Lew sounded sympathetic. "She's got the question asking part down pat."

Frankie, feeling like she'd been twisted into knots, could only agree.

"Anyway, it's quitting time for us, partner." Lew winked at her. "I'll drop you off at the duplex. Chris and Marc should've checked in for their shift by now. It'll probably fall to them to transport St. James's body to the morgue—if the ME hasn't made other arrangements. If she has, our guys can clean the ambulance and put away supplies. Give 'em something to do besides scratch their asses and bitch."

Even to herself, Frankie's laugh sounded a little forced, but she had no desire to argue. "Better them than me—cleaning the ambulance I mean, not the other."

Now, if only she could decide what to do next. Staying at the duplex horrified her, the mere thought of sleeping there made her legs go weak.

In a perfect world—heck, even a week ago— she would've asked Jesselyn for a bed. After all, she'd be at work while Frankie slept. The request had been right on the tip of her tongue as they talked. But the way Jesselyn blew her off when Frankie mentioned staying there the other day had stuck. And she'd been joking then.

"Who's Jesselyn's boyfriend, Lew?" Her former curiosity rose to the surface as they turned down the street where police cars still took up most of the space.

"Damned if I know." Lew threaded the ambulance between Gabe's Expedition and a state police cruiser. "Don't care. But probably somebody who's not good for her."

Frankie sighed. "The usual, in other words."

Stopping in the middle of the road, he waited for her to get out. "You got that right. Ask Maggie. If anyone knows, she does."

Frankie resolved to do that very thing. Maybe later today if Maggie was on shift again. But for now, she had to see to the dogs and find a place to sleep, someplace other than Jesselyn's place. Or in Gabe Zantos's spare bedroom. She couldn't—just couldn't—impose on him again.

Waving to Lew as he drove off, Frankie was relieved to see Banner with his nose pressed against the window, in no apparent distress. She hurried to unlock the door and let him jump to the ground. Shine, smart dog, waited for help.

As she looped a collar around Banner's furry neck, Gabe strode to meet her as if he'd been on the lookout for her return. Although more than likely, Frankie thought, the cop standing outside the duplex had warned him of her arrival.

"Sorry, Frankie," Gabe said, not sounding sorry at all. "I can't let you back in the duplex. Crime scene people are going over your unit along with Howie's." He eyed the bichon, who was barely able to walk, as she squatted at their feet. "This

Ms. Rider's dog?'

"Yes."

"Looks like she's in tough shape."

Frankie nodded.

"And you don't look much better." Gabe's comment didn't exactly make Frankie's morning.

"Thanks." Her sarcasm earned a narrowing of his eyes.

What difference does how I look make? she wondered a moment later. Why should she waste a second's thought? Gabe wasn't likely to become interested in, let alone involved with a woman sporting a foot prosthesis and a skull that set off metal detectors every time she went through a security gate. She figured him for a kind man, taking pity on a wounded warrior.

How she hated that phrase—almost as much as she hated being one.

"I'm just saying." Gabe leaned against the Ranger, arms crossed, his hip rubbing a clean spot in the dust. He appeared tired, too, hazel eyes red-rimmed, new lines apparent in his face.

"I know how I look," she blurted. "No need to rub it in. And maybe you ought to look in the mirror yourself."

His hand rubbing the dark stubble on his chin

failed to hide a grin. "That wasn't meant as an insult."

She shrugged

He started over. "I just meant—"

A hound baying on the hill above the duplex cut him off. Gabe's head turned sharply toward the ominous peals.

The other dog's noise raised Banner's hackles. He tugged at the leash, almost pulling it from Frankie's hand. "Stay," she told him.

Rudy Swallowtail popped from the doorway of Howie's unit. "Hey, Zantos," he called to Gabe. "Listen up. Sounds like that Freak is on to something."

CHAPTER 13

Gabe's face came alive. Straightening from where he'd been leaning against the pickup, he waved acknowledgment to Rudy. Wired, from all appearances, by Swallowtail's message, Frankie plummeted from his "pressing concerns" list.

She didn't blame him a bit.

"Give me a second and we'll go see what he's found," he called to Swallowtail. "You know where I keep the house key," he told her, dusting road-dirt off his rear. Excitement sparked in his eyes. "Take the dogs and make yourself at home. I need to talk to you as soon as I'm done here."

"I can't—" she started, but he interrupted.

"Can't what? Stay at my house? Sure, you can. Just say it's so I'll know where to find you later."

This last came from over his shoulder. He was

already taking long strides to meet up with the tribal policeman. With a brief order to the remaining deputy to keep an eye on things, he and Rudy trotted off on foot, following the bloodhound's yodel.

"Huh. Okay. But only because I want to talk to you, too."

Frankie's mutter chased the two men as they disappeared into the woods behind the duplex. She didn't much like acceding to Gabe's... um... order, but with no other likely option presenting itself, set about gathering the dogs into the pickup again.

"Starting to smell pretty funky in here," she complained to Banner.

He stared at her out of dark, almond-shaped eyes and smiled.

"Yeah," she put the Ranger in gear, "some of it's the new kid, but not all, buster."

A portion of the odor might even have been herself. God only knows she felt soiled enough.

At her grandmother's house, she carried in her traveling bag of clothes, everything dirty now. The laundry room was exactly as she remembered. Sometime in the last fifty years, a handyman, probably her grandfather, had boxed in one side of the back porch where the washer, dryer, and a huge freezer lined up side-by-side. The appliances were all leftover from her grand-mother's day.

Before tossing her clothing into the top-load-er, she rinsed the blood from her uniform shirt in cold water at the scullery sink and couldn't help smiling just a little at the old word. Scullery. It had been one of Grandma's favorites. Frankie thought it was because the old lady had read tons of Gothic romantic suspense way back when. And unless Gabe had disposed of the library, they were probably still stashed somewhere in the house.

Gabe had recently done laundry, too, and hadn't had a chance to put his stuff away. With-out thinking twice, she stole a white T-shirt from a stack sitting on the dryer to use as a sleep shirt.

A ripple feathered her skin as she slipped it on. The shirt smelled of a clean-scented detergent... and something else. Gabe. The combination pleased her.

When the wash cycle completed, she loaded the dryer, hit the go button, and dropped into bed like a wounded thing...

Frankie fell, tumbling in a riot of blood and noise. Panic flooded her system. Sweat drenched her body. Pain. Fear. Heart pounding. Lightning slashing at her brain. Explosions pulsating in her ears. Where was she? Couldn't breathe.

They were coming. Enemies with cloth-wrapped heads. The rifle. Fire the rifle. Lieutenant Jay's face twisted in agony. Drag him out of the wreckage, out of the fire.

Get to the machine gun. Shoot. Shoot them all. Him and him and him and—

Noise.

Oh, God. It hurt—she hurt—so bad.

Couldn't breathe!

The instant she hit the floor, Frankie's nightmare vision shattered. A hard landing. Painful. Bones crushed beneath the weight on top of her. She was yelling. And crying. Bewildered.

Frantic, she pushed at the weight.

"Frankie. For God's sake. Frankie!"

Who is that?

"Take it easy. Calm down. You're all right. Frankie, you're okay. You fell out of bed, is all."

Strong hands gripped her shoulders, not quite hard enough to bruise.

Whoever it was continued to speak. Quietly. Soothingly, but with an undercurrent of tension. How did he know what she needed to hear?

He?

Gabe Zantos.

She could smell him, knowing his scent from the shirt she wore. Knew his voice. Just couldn't see him. Not yet. Not until the flashing lights behind her eyes settled down. And they would when she did. But dammit. Dammit! He was right on top of her, and he'd see... he'd see the damage the war had done.

As if this episode hadn't shown him, plain as day.

Shit.

She went still and wished for invisibility. It didn't happen.

Tears seeped from between her closed eyelids, but she wasn't crying. Not really. She was just a little... leaky.

"Are you awake now?" Gabe asked, almost whispering. "Look at me."

She opened her eyes. Another flash blinded her, but then something changed. The pain evaporated, and vision returned. Another blink and Gabe's face bobbed into focus.

She nodded. "You're squashing me. Get off. What are you doing in here, anyway?" She knew she sounded combative, but damn it all.

"I heard you cry out and then a thump." He brushed the hair from her eyes. "Didn't know what was going on. Sorry."

He drew away from her as commanded, but then she almost wished him back. Because now he had a clear view of her foot without the prosthesis, an awkward club where toes ought to be. A hideous reminder of war and death and mutilation.

Frankie stuck her stub behind the whole foot, hoping to hide it. Too late, of course. He'd definitely seen. So had Howie, she remembered. And he hadn't fainted.

Neither did Gabe.

Pride, or maybe a desire to get the hurt over with, made her uncover the stub again.

"Ugly, isn't it?" It came out pugnacious, an act to show him his opinion didn't matter.

And Gabe? He didn't pretend to misunderstand. He sat beside her on the floor and ran his hand down her bare leg, ankle, and over her foot, just as if he didn't find it repulsive.

"Badge of honor, Frankie. Looks like you

earned your purple heart."

Hah! He didn't know the half of it. But who'd told him about the medal? Karl Mager, probably. She hadn't told anyone, although the information was probably in her army records for any potential employer to see.

"I'd rather have a whole foot." She scrambled to her feet, swaying until she caught her balance. The action succeeded in giving him quite an eyeful. She yanked the T-shirt down over her hips, from where it'd ridden up to expose lacy black bikini panties and a flat stomach.

Gabe, wearing jeans, though shirtless, lolled back on the floor and stared openly at the spectacle. On second thought, maybe she should say he leered.

Hell. She kinda liked it. Even when he said, "Hubba, hubba," like somebody out of the dark ages.

But then his moment of levity passed, grin fading until she saw he looked tired to the bone. She guessed her episode had awakened him and brought him running up the stairs.

Embarrassed, she sat on the edge of the bed and changed the subject. "Did the hound find anything?"

Remaining on the floor, he nodded, his forefinger tracing a loose knot in the old plank floor. "Freak's a good tracker. Best I've ever seen."

She waited. And waited some more, until he drew in a deep breath and glanced up at her.

"Rudy and I, we caught up with Boyd Holliday and the dog on the hill behind the duplex. Maybe you know there's an old logging road goes all the way to the top. Pretty overgrown these days."

"Figures. It's steep, as I remember. Kids used to ride their dirt bikes up there. Me included."

"Then you know the road ends at an abandoned stud mill. Only thing in the clearing is a falling down shack they probably used for storage." He fell silent again.

After a while, she said, "And?"

"And the dog led us right to the door. We found her—Denise Rider—inside."

Frankie knew from looking at him, but she asked the question anyway. "Dead?"

He nodded. "Funny thing, though. She hadn't been dead that long. Sometime yesterday, I'd guess. Probably near the same time as Howie. We'll know more after the autopsy."

"Was she— Did she—" Frankie faltered. "How did she die?"

"Aside from taking a terrific beating?" Gabe's voice cracked.

Rage, she thought. He was fighting pure rage.

"Shot," he continued. "At first glance, looks like the same caliber gun that killed Howie. We should know later today."

She could barely speak. "Howie knew something. Or he found something of hers—of Denise's. I told him he should speak to you or to someone. Did he call you? He promised he would."

"Howie St. James never was good about keeping his promises." Gabe paused. "Did he tell you what this something is?"

"Yes," she said, but slowly, as she was unsure. Frowning, she tried to recall Howie's exact words.

Gabe watched her, his eyes intense.

She sighed. "Well, sort of. He said he found something of hers that struck him as odd. A computer disc."

Gabe lifted himself onto the bed beside her. "Where's the disc now?"

"I have no idea. He didn't say."

"Figures. It's too bad Howie distrusted us—anyone in law enforcement—so much." He ran his fingers through his already ruffled hair. "If he'd come forward, he might still be alive."

Frankie shrugged. "He had a little bit of outlaw in him, I guess."

"More than a little." Gabe's voice was dry. "He's had a run in or two with the law even before he came to Hawkesford as a juvenile. His dad married Nell Prairie, and Howie came to the reservation to live with them. He always wanted to be as Indian as Nell's son Iggie." He stopped. "You probably already knew that."

"Now, you remind me. I'd forgotten."

On the floor below, one of the dogs, Banner most probably, started up the stairs, his toenails clicking on the bare wood. Ready to join the party now he could hear her normal voice. Her nightmares always scared him, even when he stuck it out at her side for the duration.

Sure enough, the Samoyed's black nose poked around the jamb, sniffed, then pushed his way in. He ambled over to lick her hand.

Gabe heaved himself to his feet and headed for the door. To Frankie, it seemed his every move took effort. Poor guy. Here he was, working on a double murder and not only did he have her in the house, but had the misfortune to walk in on one of her "episodes."

"You gonna be all right?" he asked, kind of skirting around the subject.

"Sure. No big deal." She found it hard to meet his eyes, glad when he consented to take her answer at face value. "I'm sorry I woke you, Gabe. I'm due a couple days off. I'll look for somewhere to live in the morning after work."

She believed his expression revealed relief as he paused at the door and gave a short nod.

"I'm glad you realize you can't stay in the duplex," he said. "Until we catch the killer, it's too dangerous. By the way, you should be able to get back in tomorrow sometime to pack your stuff. I'll let you know when."

Her thanks were aimed at his back since he was already on his way out.

***

It only seemed right, Frankie thought later, to warn Victoria Pettigrew that as soon as the all clear sounded regarding police control of the duplex, she intended to move out.

In plain fact, she'd rather pitch a tent in her neighbor's back yard than stay in that house of horrors.

Of course, there was the matter of her rent and deposit to try to recoup. She might have a fight on her hands over that. At least she hadn't signed a lease, binding her to the place for the next six months or year. The mere thought gave her the creeps.

Out of a sense of fair play, she gave Victoria a call before going on shift. Having arrived at the station a half-hour early for the six o'clock start, and finding the lunchroom empty, she propped herself against the counter in front of the sink and dialed Victoria's number.

"You again," Victoria said as soon as Frankie identified herself. "And I'll bet I know what you want."

"More than just a new mattress or the locks changed," Frankie replied. "I can't stay in the duplex after what's happened. As soon as I get clearance from the police, I'm moving out, and I'd like my deposit back. I'd like the rent prorated, too."

"Dream on," Victoria instantly snapped back. "No refunds. And don't try getting Jesselyn mixed up in this. This is between you, me, and the property owner."

No wonder Jesselyn said Victoria has been

making a lot of money, Frankie thought. She starts out huffing and puffing and turns into a steam roller. Not that Frankie felt like lying down and letting herself be run over.

"Of course this is between us. No Jesselyn. But you rented the place to me under deceptive circumstances."

"Not my fault," Victoria said.

"Not mine, either. I can't help thinking you should've spent a little more time checking Denise's departure before renting to me. You put me right on top of a murder scene."

"Well, how was I to know—"

Frankie cut in over Victoria's excuse. "All that aside, living in the duplex has put my life in danger. I just want out."

She heard Victoria shuffling papers in the background. "I'll have to ask the owner. He'll probably say 'no deal.'"

Frankie found a glass and ran water into it. Confrontational situations had a tendency to make her mouth go dry, and in this case, the tension was worse than usual. She was talking tough to Jesselyn's sister, for crying out loud. People she knew and cared about.

"Who is the owner? I'll take it up with him

myself."

"No, no." Victoria obviously didn't like this scenario. "I'll talk to him."

"When?"

"This evening, as soon as he comes in from the field." Victoria took a breath. "Forget I said that."

"You might as well tell me. I can find the owner easily enough from the property records. It just takes longer and makes me mad—madder." A light flashed through her head. She took a drink of water, the glass clinking against her teeth as her hand shook. Damn.

But Victoria capitulated. "Oh, hell. All right. What's the point. My brother Russ owns the duplex. And the hill behind it. He loaned a friend the money to buy the duplex, then had to take it over when the friend defaulted on the payment. He hates being involved with a crappy property like that. And after Denise dumped him, he really wants rid of it."

"Denise dumped him?" This felt like information Gabe should hear. Not because she wanted to get Russ, Jesselyn's brother, in trouble. He'd amused her the night of his car wreck. But still. If nothing else, he might have some sort of clue to why a woman like Denise had been living in

Hawkesford, Idaho, of all places, in substandard living quarters.

Or maybe Russ himself—No. Jesselyn's brother couldn't possibly be involved in these murders.

"Just hold your horses. You don't need to spread the news around." Victoria was back to sounding irate. "It doesn't have anything to do with... anything. I'll call you in an hour."

The phone slammed down in Frankie's ear. When she turned from the sink, Marc, Chris, and Darryl were hovering around the door, blatantly eavesdropping. Maggie, right behind them, had her chin resting on Marc's shoulder and she looked every bit as avid as the others.

CHAPTER 14

"So who'd Denise dump?" Maggie, as usual, took the lead. "Or maybe I should say, who else?"

Frankie stuck her phone back in her pocket. "You mean she made a habit of dumping old boyfriends?"

Marc, the least ghoul-like of the lot, had the most pertinent question. "Does Gabe think she dumped some guy and he killed her? Does this mean the cops know who he is and have him in custody?"

News of Denise's murder had apparently spread.

Darryl gave a relieved grin. Delighted and relieved. "You must be glad, Frankie. You'll be able to get back into your apartment."

"And quit shacking up with Gabe Zantos."

Chris winked and grinned like he'd said something clever.

Frankie reared back with her fist, ready to clock him a good one.

"Chris!" Maggie chided, moving between them. "Children, mind your manners—all of you."

Chris shrugged. "Well, what else would you call it."

"Not what you're insinuating." Frankie gave them all a narrow-eyed glare they didn't seem to notice. "I'd call it a gentleman's offer of a temporary safe haven."

"Gabe's a good guy." Marc, at least, was willing to agree with her. "Remember last winter when he invited that family from Tennessee to stay overnight?" He turned to Frankie. "These southern folks ran their car in the ditch during a big snowstorm and were not only stranded but nearly broke. Took the highway department a full day to get the road open and another for Glen Edwards to fix their car. Meanwhile, they stayed with Gabe. He does stuff like that."

Frankie could've hugged him. The information took her off the hook and gave her a new, handle on Gabe, revealing the kind of man he was. Of course, it sort of made her into a charity case, too, which she didn't appreciate.

"Yeah. A regular do-gooder," Chris said in a neutral kind way.

Darryl was quick to give his opinion. "Dangerous practice, if you ask me. Never can tell who people really are."

Not that she wanted to agree, but Frankie figured Darryl actually had a point.

"What about a suspect?" Marc asked again.

He broke off from the assembly blocking the doorway, entered the lunchroom, and set to clearing various clutter and used coffee cups off the table. Each shift someone was responsible for cleaning up the mess their duty roster created.

Frankie shook her head. "As far as I know, they haven't got one. I'm not in the 'need-to-know' category. Just a paramedic, guys, trying to do my job. Ask Gabe or Rudy next time they report in."

"Bull puckey, Frankie." Darryl turned rude again. "You're right in the middle of things. You gotta hear all the latest. C'mon. At least tell us what the cops are saying."

"They don't tell me anything. Why would they?" Frankie assumed her most innocent face. "Don't know what the police have found, don't know if they have a suspect. Really."

Maggie's lifted brow indicated skepticism. "What's this about Denise dumping someone?" She hadn't lost sight of this hot item. The one that just might hold the answer to all the rest.

"Why don't you take a guess, Maggie?" Marc grinned at the middle-aged dispatcher. "You're the one who keeps tabs on everyone's love life in this town."

Openly invited, Maggie's eyes sparkled. Even Frankie, not yet tuned into the workings of her old home town, could tell this was meat and potatoes to the woman.

"Well..." Maggie, face scrunched in a know-it-all expression, drew it out. "There's Matt Chavez—" she added at Frankie's questioning look, "—he's the executive chef at the casino's Sunset Room Steakhouse. And Russ Pettigrew. I hear he's gotten pretty serious about her. Well, he always goes head over heels, exactly like his sister Jesselyn. Let's see... how about Les Scartano, or—" She grinned wickedly. "—or you, Marc. You went out with her a few times if I'm not mistaken."

Marc shrugged. "Yeah. But Denise is a good time girl used to dinner at the Coeur d'Alene Resort, and I'm a poor EMT who can barely afford

Black Angus. We didn't work out."

He didn't, to Frankie's eyes, seem particularly broken up by the split.

Maggie's next jibe was a little more pointed. "Then there's you, Chris. We all saw you with your tongue hanging out every time she walked by."

Chris reddened. A wry expression twisted his lips. "Hell, Denise was way out of my league. She didn't want anything to do with me."

Frankie didn't think his words were quite as careless as they might've seemed. What had Denise done to him? Given him an even shorter brush-off than Marc got? She had no wish to be snide, but it made sense. Chris did suffer from a "poor baby" syndrome.

Maggie wasn't done yet. "And then, of course, there's the guy paying Denise's rent."

"Somebody is paying her rent?" Marc's mouth dropped open. "Who?"

"Don't know. All I can say is it wasn't her. My sis—the one who keeps Victoria Pettigrew's real estate company's books—wouldn't tell." Looking a little shame-faced, Maggie put a finger over her lips. "On the other hand, forget I brought that up. I shouldn't have said anything."

And if Maggie's sis had been indiscreet enough, she could lose her job if Maggie's gossip got noised around. Deserved to lose it, maybe.

As though hoping the guys would forget the slip, Maggie spun on Frankie. "So spill. Who got the old heave-ho this time?"

Frankie shook her head. In all honesty, she couldn't hold Maggie's and the guys' curiosity against them. A double murder in a small town like Hawkesford was bound to be the topic on everyone's lips. Everyone's, not just hers. They all wanted in on the scuttlebutt, on every piece of gossip, whether it had anything to do with the murder or not.

In what felt to Frankie like a reprieve, Maggie's computer display system blared to life, and she rushed to take the call. A kid down at the lake with an allergy to bee stings had stumbled upon a yellow jacket nest. Marc and Chris, still on shift, sped off to administer epinephrine, Chris grousing about the run as usual. "Well, crap! Wouldn't you know there'd be a call when there's only fifteen minutes until quitting time?"

Marc closed the door behind them, shutting off further complaint.

Darryl took off right afterward, with neither a

goodbye nor a backward glance.

"Gawd, he's rude. What eating him, anyway?" Frankie asked, eyeing his retreating back.

"Which one, Darryl or Chris?" Maggie sat back at her desk, rolled her eyes, and shrugged. "They're both impossible."

"I meant Darryl, but you're right. He's not a paid employee, is he?" Frankie, puzzled over his attitude, sat at the adjoining desk and twirled in the swivel chair. "I wonder why he doesn't choose another line of work."

"Oh, he likes the excitement and accolades well enough. Just not the job. It cuts into his private life."

"Is anything private in Hawkesford?" Given the way she caught every one of the on-duty personnel eavesdropping on her conversation with Victoria, Frankie owned to some doubts.

Especially when Maggie laughed, gave a hmph, and said, "Not much."

"I can't say as I appreciated his comments about Deputy Zantos and me, either."

"He can be kind of a jerk. And Chris almost as bad, especially when they're together."

Idle curiosity made Frankie ask, "Who is he, anyway? Chris, I mean. I don't recognize his name from around here." Or was this something else she'd forgotten?

"Were you acquainted with Herb and Aimee Forrest?"

Frankie had to think a moment. "They worked for Acton Hayes, didn't they? She the housekeeper and Herb the year around hired man?"

"That's them. Chris is Aimee's nephew. The Forrests took him in after he got in some trouble in Seattle. This was a few years after you left town. They retired to Arizona a while back, but for some reason, Chris decided to stay on here."

Nodding, Frankie had another question as long they were discussing co-workers. "And Darryl? I know he's a volunteer. How does he make a living?"

"Hah." Maggie huffed. "I swear, he's one of the most secretive men I know. He works a little for Hayes in return for rent on an old house on the property. He janitors at the elementary school, gets odd jobs, fills in at the casino and generally doesn't seem real ambitious." She made her disapproval clear before shifting focus. "C'mon, Frankie. It's just us girls here now. What's the scoop? Which of Denise's boyfriends does Gabe suspect?"

Surprised, Frankie put the onus back on Maggie. "You tell me. You're the one who knows everyone. Tell me about Russ, about this Matt guy, about Marc. And Chris, even if he wasn't a real contender."

So Maggie did tell her. A delightful ten minutes of raw and reprehensible speculation. True or not so true was anybody's guess.

***

Frankie drove the old back-up ambulance, completing a fifteen-minute run by herself before Lew and the night dispatcher arrived. The emergency hadn't been a big deal. Just a four-year-old who'd stuck a pea up his nose. She provided a quick lesson on how to teach a kid to blow his nose, and that was that.

Lew, whom she found pacing the floor when she got back to the station, actually cracked a grin when she told him about it. "Must be somebody's first child. Mama doesn't usually get in such a panic by the second or third. We get at least one of those up-the-nose calls every year."

Later, as she ran the dusting wand over the ambulance before the next call, Frankie took time to mull over what Maggie let drop about Marc's "episode" with Denise, as she knew it, and Jesselyn's boyfriend. He now had a name, and Jesselyn a legitimate reason for keeping it secret.

Turned out Jesselyn's new beau was another of Denise's old boyfriends, of which Russ was bound to disapprove. Russ's feelings were apt to be hurt when he discovered his sister dating the man who'd been his rival over Denise. Knowing Jesselyn, she didn't want to upset him if the relationship didn't pan out.

Frankie, an impish enthusiasm driving the notion as she dusted the bus's wide rear bumper, got busy concocting an excuse to meet him. This part of the talk with Maggie was fun. The other part, what she'd told Maggie in return, was what caused her feelings of guilt. She'd definitely given up more information than prudent.

In retrospect, she shouldn't have spilled the story to Maggie, the biggest rumor-monger in town, about Russ Pettigrew not only owning the duplex but about Denise conning him into letting her stay there rent-free. It wasn't Frankie's place. If anybody needed to possess the information, it was Gabe. Although he probably already knew. Anyway, going by Maggie's reaction, Frankie now regretted the deal. The dispatcher took a little too much cynical joy out of the news for comfort.

When Gabe strode into the station, commanding her attention, it had the effect of removing the flub from her mind. Freshly shaved, his uniform clean and crisp, he looked good. Too good for her peace of mind. But tired, too, as if he hadn't gotten enough sleep. Her fault?

The smile he flashed at her didn't seem accusing. "I got your note. The bichon has duly received her evening dose of antibiotic."

Lew scowled his disapproval. "Frankie duped you into taking care of those damn dogs, huh?"

Gabe nodded good-naturedly. "I don't mind."

Frankie, who'd been anxious about overstepping her bounds when it came to asking favors, blew out a relieved breath. "Shine didn't protest, did she? I hope she wasn't any trouble."

"She didn't put up much of a fight. She's a ten-pound dog and hurting to boot. Squirting five ccs of Amoxicillin in her mouth wasn't much of a chore. The only problem was Banner."

"Banner?" She could hardly believe it.

"Yeah. He wanted some too."

Lew snickered, leaned back in his chair where

he'd been checking time sheets, and tossed an empty Pepsi can into the trash. The thunk as the can hit bottom flashed a memory across Frankie's brain like the sear of a burn.

"Oh! I just remembered. Stupid!" She tapped her forehead with a finger. "Lew, the last time I talked with Howie," she said, noticing the way both Lew and Gabe's ears perked, "he told me someone from the station came to the duplex yesterday afternoon asking for me. He said it was funny because the guy went around to the back. He told me it wasn't you, but I wondered if somebody here had a message for me."

Frowning, Lew shook his head. "If they did, nobody told me about it."

"He didn't say who?" Gabe's voice was so quiet she almost missed the tension in it. Almost.

"Said he didn't know," Frankie replied, watching Gabe.

"Kind of strange, all right." Lew shrugged, missing Gabe's response. "Ask Karl when you see him. Or better yet, ask Maggie."

"I will." But Frankie couldn't help thinking if someone gave Maggie a message to pass on, not only would've it been promptly delivered, but she would've demanded to know every detail regarding the contents. Ergo—Howie's report of a message was somehow wrong.

She wasn't the only one who thought so. Gabe honed in on her unease. Well, she felt a weird vibe all right, and what it did was send chills down her spine. Who had the person really been? The killer?

But, the next moment, she accused herself of having an overwrought imagination. If Gabe reacted before, any sign of it had gone. His phone rang. Putting it to his ear, he said, "Zantos," then stood listening. After a moment, he nodded. "Yeah, on my way. And, Shane, thanks." He clipped the phone to his belt again and motioned for Frankie to walk out to the SUV with him.

"That was Shane, from the CS unit," he said when they were out of Lew and the dispatcher's earshot. "He said they're done working the scene and have locked up. You're free to clean out your stuff anytime you like, if that's what you decide to do. Otherwise, you can move back in if you want." He stared toward the hill outside town—the one behind the duplex. "I wouldn't recommend it. We still don't know if the killer found what he was looking for."

A hot, glowing flash lit the nerves behind

Frankie's eye, pain wiping the question she meant to ask from her mind. Hoping to forestall a stronger reaction, she pressed two fingers against her right temple—and noticed Gabe tracking the action. Damn him. Sometimes he saw too much.

"You okay?" he asked.

Frankie lowered her telltale hand, clenching it into a fist instead. "Sure. Just a little…" She trailed off, unable to explain.

He took her arm, urging her toward his vehicle. "About the duplex—I don't like the idea of you going there on your own."

Another flash. "Have you forgotten I'm an army veteran, Deputy Zantos? I've been in combat. I can take care of myself." Or could, if only she didn't feel so fragile most of the time.

"Without a gun in your hand, you're a lightweight."

Gabe's words were such an echo of her own thoughts she almost wondered if she'd voiced the part about being fragile out loud. Anger jabbed, making her go tense, until she realized he wasn't insulting her, but referring to physical attributes.

"I'm tougher than you think," she said. "I've had to be." God, how she hated even oblique mention of those cursed war wounds.

"But you'll find another place in the morning after work, right?" he pressed.

At least he hadn't forgotten what she said earlier. "I'll try. Believe me, I don't want to go back into the place. If I could afford to abandon my stuff, I would."

This made him smile. "Ask somebody—one of the guys from the station—to go with you."

"Safety in numbers?"

"Exactly."

A light came on as Gabe opened the door to his SUV. Frankie noticed the sun was sinking beneath the horizon, casting long shadows over the town and touching distant fields with gold. The day's heat had begun to dissipate, leaving gasoline fumes and the scent of crushed weeds in its wake.

Before Gabe could climb into the SUV, another car, headlights stabbing over them, sped into the parking lot. Frankie leaped out of the way as the car stopped, driver's-door-to-driver's-door beside Gabe. The car, a new metallic black Mercedes-Benz SL63 AMG, had a woman at the wheel.

"You," the woman called to Gabe, ignoring Frankie as if she were invisible. "You're the law around this burg, right?"

Gabe touched the brim of his hat. "Yes, ma'am. Resident deputy for this side of the county. Is there a problem?"

"My husband tells me there have been two—two!—murders in town within the last couple days. I want to know what you're doing about it. I want someone patrolling the beachfront properties twenty-four/seven until this killer is caught. You are trying to catch him, aren't you?" The woman looked down her nose at Frankie. "Or is part of your job standing around blathering?"

Hmm. Not invisible after all. What a relief.

The looking-down-the-nose thing should've been impossible since the driver was sitting in an expensive car and Frankie was standing, but there you go. Frankie thought it must be a trick a certain type of woman learned early on. The air of command, the assuredness her every whim would be catered, the self-confidence a great deal of money could buy. The car, the diamonds in her ears and on her fingers winking under the newly lit parking lot lights, all told a story of privilege Frankie couldn't hope to match.

Not that she wanted to. Shamelessly, she eavesdropped on what the woman was saying.

To Gabe's credit, he didn't flinch, not even with the woman's stare stripping him down to his BVDs. No mistaking that look. And he knew it, too.

"We're doing everything we can to apprehend the person responsible, ma'am."

"I want an officer protecting my property at all times," the woman said again. "God only knows who this creature will come after next."

"Ma'am, I can step up patrols., but I don't have the manpower to keep someone there around the clock. We need every available officer working the case," he said, sounding perfectly polite.

"Really?" the woman sneered, a faint lifting of her plumped lips. "We'll see what the district attorney has to say. I'll have you know Abel Conner is a personal friend of mine. You'll be hearing from him."

Before Gabe could say another word, she sped away, her car kicking parking lot gravel onto Frankie's legs.

Blinking, Frankie stared at Gabe, who smiled faintly and shrugged.

"Who was that?" she asked openmouthed. And then, without conscious thought, "Where is Denise Rider's BMW?"

CHAPTER 15

If Gabe answered Frankie's question, the klaxon that blared inside the station just then drowned him out.

Simultaneously, Gabe's shoulder mic began spewing unintelligible words. He listened, told her "Later," and took off. By the time he got to the end of the parking lot, his siren was screaming its eerie wail into the dusk.

Lew, already in the ambulance, pulled out of the garage ten seconds later. Frankie ran to join him. Inside the garage, the two on-call volunteer firemen were scrambling into the pumper truck.

She got into the bus and swung her door shut. "What's up?"

"Combine accident." Lew popped the clutch. "Out at Acton Hayes's place. Hydraulics line running the leveler broke. Machine tilted, threw the operator off and managed to start the field on fire."

Frankie, still fastening her seat belt, glanced over at him. "Hayes place. That's where Chris lives, right?"

"Yep. He'll have any injuries under control."

Contrary to Lew's expectation, Chris wasn't on scene when they arrived only a minute or two behind Gabe. Presently, the fire truck drove up, the volunteers jumped down, and, dragging hoses, started spraying water to knock down the fire around the burned-out combine. Glowing flames lit the field beyond the machine. Sparks leaped into the darkening sky like swarms of tiny LED Christmas lamps.

She spied one heroic man on a Caterpillar tractor plowing a firebreak close to the burning wheat while a pickup with water barrels in back ran interference for him, spraying embers as they landed. A line of men and women with shovels and sacks beat at the edges of the fire line.

Apparently, every person in and around Hawkesford had turned out.

Lew and Frankie, with Frankie keeping a close eye on the field closest to them in case the conflagration spread, dragged equipment through choking smoke and hot, blackened stubble to reach their victim.

Barely conscious and incoherent with pain, the injured man lay helpless, surrounded by hot ash. Frankie dropped to her knees beside him, wincing as overheated earth burned through her pant legs.

"You're okay," she said to him, unsure whether he was even aware help had arrived. "We've got you. You're fine. Lew and I are going to take good care of you."

He moaned, choking for air.

"Hold on, sir. We'll have you out of here in a jiffy."

"Not my fault." His words were barely audible over the roar of machines and shouting men. "Cut. Not my fault."

Frankie exchanged a questioning look with Lew. What did the guy mean?

"Talk later." Lew leaned over him, adjusting an oxygen mask over his mouth. "Save your breath."

A quick examination revealed a shattered tibia along with a fire-bitten arm and an obvious case of smoke inhalation. Frankie inserted an IV. Lew took vitals and reported to the emergency physician at Kootenai Medical in Coeur d'Alene. Presently, he inflated a splint around the man's leg and applied a wet cover to the burned arm while Frankie injected fentanyl. With quick efficiency, they got the patient stabilized and ready to roll within a few minutes. Lew nodded his approval.

Groaning a little herself, Frankie got up and brushed soot from her knees. Their patient was not a small man. Lifting him onto the stretcher took all the strength she had.

Back in the ambulance, Gabe, on traffic detail, directed them to the main road. Dodging gawkers and firefighters, Lew hit the siren and soon put on a burst of speed. Frankie, surrounded by the stomach-twisting odor of burned flesh, sat in back monitoring the patient. Regardless of fentanyl, as soon as the shock wore off the pain would start, poor guy. She knew. Been there, as a caregiver, as an observer, and as a patient.

Out the rear window, she saw the firefighters were gaining control. The flames were lower now, more smoke than fire. As they sped away, those remaining shrank to a faint glow on the horizon in the deepening night.

It wasn't until they were on the way back to the station after the run to the hospital that Frankie remembered the woman in the Mercedes and questioned Lew about her. "You saw her talking to Gabe at the station, didn't you? Who is she?"

Lew dimmed his lights against an oncoming car. "You've met her husband."

"I have?"

"Yep. And as I remember, you weren't impressed."

Frankie got the connection. "Dr. Muncie's wife, by any chance?"

"Smart girl. Got it in one. Only don't ever refer to her as Mrs. Muncie. You might not come out alive."

"Who made that mistake?" That sounded like a good story was in the offing, and Lew didn't disappoint.

"Karl Mager." Lew's grin reflected against the dark windshield. "You never saw a man's face turn so red in your life. I couldn't decide if it was because he was mad as hell or just mortified."

"Oh, dear." Frankie snickered. "I hope this was a private meeting."

"No such luck. It was at a Christmas dance to raise funds for Hawkesford emergency services. You'd be surprised at how many of the summer folk turn out to support us. Gives them something to brag about."

"Good to know. But what did Karl do?"

Lew shrugged. "What could he do? Turned around, went over to the bar, and inhaled Jack Daniels until the lake contingent had enough of consorting with the yokels and left."

"Poor Captain Mager."

"Yep. The woman's not much for the little people. Don't want to get in her way, and that's for sure."

They were silent as Lew hit the brakes to avoid a deer—and then another since where there was one, there nearly always were two—dropping his speed as the highway passed through a wooded section.

"So what do people call her?" she asked when they came out the other side.

"Besides bitch?" Lew huffed out a breath. "Her professional name is Ms. Barwick, and don't you forget it. Ms. Alexis Barwick, to be exact."

"That was Alexis Barwick?" Even Frankie had heard of her. The woman had been in all the papers, on CNN, FOX, and about every other big news venue of late wrapped up in litigation regarding the US Government vs. Hanford Nuclear Fallout Victims. Ms. Barwick was not litigating on the side of the survivors, who grew fewer every day. Soon they'd all be gone, and whether the government won or lost, the claim would be moot. The attorneys, of course, would still collect their obscene fees.

At the station, Lew backed the ambulance in beside the pumper truck, which had already been freshly washed free of soot, smoke, and water spray. The duty staff gathered in the break room, drinking coffee and rehashing the fire for the rest of the night.

"An arson inspector is coming out in the morning," one of the firemen reported.

"Arson?" Frankie's eyes widened. "Oh, no. Seriously?"

The fireman nodded. "Gabe Zantos got to looking around the combine. Said he didn't believe the hydraulic line burst of its own accord. He thought it'd been cut. So he's got a call in to the inspector."

"The guy, our patient—" Frankie fell silent, trying to pluck an elusive memory out of the air, then she got it. "Our patient said something odd." She glanced at Lew. "Remember? He said, 'Not my fault.' Actually, he said it twice."

Lew nodded." I heard him. So he was right."

"Who the hell'd do a thing like that," The fireman's cheeks reddened with anger. "Or why did he do it. Doesn't make much sense."

"Vandals," Lew growled, but Frankie stirred uneasily, events around the duplex too fresh in her mind to reduce any mayhem to something as simple as vandalism. Yet, what other reason could there be?

The rest of the night passed in calm. So much so that boredom set in, and Frankie, filled with restless energy, at three a.m., got the ambulance out again and washed it down from top to bottom.

In the morning, she drove to Gabe's place—hard to call it his when it would always be her grandparent's home—and slipped into the house, prepared to give Shine her first meds of the day. While Gabe was clearly home, his SUV backed into the drive ready for a quick take off, for some reason she hadn't expected to see him up and about. But she walked in, and there he was, in the kitchen, cooking breakfast.

The table was set for two. A glass of orange juice resided at each place. An aroma of freshly brewed coffee mixed with frying bacon filled the kitchen. Frankie's mouth watered, her empty stomach growling with hunger.

Gabe, dressed in jeans and a plain blue T-shirt, leaned over the stove whipping eggs for an omelet. Grated cheese filled a bowl, ready to scatter over the eggs. Banner sat beside Gabe, licking his chops in anticipation, leading Frankie to believe he'd already snagged a treat or two. Shine, more leery of the man, her hurt leg raised, hovered within smelling distance, but not so close as to be underfoot.

The bichon, Frankie noted with relief, looked much more alert and vigorous today. Dr. Kelly would be pleased with her progress.

Hesitating in the doorway to study the tableau, Frankie flushed in embarrassment. "I'm sorry. I didn't mean to bust in on you. You're expecting company, and my dogs are pestering." Or maybe someone was already here, in another room. The bedroom?

She snapped her fingers, banishing the twinge of... well, who knew what? "Banner," she commanded, "come here. Shine—"

Banner obeyed, Shine didn't budge.

"She doesn't know me yet," Frankie excused her. "We'll get out of your way." Moving forward, she picked up the small dog and cuddled her.

Shine licked her chin.

Gabe waved the spatula above the frying pan. "Looks like she's taken to you, though. They've both been waiting for you at the door. Me too. Now you're here I can cook the omelet." With a minimum of fuss, he poured eggs into the skillet. "Sit. Breakfast'll be ready in a few minutes. I'm starved."

He'd been waiting for her? Why? Not to cook eggs, she'd be bound, although the idea was intriguing. Weakly, she let herself be persuaded. "I'm starved, too."

Erk! Her voice must be failing. Breathless, like she'd been running.

Or maybe from the smoke she'd breathed at last night's fire.

Gabe lifted the eggs, allowing the liquid to run beneath the cooked portion. "You had something to tell me, I think. Before we were interrupted last night."

So that's why he waited for her. Breakfast was a nice touch. A real bonus. For the first time in months, she felt truly hungry.

Seated in her accustomed place at the table, Frankie relaxed. Gathering her thoughts, she held Shine on her lap and took a sip of orange juice.

"Cops look for motive first, don't they?" she asked. "Motive, means, and opportunity?"

He turned from the stove and grinned at her, eyes crinkling with amusement. "You been watching cop shows on TV?"

Frankie shrugged. Guilty as charged. "Maybe a few. But just because they're on TV doesn't mean they're all wrong, does it? So, do you have a motive for Denise's murder?"

Omelet ignored for the moment, he stared at her. "My idea is that it had to do with the computer disc you told me about. I'd sure like to get my hands on it and take a look. My crew damn near tore St. James's apartment to pieces, searching for the damn thing."

"You didn't find the disc?"

"No. Could be the murderer got there first." He shot her a glance. "Why? Have you heard any other reason someone might want her dead?"

Frankie wished he'd mind the eggs. She preferred her omelets without scorched edges, thank you, even though she was hungry enough to eat charcoal.

"Well?" Gabe urged.

"Not really. It's just—" She knew this was going to sound awful. "I called Victoria Pettigrew yesterday. I told her I can't stay at the duplex after all this and asked for my rent money back—prorated, of course. I'm not out to cheat anybody."

He moved impatiently, as though to hurry the story. "And?" Nose wrinkling, he shifted his attention back to cooking.

"One thing led to another. Victoria let drop about her brother, Russ, owning the duplex."

Gabe nodded. Apparently, he'd known that.

"Victoria also said that while 'someone' started out paying Denise's rent, Russ has been letting her stay there without charge the past couple months while they were going out together. But then Denise dumped him. From what I've heard, she has—had—a history of... um... short-lived romances."

She had Gabe's interest now.

"Amicable partings of the way?" he asked.

"I don't know. It's just gossip. Mind you, I haven't been in Hawkesford long enough to have first-hand knowledge of anything." This is where she got a little scared. Passing along this kind of rumor wasn't her thing. "Except for what Victoria said, of course. But some of us were talking at work yesterday, and... Marc... well, it occurred to me... to us..." Stammering out her report, she played with Shine's good ear as the little dog pressed into the caress.

"Interesting." Gabe, an abstracted expression on his face, added sautéed onions and green peppers to his cooking, scattered grated cheddar over all, and folded the omelet neatly. He divided the puffy mass into halves, plated them, and laid bacon and whole wheat toast alongside.

"Maybe I shouldn't have said anything." Frankie set Shine on the floor and reached for her fork as he set a plate in front of her. "The whole idea is probably meaningless."

Gabe sat across from her. "You never know. Was anyone else mentioned in connection with Denise's love life?"

"Yes. Several men." Frankie ticked names off on her fingers, almost relieved to have more than one to pick on. "Among others, a chef from the casino restaurant, Marc, our EMT, and even Chris Adkins, although he says he was a non-starter."

"Interesting," he said again. His eyes took on the blank expression of someone committing information to memory. Then he selected a piece of crisp bacon, broke it into three pieces, and doled bits out between Banner and Shine who snapped them up like they hadn't eaten in a month. The third bite he stuck into his own mouth.

Frankie gobbled her cheesy omelet, giving herself time to absorb his apparent interest. So this must have meaning. Either that or Gabe was coming up empty in the suspect department and needed something—anything—to pick up the pace.

"Do you think any of this is important?" She took a bite of her own perfectly crisp bacon.

"At this point, every detail is important. The more we know about the victim, where she went, who she knew, what kind of person she was, the better chance of discovering who murdered her. And don't forget St. James. It seems clear he was killed as part of her trouble."

"Collateral damage."

"I'm afraid so. And anyone willing to kill a second person may not stop there. Some people find each subsequent killing easier than the last. That's why—" It was his turn to stop abruptly.

Frankie got what he was trying to say, though. He looked upon her as another potential victim. Who else had been living in Denise's only partially cleared quarters? And been right behind a thin wall when Howie was shot?

No longer hungry, she pushed away her half-empty plate.

***

An hour later, Gabe left to go on duty, telling Frankie he'd mull over what she'd learned about the men in Denise Rider's life. Or what the rumors said, anyhow. Which wasn't, when you came right down to it, much. Was Gabe just pandering to her, or did he really think the gossip and innuendo truly meant something?

With her host out of the way, Frankie cleaned the kitchen in payment for breakfast, then took off for the duplex. On foot, as it happened. Banner needed exercise, and so did she. Something physical, to help clear her head.

The boxes used to transport her stuff when she moved into the duplex were still there, some of them not yet unpacked. She planned on boxing up everything loose, then walking back and driving the Ranger over for the actual move. After that, who knew?

With her destination a pleasant mile and a half's walk away, she looked forward to using her muscles, sadly neglected since she'd been in Hawkesford. According to the way Banner bounced along, he felt the same. They left Shine at the house, stretched full-length on the cozy dog bed her former owner had bought for her.

Frankie loved this time of year—the shimmering heat, the acrid smell of gone-to-seed weeds. Even the grasshoppers flying up in her face as she jogged along. Banner didn't care for the bugs so much, and every now and then he pounced, in a vain attempt to catch one. She was laughing as they approached the duplex. The mail carrier's car was stopped at the box at the end of the drive while Susie Ray, another old friend of high school days, sorted through some mail.

"Hey, Frankie." Susie Ray waved, a cheery smile on her face. "Long time, no see. That's a beautiful dog." She nodded at Banner and went on without pausing. "What are you two up to this fine day? Kind of hot to be out walking, isn't it?"

"Nah, it's fine," Frankie said. Banner's tail wagged.

"I was tickled when I heard you hired on as a paramedic," Susie Ray said. "It's great to have you back in Hawkesford, alive and well. How do you like working with Lew? He's sort of known as our local curmudgeon, you know."

"Some people may think so. I know he's a hard worker and meticulous in caring for our patients."

Susie Ray fluttered the stuff—which looked mostly like junk mail—she'd been about to put in Frankie's box. "This place. Aren't you afraid to live here, Frankie? You couldn't pay me to go inside."

"I'm moving out today." Tacit agreement, she guessed. "Is that my mail?"

"Oh, yeah. Nothing for you but a couple advertisements addressed to occupant." Susie Ray grimaced. "Got some mail for Howie. Guess I'll have to take it back to the post office. I can't just leave it moldering away in the box."

"True." A point occurred to her. Meeting Susie Ray worked out just fine and might clean an item from her to-do list. "If I do get any mail sent to this address, can you hold it at the post office for me? I'll drop by and pick it up when I find a permanent address."

"Sure." Susie Ray actually seemed relieved. "No problem. I don't blame you for not wanting to live here after two murders and God only knows what else. If I were you, I'd move out too." With a quick wave, she drove off to the next house, leaving Frankie choking in the cloud of dust that rose up to clog her nose. Banner sneezed.

Sweat dampened Frankie's face as she walked

up the driveway. At the front door, she paused before shoving the key in the lock. Something kept telling her not to do it. Collywobbles, she told herself. The police had been looking after the place. Nothing here to be afraid of. So why didn't she believe it?

Something in her brain was telling her to check out the back first.

Oddly enough, as though infected by her fears, Banner turned cranky. As they walked around the house, he pitched a fit, rearing back on his leash and trying to go the other way.

"Banner," she snapped, too impatient, too freaked, to deal with an uncooperative dog. "Behave yourself."

An archway with a spindly clematis vine growing over it topped the gate. The gate itself sagged partly open, into the yard. Frankie paused to wave away a fat bumble bee. More than a little irritated at Banner for struggling on the end of the leash like a hooked bass, she gave the gate a shove.

Banner's sudden jerk brought her down on her butt.

"What in the world is the matter with you, Banner?"

His eyes rolled wildly, his black nose twitched. He uttered an uncharacteristically loud bark.

"I'm going to check you over for ticks when we get home." Frankie rose to her feet. "You're acting like you've got bugs in your britches."

Her prosthesis had shifted. She stomped her foot, getting it back in place, and reached for the latch, lifted it, and opened the gate. Forcefully, as the bottom scraped over a layer of river rock. Only then did the odor of rotten eggs register on her mind. Rotten eggs.

Oh no, she had time to think as her senses finally telegraphed the danger. Banner's desire to flee succeeded. He lunged away from the open gate, yanking Frankie along with him. A few seconds later, the house erupted in a ball of fire. Even as the blast reached them, he dragged her onto her hands and knees, charging down the driveway towing her behind him.

A concussion raised the roof on the duplex, knocking them both flat.

Frankie retained just enough sense to beat out the sparks that fizzed in Banner's fur before she blacked out.

CHAPTER 16

"Frankie! Frankie! Wake up. Hello. Hello, yes, it's Susie Ray here. Ouch! I'm at the duplex on South Sixth with Frankie McGill. Ow! The duplex just blew up, and Frankie is hurt. The house is on fire. Ow, ow! Hurry!"

Dazed, Frankie cowered, feeling the ping of bullets passing over her head. Her foot. Oh, God. It hurt so bad.

No. No bullets. This wasn't war. Was it?

Frankie struggled to make sense of Susie Ray's words. Who was she talking to, anyway? And where had she come from? Had she said the duplex was on fire?

Frankie blinked her eyes open. Susie Ray flung up an arm, batting at something that looked like a chunk of flaming roof material. It landed only a couple inches from Banner's tucked-under tail.

Aha. Susie must be talking to dispatch and thank goodness for that! Not Afghanistan. No al-Qaida or Taliban or ISIS fighters. No gunfire. No frigging terrorists.

Frankie fought to breathe as the world whirled around her.

"Ouch! Ouch!" Susie Ray yelped, shaking her hand. "Come on, Frankie. Wake up. We've got to get out of here."

Susie's screeching roused Frankie from her stupor, the noise bouncing in and out on pulsing eardrums. Something soft, slimy, and wet dragged across her face. Uh! She recognized the feel of Banner's tongue. A siren began wailing a few blocks away. Struggling against weighted limbs, she realized she lay flat on the ground with Banner bucking up and down beside her.

"Run," she yelled.

At least, she tried to yell. Her tongue seemed cloven to the roof of her mouth, unable to break free. A huge knot was stuck in the middle of her chest. Winded, she thought. Thrown down flat and all her air knocked out.

"Frankie, get up," Susie yelled like she suspected Frankie was deaf. "Ow! Damnit, come on."

The scene looked like something straight out of hell. Susie was leaning over her, protecting her from at least some of the sparks, which explained all the "ouches" she'd been uttering. Beyond her, the house turned into a raging inferno. Flames shot through broken windows and the blown-out doorway. Black smoke roiled into the sky. A wall of heat radiated off the fire, seeming to suck all the good stuff out of the atmosphere. Burning wood crackled.

Frankie failed to muster the balance to rise to her feet, but at Susie Ray's urging, she rose on her hands and knees and crawled in the direction Susie pointed her.

Banner came to her rescue. He wanted desperately to escape, and the only way to prevent him from dragging her on her belly through the sparks and debris was to get up. Susie, the brave soul, stayed with her, giving her a needed boost as Frankie finally lunged to her feet. The three of them staggered toward the road where Susie Ray's mail truck sat idling.

"Get in." Susie boosted Frankie into the back seat of the Jeep Cherokee and held the door for Banner to jump in as well. She ran around to the driver's side and slid under the wheel.

"We can't leave," Frankie protested, finally regaining her senses. Most of them, anyway.

"We're not. But I'm not parking my car where it can get blown up, either, and I'd better not block the street. The fire engine will be here in a minute."

They could hear it now, the heavy diesel engine thundering, the ululating siren growing louder and louder. Debris from the explosion littered the road and nearest yards; windows had been shattered.

Neighbors, mostly women and kids at this time of day, gathered outside, many still screaming and crying. A hardy few headed in their direction, either for a closer look or to help.

Feeling like a fool, Frankie agreed. "You're right. We don't want to get in the way. I think my brains are addled."

"I wouldn't doubt it," Susie said kindly. "What in the world happened, just now?"

Frankie stared at the other woman. Susie Ray's bright summer blouse had charred holes here and there. Blisters rose on her tanned arms.

"I'll be darned if I know." Horror struck. "Oh, my God, Susie Ray. Howie's cat. It's in there. They have to get it out."

Susie Ray's breath caught. She eyed the burning house. Her mouth turned down. "I don't think the cat stands a chance," she said, then, "Jeez. This looks almost as bad as Denise's car."

"Car?"

"Yeah," Susie Ray said. A half block away, the fire truck turned the corner and rumbled toward them. "This must be my day for fires. I found Denise's car a little while ago, down by Lake Shore road. Gabe Zantos about had a fit. Anyway, it's about as wrecked and burned up as this house. Shame, a nice car like that."

***

The duplex had burned to a smoldering ruin before Karl Mager found time to talk to Frankie.

"Exciting times, eh, Frankie? What set the gas off?"

"Gas? Is that why the house blew up?" She blinked, her vision squirreling into an unexpected blackout. Her head pounded.

"Yeah. The propane tank exploded—and took the house with it."

Frankie could only repeat what she'd told Susie Ray. "I don't know how it happened. I came over to pack up my stuff and move out of that godforsaken place—and had just opened the gate when, kerblooey! I can't even describe it, Karl. Everything is a blur. No warning, no nothing." Tears gushed from her smarting eyes. "Howie's cat was in there, you know. That's the worst part."

They were standing a half block away from the house, out of what was still intense heat. All the near neighbors now gathered on the verge of the road, talking in hushed groups. Kids ran around with their faces showing excited glee—callous little twits. Karl sweated like a racehorse in his heavy turnout gear, big drops rolling down his face. Like Frankie, Susie Ray's spark burns had been laced with an antibiotic salve out of the EMS truck, and she'd gone on to finish her mail route. Frankie's profuse thanks and promise of a new blouse followed her.

"The mail must go through and all that malarkey," Suzi Ry had said, still big-eyed from her fright and wincing as her back touched the scorching hot driver's seat of her car. "And here I always thought they were talking about the weather."

Karl surveyed the destruction, absently wiped at a trickle of sweat running down his neck, and nodded toward the house. "This is the first time I've seen anything like this. Read about it, though." He leaned past her to bawl a new instruction to his crew. "Keep your eye peeled for a cat. Supposed to be one here." Then, as an aside to Frankie, "Don't know how it works, but sometimes a critter will survive a fire."

She guessed he was lying.

Tears gathered in Frankie's eyes, fortuitously washing out some of the ash and dirt that had migrated to the inner corners. "Poor old kitty. I hope he got out." She knelt beside Banner and hugged his neck. "If I'd been listening to my dog, we would've been long gone when the house went up. He tried to warn me of danger, best he could."

Karl patted Banner's head, the dog smiling up at him. "Dogs got good noses, even a hairy snow dog like this guy." Seeing something that met with his disapproval, he yelled over at a volunteer not to be tossing his fire ax around, as he was apt to whack off his own foot.

Frankie knew the second he remembered her prothetic because he glanced at her and blushed a vivid red. Color fading, he turned to her again. "So you didn't smell the rotten egg odor, huh? But the dog did. Funny. It should've carried to you, too."

"It did, but not soon enough. My nose was all clogged up with the dust and pollen." Innards quivering, she went back to that moment. "Or I wasn't paying enough attention." Karl thinking of her foot was bad enough. She wasn't about to mention the mixed signals she sometimes got from her brain. "I was trying to lift the gate over the doggoned hump in the path at the time. I caught just a little whiff, but by then Banner already had me in tow, hauling me down the driveway. Almost too late." She surveyed the torn skin on the palms of her hands. "I'm going to nominate Banner for Dog Hero of the Year. He saved my life. Him and Susie Ray."

"Yeah. They sure did." Karl walked away as he spoke, his attention riveted on the aforementioned gate.

What had she said? Something, judging by his determined stride. Curious, she followed him, watching as he bent down to examine the ground under the gate. With a thick, blunt finger, he scratched through the gravel. When he straightened, a fine wire dangled from his hand. He gave it a slight tug. The wire pulled loose from a shallow, well-hidden trench. He followed the wire all the way to the rear of the house, Frankie right on his heels.

"Damn! A bomb?" Her mind whirled. "Seriously?" Good Lord. Apparently, she hadn't left war behind when she mustered out of the service.

Karl's walk came to a halt where a pile of smoking black char showed where the back door had been. "Well, now we know why this place blew up—and it sure wasn't any accident. Bet we find traces of an accelerant inside, too." He pulled a cell phone from under his turnouts and punched a number on his speed dial. "Looks like it's up to the cops to find out who rigged it.

"Yo, Zantos," he said into the phone. "Get your butt over here. I need your help."

✳✳✳

Frankie sat on the running board of the fire truck, Banner on the ground beside her. She heard Gabe's SUV coming before she saw him. He roared up and hurled himself out of the rig without stopping to close the door. He must have set a new speed record to arrive this quickly, she thought, a smile stretching her heat-cracked lips.

His eyes on the ruined house, he didn't see her immediately. Not until Banner gave a little "woof" and called attention to their whereabouts.

Gabe changed direction and headed toward her, his face shockingly pale. Wordless, he reached out and drew her to her feet, his arms going around her. Carefully, so not to aggravate her burns.

"You okay? Karl said you came within a breath of getting blown up."

"I'm fine." A lie. She clung to him like a dirty piece of Saran wrap; her voice muffled against his chest. "You got here fast. You must've been driving like a maniac."

What was he doing, hugging her like this? What was she doing, hugging him right back?

"I was only a couple miles out of town when Karl's call came through. Denise Rider's..." He stopped before imparting information she already knew, thanks to Susie Ray. "Dispatch notified me right away of an explosion at this location. Something told me—" He pushed her away and studied her sooty face. "You sure you're not hurt? You've got burns."

She drew a shaky breath. "Minor ones. I was lucky, aside from a few scrapes and bruises." Minor stuff that hurts like sin, she added internally. "Banner is all right, too. And so is Susie Ray, who rescued me. Only Howie's poor old cat—"

His grip pulled her against him again. "A cat?"

She pressed her ear to his chest, the better to hear his heart beating over the deep rumble of the fire truck's diesel engine. "Yeah. They found his body in the rubble a while ago."

He buried his face in her hair, never once recoiling from what she knew must be a horrible stench. That she had any hair was a matter for rejoicing, although she had an appointment at the beauty salon marked on a mental to-do list.

"It could've been you. If you'd gone inside—"

He shuddered and, using one finger, tilted her face up to his. His kiss was long, deep, and heartfelt. Without thinking, she kissed him back. Threw herself into it, actually. Gabe drew away and studied her, a grin finally tweaking his mouth.

"What?" She knew that look. It meant some kind of devilment.

"Did you know your eyebrows are singed? They're drawn up like itty bitty Slinkies."

"Slinkies?" She brushed at one. Singed hair floated down. "Must be charming."

It was probably a good thing Karl Mager finished whatever he was doing over by the fire just then and came to greet Gabe. Pretending he hadn't noticed a thing, he kind of twinkled as he eyed them. "Frankie tell you how the fire started?"

Gabe threw her a swift glance. There was a wary quality in the look. "Not yet. How about you fill me in?"

With a lift of his thumb and a jerk of his head, Karl beckoned Gabe over to the gate where he'd found the wire running under the gravel. "You'd better take a gander at this." His thick finger pointed at the thin flash of metal.

Gabe frowned. Without touching the exposed wire, he and Karl followed it around the corner of the duplex, leaving Frankie and Banner standing by the fire truck. Most of the neighbors and fire engine chasers drawn to the site had departed. Too hot to stand around in the sun. Frankie was just as glad to be alone for the moment. She sank back onto the truck's running board.

Sighing, she squeezed another drop of artificial tears into eyes still smarting from the heat.

A sudden breeze stirred the smoke, luckily blowing it in the opposite direction, out of her face. The fluttering of an unstuck flap on a mangled envelope caught her attention. Lying close to the truck, the envelope, a large one with a see-through window, was fire scorched and torn. She guessed it had been tossed from the duplex by the explosion. Something of hers, or something of Howie's?

As weary as though she'd run a marathon and with every muscle aching, she reached down and picked up the envelope, shaking the contents until they showed through the window.

Inside, in a clear case, a DVD in a paper cover appeared.

Hand-written with a Magic Marker, the disc bore a title. Smoke Signals. What had Howie said about it?

Her breath caught.

"Gabe," she called, too late because he and Karl had already disappeared behind the burned building and were beyond hearing. Just as well, she thought. While this must be the disc Howie told her about, who knew the contents? What if this wasn't a mysterious list, but a compilation of movie credits. Wouldn't she feel like a fool interrupting the investigation with a totally meaningless piece of debris? Best she look for herself first.

Grasping the end of Banner's leash, she stood up and tucked the envelope into the back pocket of her jeans. Everybody was busy right now. Although she'd set out this morning filled with energy, the explosion had taken every bit of vitality out of her. Her foot, what there was of it, ached within the confines of the prosthesis's grip. Her head blazed with pain. The mile and a half home seemed almost insurmountable.

"One foot in front of the other," she told Banner as they started off and then couldn't remember if the old saw came from the bible or a cartoon—or neither.

They were past mid-way when the ambulance came tooling up beside them.

"Hey," Marc, at the wheel today, called. Chris sat beside him.

She stopped when they did. "Hey, yourself."

Looking shaken and pale, Marc leaned across to speak to her. "Heard about the duplex blowing up. Lucky you weren't inside."

"Came close," Frankie said, putting on her stoic face and firmly quelling the little shake in her voice. "If it hadn't been for Banner—" At the sound of his name, the dog wagged his plumy tail. "—and Susie Ray, I would've been toast." She paused. "Burnt toast."

No. It wasn't funny.

Marc didn't think so. "What happened? The propane tank spring a leak?"

Beyond pretending, Frankie forced a smile. "Nope. Apparently, the explosion was rigged. Karl found a wire. He and Gabe are investigating it as arson."

Marc's eyes opened wide. "You mean somebody tried to kill you like they did Howie and Denise?"

"Not quite." Frankie's quip came out dry. "He didn't shoot me."

"How you can make a joke of something like that, I'll never know," Chris said like he disapproved. "Was the house destroyed?"

"Oh, yes. Totally. And all my things along with it. Clothes, household goods, linens. Damn. My army records." Demoralized and impatient to get home—to Gabe's, rather—and shower away the smoke and road dirt where she'd been dragged on her belly, Frankie started walking again.

"Get in," Marc said. "I'll drive you to where ever you're going. Zantos's place?"

Relieved, Frankie could only nod as she went around to the passenger side, and Chris made room for her and Banner to crawl in beside him.

Without thinking, she pulled the disc from her pocket and held it in front of her.

"What's that?" Chris peered down as though to see the title.

Frankie placed her thumb over the writing. "A memento," she said.

CHAPTER 17

Frankie flopped the age-stiffened curtain aside and stepped out of the second-floor shower. The plastic rattle reminded her that she should buy a couple new curtains, cloth this time, as a thank you gift to Gabe for allowing her a room in the old house. Wrapping one bath towel around her hair, she patted herself dry with another. Dang! No soothing lotions or face creams, no goop for her hair, no makeup. Not even any deodorant. Well, she could solve that problem at least. She'd just borrow some of Gabe's from the downstairs bathroom. He'd never know.

Worse, as she started to dress, all she had clean to wear were paramedic duds. Her only regular clothes were those she'd been wearing and, if not totally ruined, they were much too filthy to put back on.

A shopping trip moved to the top of her to-do list, even before scouting out a new place to live. But the shopping thing proved a bit of a dilemma. She wasn't up on the latest styles.

After five years in the military with little call for civvies, jeans and T-shirts had been her thing. Now, for some reason, she felt a little more adventurous. Not to compare with Victoria Pettigrew, of course, or even Jesselyn, but a fresh opinion on her wardrobe seemed called for immediately.

"Somebody," she told Banner who was watching his mistress eye herself critically in front of the floor-length mirror, "not mentioning any names, could use a little fashion advice. And I know just the person who'd be delighted to give it."

Frankie picked up her phone, punching in Jesselyn's number. Jesselyn answered on the first ring.

"I just got off the phone with Vic." Jesselyn omitted the normal 'hello' and spoke in a rush. "She told me about the damn duplex blowing up. Smithereens. Ruined. And you were there." This last sounded almost like an accusation, until she added, "Are you all right? Were you hurt? Did it—" She took a breath before whispering, "My

God, what's going on in Hawkesford, anyway? I can barely recognize the place anymore."

Frankie forced a chuckle. "Join the crew. But aren't you the one always complaining nothing ever happens here? Are you sure you just haven't been paying attention?"

Jesselyn snorted. "Excitement is the word I've been trying for, woman, not mayhem. So I gather you weren't killed."

"Not this time." Frankie hoped she came across as insouciant and cheerful, but she wasn't any too sure of her acting job. "Anyway, all I've got left to wear is what I'm standing up in."

"Can't help you out," Jess said promptly. "You're too tall and skinny for my stuff."

Frankie laughed. "And I never wear pink. But I hoped you might want to help me shop on your lunch hour. Please?"

"Ooh. My favorite thing. Spending other people's money. Done. Pick me up at noon, and we'll hit the mall. Oh. Bring me a cheeseburger, will ya? I'll need to stoke up for a forty-minute shopping marathon."

"It's a date."

As she hung up, Frankie noticed a new text message waiting on her phone. It was from Dr.

Kelly. Hitting recall, she learned the vet wanted her to bring Shine in for a check-up. Yes, the receptionist told her when rung back, she could leave the dog at the office and retrieve her later. "As long as it's before five p.m."

Frankie glanced at her watch. If she put on her skates, she had plenty of time to drop Shine off, visit the salon for a haircut, and pick up a burger for Jesselyn. Swiftly skinning into her uniform, Frankie affixed her prosthesis, gave her hair a lick and a promise, and called it good.

Starting out of the room, she glimpsed the Smoke Signals disc lying where she'd tossed on the dresser. Case smudged with several sets of dirty fingerprints, it seemed to be calling her name. Was this the same disc Howie told her about? Was it the reason he'd been killed? She should, by rights, turn it over to the sheriff's department sight unseen, but what the heck. She had to know.

Gabe's computer sat in plain sight on a table in a corner of the living room, she remembered. A spiffy all-in-one jobbie with a screensaver of a night sky twinkling with stars. Snatching up the case, and with Banner padding along beside her, she hurried downstairs, plopped into Gabe's comfortable leather office chair in front of the computer, and shoved the disc into the DVD drive. One click and the machine came to life with a whirr and a buzz.

Holding her breath, Frankie opened the single Excel file the disc showed. Another touch to the mouse and the document expanded. Several pages unfolded, each broken into columns titled date, name, one called "age," invariably in the 60s, 70s, and 80s, with a couple 90s for good measure, some kind of digit codes, and dollars. There were a lot of names—and a lot of dollars.

Scanning down the columns, she saw the names started repeating at approximately two-week intervals.

"What the heck?" She stared at the document. Banner's curly white tail thumping against her leg made her realize she'd spoken out loud. "Not you. I know you're all right. I'm not so sure about this stuff." Slowly, she scrolled through four of the several pages. The dates spanned a period of approximately two years. There were about forty different names. Sometimes the codes repeated, and the dollar total made her blink and look twice.

"This is what Howie was talking about all

right." She looked down at Banner. "But what does it mean?" A glance the computer screen clock showed she didn't have time to puzzle over it now. She had to get going. And yet, it reminded her of something. Something she should know.

Frankie pressed two fingers against her temple. Just when she needed to remember something important, the damn brain blanked out. Typical.

But one thing she recalled clearly. Howie had very likely been murdered because of Smoke Signals. Thank God, nobody knew she'd picked it up. She couldn't wait to show the DVD to Gabe.

Before she shut the computer down, Frankie downloaded the file onto the hard drive and gave the new document an innocuous name; one Gabe was bound to discover. She took the disc with her. It just didn't seem right to leave it lying about.

***

Even after a quick haircut and delivering Shine, who greeted Dr. Kelly's receptionist with a wagging tail, and agreeing to pick the dog up in a couple hours, Frankie was a few minutes early in meeting Jesselyn. On the dot of twelve, Jesselyn came striding out of the ad agency where she worked. Her strawberry blonde hair was perfect, her makeup fresh, her trousers fitted smoothly over slightly plump hips. Her shoes, for God's sake, had three-inch heels.

For a moment, Frankie hardly recognized her. "Lookin' good." She handed Jesselyn her burger. Catsup and pickles only, no onions. "Do you think you can do something for me? So I'm not quite so…" She made a helpless gesture.

"Of course. You won't recognize yourself when I'm done with you. I see somebody chopped your hair." Jesselyn scowled at Frankie as she took the Five Guys sack and dove in. "Aren't you eating?"

"Already did." It was true. Partially, anyway. Wondering about the disc worked to kill a large portion of her hunger.

"Let's get going then. I only have an hour. Or an hour and a half if I stretch it."

Frankie blinked at her. "Will you be in trouble if you're late?"

Jesselyn only shrugged. "Barney'll get over it. He always does."

The careless answer sounded strange to Frankie, who, after six years in the military, was accustomed to a stricter adherence to the rules.

"So…" Jesselyn managed to say around a bite

of burger, "any news about the explosion. Have they caught whoever did it?"

"I haven't heard a word. If they have caught anyone, nobody's told me. How'd you know it was deliberate, anyway? Who told you?"

Jesselyn snorted. "It's all over the news. Since everyone at work knows I live in Hawkesford, it's the main topic of conversation this morning. Barney had a television going for the breaking news. Susie Ray did an interview."

"She did? Yikes." Frankie grimaced. Gabe was probably fit to be tied. "I hope she looked good on TV." As a joke, it wasn't much, but it served to sidetrack her friend from the main topic.

Jesselyn laughed. "We should all be as photo-genic. So what's the story?"

"Did she talk about being a hero and tell that between her and Banner, they saved my life?"

"She may have mentioned it a time or two. And something about a car. I didn't quite get that."

Frankie's explanation took up the couple of miles between Jesselyn's workplace and the mall. She wheeled into a parking space only steps from Macy's front entrance.

Jesselyn, still licking catsup from her fingers, hopped out of the Ranger more gracefully on her high heels than Frankie managed with her prosthetic foot. They dashed into the store, Jesselyn in the lead, carrying a list in her hand.

A long list, Frankie thought, eyeing the page-length document with unfeigned alarm.

"Bras, panties, socks. What size do you wear? What size jeans? I'm going to pick out a few things for you to try on, then while you're in the dressing room, I'll select some underwear. Do you still wear pajamas or have you gone over to nightgowns—or commando? Well, no. Probably not. You always were a Miss Modest." Jesselyn, her pretty face intent, was all business. "We'll hit Sephora for your makeup, and that'll do for today. When you find a place, you can replenish your household stuff. Doubt if you'll need any tonight. Personal gear is most important. Besides, we can only do so much in one lousy hour."

Frankie felt like a drowning person, underwater and out of breath. She hissed out answers, and by the time she made it into a dressing room, Jesselyn already had a dozen garments hanging over her arm to choose from. Resigning herself, Frankie removed her uniform and donned the first pair of jeans. Way too loose.

Wise Jesselyn, prepared for all contingencies,

had added a smaller size in a style with fancy back pockets guaranteed to add bulk to her skinny rear end—or so she said. Perfect. The keepers piled up on the dressing room bench, along with the cost. Her poor Visa. Frankie couldn't prevent a whimper or two.

A little more than an hour later, they were done—or, as Jesselyn told her, "At least we've made a small start."

The space behind the Ranger's bucket seats was stacked high with bags and boxes—including two pairs of shoes Frankie somehow managed to purchase without either the clerk or Jesselyn commenting on her foot.

"I'm exhausted," Frankie announced as she climbed into the driver's seat.

Jesselyn grinned at her. "You've just experienced what we dedicated shoppers call 'retail therapy.' You're supposed to be tired—and exhilarated. It was fun, wasn't it?"

Frankie's lips twisted. "Would've been maybe, if it hadn't been for the reason behind the necessity."

"Um. There is that."

"Anyway, thanks, Jesse. I wouldn't have known where to start without your help."

"I know." Jesselyn's smile was smug.

They tooled down Sullivan and turned west on Sprague, pulling up at the office where Jesselyn worked. The pickup's air conditioner ran full blast, blowing Frankie's short hair into a halo around her head. Jess, in the passenger seat, fiddled with the air ducts, directing the strongest stream into her face. They had five minutes left of Jesselyn's stretched lunch hour.

"I found out your boyfriend's name," Frankie said, aware of how abrupt she sounded. "Matt Chavez. He sounds cool. I don't know why you didn't tell me about him."

Jesselyn's lips pursed. "Maybe because I didn't want anybody to know."

"Oh, please." Frankie cast Jesselyn a mock scornful glance. "This is Hawkesford. Maggie knows. From what I understand, that's enough for everyone. How do you think I found out?"

"Damn," Jesselyn said, but without real heat. She must have been aware the news would soon spread.

"I don't understand why you wanted to keep it secret. It's not like he's an out-of-work gigolo trying to live off you. Executive chef at the casino is a pretty impressive job. I heard he's been invited to cook in New York at one of the best restaurants." Frankie kept the words and tone admiring, which is why she didn't understand when Jesselyn turned pink and avoided her eyes.

"What?" she demanded. "Am I wrong?"

Jesselyn fiddled with the air stream again. "No. You're right. Matt does have a good job, and it pays well. He's an ambitious man with lots of opportunities, and he's certainly not trying to live off me. But…"

"But what?"

"Well, there's Russ. My dear brother was pretty pissed at Matt when he—Matt—started going out with Denise Rider right after she broke up with him. And…"

Ah, the jealousy factor. Never good. Frankie frowned. "And what else?"

Jesselyn's hand sneaked onto the door handle, as though she couldn't wait to be gone. "Oh, it's just that Russ would have a total fit if he knew where Matt learned to cook."

"He would?"

"Yes."

"Why?"

Jesselyn pushed the door handle down, opening the pickup interior to a rush of hot outside air. She stepped down, finally meeting Frankie's eyes. "Here's something I don't think Maggie knows and I trust you not to tell her." Her pause was dramatic. "Matt was in prison. That's where he got his initial chefs training. When he got out, he went on to culinary school. Anyway, I wanted Russ to have time to get over the break-up with Denise before this fact came to light. You know. Since Matt took over where Russ left off. Then it didn't work out between them, either." Her voice rose into a wail. "And now Denise is dead. And Russ…and Matt…What if he leaves and doesn't ask me to go with him."

"Who, Matt?" Frankie's mind stuttered.

"Of course, Matt. Who else?"

"Would you go with him if he did ask?"

"Like a shot." Quite suddenly, Jesselyn slammed the door closed and fled into the office building, quick as her stilt-like shoes would carry her.

Frankie winced. Wow! That had been awkward. Her fact-finding mission had met a rather momentous bump in the road.

She could always rely on Jesselyn to bestow her affections on the least deserving man in the area, laying herself open to unhappiness. Her previous history was checkered with broken hearts. Her heart, at least. Jesselyn always cared too much.

Of course, Frankie had an equally checkered history when it came to blundering into her friend's affairs. No wonder Jess hadn't wanted to talk to her about Matt.

But she couldn't help wondering what crime had put Chavez in prison? Some investigation seemed in order.

***

When Frankie got to the veterinary clinic, Dr. Kelly made time to see her. The vet smiled, observing the eager way Shine greeted Frankie. It was as if a load lifted from the doctor's mind. She gestured Frankie into her office and offered a chair. "Do you have time to talk a minute?"

Frankie couldn't help a niggle of worry. Dr. Kelly's smile seemed off. Had something gone wrong with the bichon?

"First of all, Shine is receiving a clean bill of health." Dr. Kelly alleviated that concern right off the bat. "The wound is healing well, and there's no trace of infection. You've done a good job with her."

Instant relief swept over Frankie. She thought

of Gabe. "I had help. A…a friend, and Banner, of course."

"Have you decided to keep her in a forever home?"

A small foot pawed at Frankie's leg. Shine, wanting a lap to sit on. Frankie picked her up. "Yes. I don't know if there are hoops to jump through, but if there are, I'm willing to do the jumping."

"I'm so relieved." Dr. Kelly's blue eyes brightened. "I don't think there'll be any problems. I'll just see to changing the information on Shine's microchip, shall I?"

"Fine."

"In fact, I'll do it right now." She brought up a form, asking Frankie questions and typing in answers. Finished, she turned the screen for Frankie's okay and sent the document off into the ether.

"Also, I wanted to ask," the vet continued, absently closing out the microchip change program, "have you, or the police, discovered anything new about Denise's murder?"

"The police are working non-stop, trying to find the killer." Frankie hunched her shoulders. The vet evidently hadn't heard about the notorious exploding duplex or finding Denise's car. Yet. "There have been other things happening around Hawkesford. It's gotten…dangerous."

Dr. Kelly frowned. "What other things? Dangerous to whom?"

"Me, among others." Frankie spilled the story. Most of it, anyway. It was as she spoke that the program now showing on Dr. Kelly's computer drew her attention.

She pointed at the monitor. "What is that?"

"What?"

"The document on your screen. What is it telling you?"

Dr. Kelly slanted the monitor, so Frankie no longer had a view. "You shouldn't have seen that. Private contents."

"Yes." Frankie moved impatiently, disturbing Shine's nap. "I'm sorry. I don't care who it's about, but I need to know what it shows."

"Why?"

Oh, Lord, Frankie thought. What should she do? Was it wise to talk to Dr. Kelly? It seemed a bit like stomping on Deputy Gabe Zantos's toes. But if the vet had answers, a short cut to information, wasn't this more important than a few toes? Besides, Dr. Kelly's concern over Denise Rider and Shine seemed genuine.

Frankie took the plunge. "I have in my posses-sion a DVD. I'd like you to take a look at it and tell me what you think about the contents." She spoke slowly, picking her words to avoid telling Dr. Kelly where she'd gotten the disc, or what she suspected it contained. If the vet was able to offer a plausible explanation of the contents without knowing the background, it made her summation all the more authoritative. And then, just maybe, Frankie would have something solid to aid Gabe's investigation.

"A computer disc? What is it?" The vet tapped her fingernail on the desk. "I'm a little busy, Frankie. Maybe you can—"

Frankie cut across Dr. Kelly's excuse. "I wouldn't ask if it weren't important."

"Does it pertain to Denise?"

"Please. I don't want to say anything yet. Not until you've made an evaluation."

Dr. Kelly stared across at her for a moment, then slowly nodded her head. "Do you have the disc with you?"

"Right here." Lowering Shine to the floor, Frankie rummaged in her handbag and drew out the grubby case. She handed it to Dr. Kelly.

"Let's make it fast." The vet opened the case, glanced at the title, and, with a puzzled crease between her eyes, slipped the DVD into the drive. After a few seconds, the spreadsheet blossomed onto the monitor. Silently, Dr. Kelly studied the columns, scrolled down to the next page, then more swiftly to the end, and back to the start. Biting her lip, she looked at Frankie. "What do you think all this is?"

Instead of answering directly, Frankie asked, "Can you interpret those number codes?"

Reaching for a book on the shelf behind her, Dr. Kelly lifted the heavy volume and flipped through a few pages. Finally, she slammed it closed. "Well. Definitely not smoke signals, but something on the same order. They're CPT codes. All health insurance companies require physicians to use CPT codes to expedite payment. Even us lowly veterinarians use them for our patients who carry insurance."

Light dawned in Frankie's head. Of course. God knows she'd seen enough of those on her own medical statements. She should've caught on immediately. "No wonder they looked familiar. So the names must be patients, the dates are doctor appointments, and the dollars are the amounts their insurance paid."

"Yes." Dr. Kelly was frowning again. "Maybe your deputy sheriff can check, but I'd say—" She hesitated. "No. I don't want to presuppose anyone. Just have the police see if they can find the doctor involved and check the statements."

"All right." Heart-lifting, Frankie felt vindicated. "But just between you and me, what is it you think you see?"

Dr. Kelly blinked. "Fraud."

CHAPTER 18

As though on auto-pilot, Frankie drove into her grandmother's driveway and stopped. Only after helping Shine to the ground and opening the crew cab door to retrieve the bags holding her purchases did she realize she'd spaced one of the main goals set for herself today.

Rent a new place.

For heaven's sake! How could she have forgotten? Finding an apartment had been number one on her list. Or number one after Shine's checkup, anyway. And dead even on the checklist was buying clothes. Then it had been important to ask Dr. Kelly about Smoke Signals. A glance at her watch did nothing to dispel the guilt. It was too late now to begin a search in either Spokane or Coeur d'Alene. But after her promise this morning, she wouldn't blame Gabe if he kicked her out.

What was worse, she thought viciously, her damn foot was giving her fits. She stumbled, burdened by an armload of heavy packages, over the paved sidewalk to the front porch. Something had tweaked when Banner dragged her away from the exploding duplex, and the muscles in what was left of the foot kept spasming. Tromping around the mall and trying on shoes hadn't helped any.

Banner waited at the door, bouncing his front legs up and down as though anxious his newfound friend might've pulled a disappearing act. Disgruntled, Frankie thought he seemed more relieved to see Shine than he did her.

"Two-timer," she accused as she dumped her packages on the dining room table. The table sat bare, without centerpiece or cloth to accent the cherrywood's beauty, dull now from lack of polishing. Dust-free, but in need of a coat of wax. Remembering all the Sunday and Thanksgiving and Christmas dinners of her life, her hands itched to remedy the condition.

Meanwhile, Banner, ignoring her epithet, led the bichon into the kitchen where he held the doggie-door open for Shine to pass outside under his belly. Frankie had to laugh. "You're a regular gentleman, aren't you? So helpful."

Kicking off her shoes and prosthesis, Frankie scrounged under the sink until she found the bottle of furniture polish Grandma McGill had kept there since time began. Selecting an old kitchen towel from a stack of rags in the utility room, she started on her self-imposed housekeeping duty before she could forget.

The fresh lemon scent of the polish, still strong after her grandmother's death eighteen months earlier, combined with the repetitive motion of rubbing the table, soothed her soul. As she stroked, Dr. Kelly's assertion came back to her.

Fraud, the vet had said, her blue eyes narrow with what looked like disgust. According to the parameters laid out in the date column, over a two-year period, the dollar amounts added up to several hundred thousand dollars. Definitely a motive for murder. So what had been Denise's part in the setup? She had to figure in the equation somewhere. Even Dr. Kelly had admitted that.

Furniture well-polished, Frankie limped into the kitchen to put away the cleaning materials.

In need of coffee, she ran fresh water into the pot and flipped up the toggle switch, preparing to wait on a caffeine revival.

Having put off the moment, she was working herself up to call Gabe. Tell him what she'd learned and, in the process, no doubt, earn a butt-chewing for delving into matters without his say so. Well, tough. When the coffee finished brewing, she sat at the battered old kitchen table, took out her phone and dialed the number Gabe had given her.

Closing her eyes, she waited, a little catch of anticipation roiling through her.

"Zantos." His voice sounded strong in her ear. "Have you got the list ready? We learned Pettigrew has an insurance policy for his renters, so you may be able to collect. The good news is we found a small fire-proof lock-box in the rubble. Is it yours?"

Frankie blinked. List? Insurance? Lock-box? What in the world is he talking about?

"Hello? Frankie? You there?"

Gabe's impatient question alerted her.

"Yes. I'm here. It's just—" There, on the table in plain sight, was a piece of typing paper half covered with a looping scrawl. "Sorry. I just now got your note."

She tried to read it while listening to him say, "Where were you? I've been trying to reach you all afternoon."

"I was in Spokane. Sorry. I forgot to turn on my phone." Hadn't she told him her destination this morning?

He was silent a moment, then said, "Did you find another apartment?"

"I'm afraid not. I had some shopping to do—nothing to wear, literally—and Shine was due for her check-up, so—"

"That's fine." He cut across her stumbling explanation. "No rush. I think—"

Now it was his turn to stammer.

"What?" she asked.

"I think I'd just as soon you stay where I can keep an eye on you. So, is the lock-box yours?"

"Unless Howie had one just like it, I expect so. A Sentry eleven hundred?"

He verified the model.

"I hope it's as fire-proof as the manufacturer advertised." Reminded of her loss, she couldn't help fretting. "My army records are in there. And some family papers from Grandma's estate. Pretty much irreplaceable."

"I'll bring the case home with me. How about the list? How soon can you get one worked up?"

By now she'd read through the note. Apparently, he—or Russ Pettigrew—wanted an itemization of her possessions destroyed in the explosion for an insurance claim. She couldn't even describe the sense of relief she felt on hearing that. The Hawkesford Fire Department's pay scale wasn't especially munificent, and she'd been worried about meeting her bills.

"I'll work on it," she told him. "But that's not why I called."

"It isn't?"

"No. I've found something you need to see."

"Is this about the murders? What is it?"

"A possible—no, a likely motive."

"Are you sure?"

Well, no. Not quite. But that didn't stop her from saying, "Yes."

Gabe was silent a moment, then said, "I'm checking some leads right now and hate to break off mid-stream. I'll be back in Hawkesford in a couple hours. I'll see you then. That okay?"

What the heck? Only by a fluke had the DVD survived an exploding house anyway. What difference could a few more hours make? "Sure. I guess so," she said.

"Good." He hung up without saying goodbye.

Like in the army, she thought. Communication didn't require politeness. Only clarity and getting the point across.

***

Gabe's two-hour time frame, plus an added sixty minutes for good measure, passed without him showing up. Frankie occupied herself in the meantime in removing price tags from her new clothes—adding up the cost item by item and nearly having a heart attack—pressing everything but the underwear, and hanging stuff in the closet. An awful lot of space was left on the rod considering the amount she'd spent. A list detailing her loss at the duplex took only a matter of minutes. She couldn't see putting in a claim for a few battered pots and pans acquired from the second-hand store—except for that old cast iron skillet and the dutch oven. Antiques, or so she'd been told. Taken together, though, the replacement cost even of stuff added up.

Shortly before dinnertime, she gathered her menagerie into the pickup and trekked off to the grocery store. It only seemed fair since Gabe had fed her more than once, telling her to help herself to whatever was in the refrigerator. Frankie believed in paying her debts. Also, she couldn't help thinking he would be in a better frame of mind if his belly was full of good food. Chowing down always worked for the troops.

Seeing one's neighbors while grocery shopping is kind of like being at a community-meeting center. Frankie spied Maggie pushing a cart up and down the aisles as she headed over to the produce department for mushrooms. Chris and Darryl were buying beer and potato chips in the junk food section. Hoping to evade her co-workers, Frankie threw a handful of 'shrooms into a paper bag, a few seconds too late to escape, when Maggie touched her arm.

"There you are," Maggie said. "I was hoping you'd stop by the station and fill us in. Karl said you were okay, a few superficial burns, but I, for one, would rather hear it from you. Men sometimes don't realize—"

Frankie cut across what might become a full-on attack. "I'm fine, Maggie, thanks for caring. Howie's cat was the only casualty—aside from the duplex, of course."

Maggie eyed her. "Chris was telling us you looked rough when they gave you a ride home."

"Us? Who else has Chris been talking to?"

"Just Darryl and me. And Benton. That's all. We were concerned, all of us."

Maggie didn't seriously expect anyone to be fresh as a flower after being dragged down a gravel driveway, did she?

"I'm fine, Maggie. Really."

Frankie paid for her groceries and made her escape.

***

Shine and Banner, toenails clicking on the hardwood floors, rushed to meet Gabe as he backed his SUV into the driveway.

The coil of worry Frankie had been harboring about his safety released. Then she scoffed at herself. Why wouldn't he be safe?

Frankie heard him talking to the dogs as she shoved a couple ribeye steaks under the broiler and got out salad fixings. Turning to meet him as he walked into the kitchen, her heart beat a little faster. Though not a large man, he had presence.

Of which she was very aware.

"Hi," she said. "I'll bet you're hungry."

He sniffed the air. "Garlic and mushrooms, which must mean steak. What are we celebrating?"

Instantly, Frankie felt heat rise in her cheeks and imagined turning three shades of red. Not celebrating—laying a blanket over her guilt. He was going to be pissed when he learned she'd looked at the disc before turning it over to him. With good reason.

Hoping the open broiler door on the stove provided an excuse for coloring like a schoolgirl, she said, "Being alive. Reason enough for a good meal?"

"There is that." He leaned against the doorjamb and studied her, then smiled. "But I think something else is bothering you. Spit it out, Frankie. But let's get this over with first." He clumped over and dumped an extremely sooty and battered looking lock-box onto the table.

"Here you go. Looks like it survived the fire and explosion in good shape."

"As long as the papers didn't turn brittle and crumble."

"One way to find out. You do have the key, don't you?"

The faintly derisive question raised her dander,

a good thing. "Of course," she replied coolly. "I keep it with my car keys." In proof, she fished the simple ring out of her jeans pocket and unlocked the box. Everything, she discovered, was whole, if slightly browned in color. As she lifted the file folders out to examine, the casket containing her medals spilled out too. Lid knocked askew, they glinted under the kitchen light.

"Purple heart." Gabe touched the ribbon before she could sweep the medals back into their container. "And—" His astonished gaze wrenched up to meet her eyes. "Good Lord, Frankie. Is this a Bronze Star? My granddad had one. That means—"

She couldn't bear the sight of those medals. Men had died. She almost died. Why did people say soldiers "won" or "earned" combat medals. There was no win or earn about it. The whole episode owed to blind luck.

"It doesn't mean anything." She slammed the lid down and threw the casket into the lock-box. "Supper is the same as ready. Why don't you wash up? Your hands are dirty."

They were, too, soiled from handling the lock-box. Lucky, also, to have avoided being crushed by Frankie's safe lid.

Somehow, they managed to get through the meal with no further outbursts. The dogs helped ease the tension arisen between them. Banner sat beside Frankie, graciously accepting the two chunks of beefsteak she allowed him.

Shine crouched near Gabe. The bichon was still leery of approaching him but allowed herself to be enticed by tiny bits of meat.

"What about it, Frankie?" Gabe asked her once. "Do you think this dog has been abused by a man at some time? She's not warming to me very fast."

He sounded hurt by it.

She wiped her fingers on a paper napkin. "Well, somebody shot her, and I'm betting it was a man."

"You're probably right. Shooting a dog doesn't strike me as a woman's act of violence." Thoughtfully, Gabe chewed a bite of succulent ribeye.

The food, to Frankie's way of thinking, turned out darn good, something of a minor miracle since she hadn't cooked a real dinner for anyone in ages. Gabe wouldn't hear of letting her clean the kitchen by herself afterward, pitching in to load the dishwasher and scrub the broiler pan. But this couldn't last and finally, with the towels hung on a rack to dry, he led the way into the living room.

Frankie grabbed the computer disc out of her purse and presented it to Gabe. "Here. This is what I found."

She held her breath.

His eyes lit. He turned the case over while examining it as though trying to garner information through his fingertips. "This is the DVD Howie told you about?"

"Yes. See? It's marked Smoke Signals, just like he said."

Gabe's voice was patient and soft. "And just how did this come into your possession?"

"I found it after the duplex blew up. I was sitting on the pumper's running board before I started home when an envelope came tumbling right at me. The disc was inside. Evidently, the explosion blew it in from somewhere."

His eyes narrowed. "You mean you've had it in your possession for hours and didn't bother to tell me?"

Uh, oh. Sounded as if she'd given the wrong answer.

"I tried, but you'd already begun talking to Karl and checking stuff out. Then, later, I got busy with other things and didn't remember I had it. I—I forget things, sometimes." Not wholly a lie.

Smoke Signals had faded off her radar for whole hours at a time today.

"You forget things?" He sounded incredulous, disbelieving.

Her head hurt. Mortification burned through her. Without thinking, she pressed two fingers against her temple, fighting the sudden pain. "Yes," she said defiantly—or maybe belligerently. "Sometimes I forget things. So shoot me."

Gabe's expression changed. "I'm sorry. I didn't mean to snap at you. You—I—"

Damn all war wounds. Now she had him stammering like an adolescent. Frankie waved his apology aside.

"Have you looked at what's on the disc?" he managed to say after an awkward pause.

"Yes. In fact—" This admission was going to be hard. "—I downloaded it to your computer before I took the dog to the vet."

He scowled. "So I guess I don't need the disc at all."

She felt like chewing off her tongue. "If anything happened to me, I wanted to be sure you had the information. But the main thing is, after I looked at the file, some of the stuff struck me as familiar."

"Familiar?"

"Yes. But my memory—" Here she went, playing on his sympathies again. "So I showed it to Dr. Kelly."

"Who?" Gabe's dark eyes snapped fire. His face turned hard as stone. His cop face.

"Dr. Kelly is Shine's vet. I told you, she contacted the sheriff's office about Denise's disappearance. She's the one who convinced me Denise's absence was suspicious."

"I remember. But why show this to her. This disc may be evidence, Frankie. You can't go around—"

Frankie interrupted before he could go into a full tirade. "I thought she might decipher the part I couldn't remember."

His jaw clenched. "And did she?"

"Sure did." She couldn't help the smile—or maybe smirk—breaking over her face.

"Are you going to tell me what the two of you found?" His patience seemed exaggerated.

"Certainly. We think it's about insurance fraud. A whole bunch of insurance fraud."

With long steps, he strode to the computer and dinged the keyboard. The monitor flared to life.

"And blackmail," Frankie added, peering over

his shoulder.

Turns out Gabe had a highly inventive vocabulary of cuss words at his command. It was just like being back in the army.

CHAPTER 19

For Frankie, morning came all too soon. Eyes gritty, yawning and stretching, she slouched downstairs, following the scent of coffee.

Gabe, like a terrier at a rat hole, had kept at her for what seemed like hours last night after she dropped the blackmail bombshell on him. The experience kept worrying at her this morning, just as it had all night.

Quote: What the "expletive" did she think she was doing, pulling an outsider like the dog's vet into the equation? Why the "expletive" hadn't she brought the disc straight to him? "Expletive." Hadn't she ever heard of a person using her own initiative? She wasn't in the blankety-blank army anymore. In the real world, people had to think for themselves, make good decisions, and she hadn't done much of a job of it. She was an idiot! Unquote.

Oh, yeah. He definitely went off on her. And he had a point, as she'd known all along. He also didn't know how close she'd come to popping him one. Or maybe he did. He'd seen something that suddenly called him to lay off.

All of which didn't help her surly mood as she peeked around the corner into the kitchen. Except for Shine, rising from her dog bed when she saw Frankie, and Banner noisily lapping water from a bowl, the room was empty. Emboldened, Frankie entered.

"Where is he?" she asked Banner in a whisper, not ready to face Gabe just yet.

The dog looked up, flicked his plumy tail back and forth a few times, and dripped water on the floor from his muzzle.

"You're not helping," she told him. "Is he gone?"

She spied the note then, on the table, weighted down by a bakery bag. Peeking inside, she found a fresh apple fritter within. Her heart did a little jump. An apology, by any chance? Pouring a cup of coffee and downing half of it in a mouth-scalding series of swallows, she munched the fritter and picked up the note.

You'll be glad to know we've got a lead on Denise Rider's former employer, it said.

Humph. She wasn't surprised. Gabe's first scan of the files last night had him punching numbers into his phone and, as soon as someone on the other end answered, he reported in a terse, shorthand kind of way. He finished by snapping suggestions that sounded more like orders, just like her old drill sergeant. Funny really, since he said he'd never been in the service.

Looks like you and Dr. Kelly were on the right track. Now lay off. The sheriff's department will take it from here, the note continued.

Frankie blinked. Well, that was clear enough and suited her fine. She'd emptied her mind to him last night. Hadn't forgotten a thing, of that much she was certain. Repeated every word Howie ever said to her. Relayed Dr. Kelly's impressions of Denise, which he said he'd ask the vet about himself, thanks. Did her best on an inventory of what she'd found in the apartment when she moved in. Accounted for all of Denise's old flames, what she knew of them, admittedly not much.

"Ask Maggie about any other rumors," she told him, "because I'm all done."

To which he replied, "You bet your sweet cheeks you are."

Gabe's note closed with, Call Karl Mager. Meticulously, he time-dated the note. He'd written it—she looked at her watch— only ten minutes ago. She'd just missed him, and thank God for that.

Now what? Did the department need her to work? Or did they want to fire her?

Telling herself not to be ridiculous, she poured a second cup of coffee and dialed the station. Benton, on dispatch this morning, transferred her to Karl with almost too much alacrity.

Karl barked his name into the phone like he'd been taking lessons from Gabe.

"Good morning," Frankie said, cheerily upbeat as all get out. "I got your message to call."

Karl huffed. "Deputy Gabe Zantos is a helluva fast worker by God."

She wasn't quite sure how he meant that, but it struck her as kind of double entendre-ish. Since he couldn't see her, she glared at the phone and said stiffly, "I beg your pardon? I hope what you're saying is that Deputy Zantos is extremely efficient."

Karl got a kick out of her answer. She could

tell that by the way he chortled in a smothered sort of way.

"You called," she said again.

"I did. I wanted to let you know Lew is satisfied you know your beans. You're cleared for duty as paramedic in charge. He's going back on days with Chris, and you and Marc will be carrying night shift. That leaves Hal and Mary Lou to take up the slack with whatever volunteers have enough training. Sound good? Think you can handle it?"

Relief flowed over her like a gentle breeze on a scorching day. Frankie barely avoided laughing out loud. "Of course, I can handle it. Sounds great!"

"Means your weekend is cut short. We'll need you back on tonight, but after this little bump the schedule will be set."

"Fine with me. Thanks, Karl."

"Don't thank me. Thank Lew for the passing grade and the US Army Medical Corps for the training. Get some sleep before your shift, hear?" He hung up as someone in the background asked him a question.

A sense of well-being swept over Frankie. Somehow, her physical condition hadn't interfered with carrying out her duties, and apparently, she hadn't forgotten any critical medical process or harmed any of the patients. She'd passed everything she knew about the murders into Gabe's capable hands. No more worries on either score.

Only one thing marred her euphoric state. At this rate, she'd never have the time to find a place to live.

Her jaw hardened. Looked like Gabe was stuck with her and her menagerie for another day or two whether he liked it or not.

***

The clock wound slowly down to midnight, not that Frankie was watching the hands move. Not exactly, anyway.

So far, the shift had gone smoothly with only a single call entering the system, a farmer reporting a prowler around his combine, which was parked in the field next to his house. Maggie, on night shift this week, passed the call on to the deputies, and then she, Marc, and Frankie went back to relaxing.

No fire, nobody hurt—just the way Frankie

liked it. Sort of. The only challenge so far included any of them staying awake.

She grinned, thinking of how savvy farmers were these days. Even old-timers like Clyde Pettigrew, although she suspected that was mostly due to the influence of younger men like his son Russ. Nowadays techno-appropriate alarms warned them of fuel thieves before they could be cleaned out. It was a safeguard they'd taken for themselves, being unable to rely on sparse police protection in wide-open farmland. Gabe or another deputy would probably take the farmer's statement in the morning.

Anyway, this had been the slowest night since she'd been here, and there were still six whole hours to go. Marc had given in to his boredom and was dozing on a cot next to the fire engine. At the dispatch desk, Maggie daubed a third coat of polish on her nails. Once she yawned so widely, Frankie wondered if her next patient would be the dispatcher with a broken jaw.

To Frankie's dismay, the book she'd chosen to read had lost her interest and threatened to put her to sleep, too. She rose from a desk chair grown a little too comfortable and stretched, her back popping. Punching air like a boxer, she skipped—if one could call her awkward shamble a skip—into the break room to draw a glass of water.

Automatically, she glanced out the window to where her Ranger sat parked side-by-side with Maggie's old Subaru. Marc had followed his custom by walking to work, saying he needed the exercise.

It was as she turned the faucet off that a quick movement near the cars caught her attention.

Visions of the duplex exploding flashed across her mind.

She froze, hand gripping the glass.

The station stood right next door to Patterson's Bar. It stood to reason a drunk might be wandering around looking for a ride.

Or so she tried to convince herself. But there was something... something furtive about the figure she saw. And comfortable complaisance belonged to an earlier era, before Howie and Denise.

Alarms went off inside her head.

Reaching for the switch, she doused the overhead lights. The room dimmed, making her, she hoped, less visible to anyone outside. She peeped around the side of the window and squinted.

"Frankie? What's with the lights?" Maggie

called from the outer room. "You in 'save the planet' mode?"

Frankie didn't answer.

At first, until her night vision developed, she couldn't see a thing, but a sudden sharp clang of metal on metal suggested vandalism. Anger flaring, she started for the door, meaning to shout a challenge—until renewed caution cooled her temper. The noise wasn't quite loud enough to denote heavy damage, she decided. Perhaps it could wait.

With her eyes adjusted, she made out an almost invisible, dark-clad figure darting through the open space between her car and the station. The glimpse showed a big man. Thick in body, tall, heavy-footed. The figure was carrying something metallic in his hand. It glinted under the moon. A pistol? It had that general shape.

Her body took charge of her brain, a sense of self-preservation coming to the fore. Side-stepping the yard or so to the door, she snapped the lock on. Then, feeling as if she were moving in slow motion, she hurried across the station to the front and did the same. Her heartbeat thrummed in triple rhythm as if she'd been swimming upstream.

Astonished, she discovered she was shaking

like a palsied old lady. Pain shot through her temple.

"Frankie? What's the matter? Why did you lock the door?" Maggie, nail polish brush poised in mid-air, stared at her, brow furrowed.

Frankie put her finger across her lips. "Douse your light, Maggie. I think we've got trouble."

"What?" Maggie stared at her blankly. "What kind of trouble?"

Without answering, Frankie rushed back into the break room. Stood to the side and peered out the window again. There. A flicker of movement at the corner of the station.

Should she call for help? Instinct urged her to do so, except what a fool she'd look if she reported a false alarm. Her first night here in charge. She'd be so embarrassed. And Gabe—

They should call Rudy Swallowtail, Frankie decided. Ask him to come. He was probably somewhere fairly close.

She reached for her phone, only to discover that instead of being clipped to the waistband of her jeans, the instrument sat out of reach on the work-station desk in the other room. Plugged into an outlet charging. Dandy.

"Maggie," she said quietly, "don't ask questions.

Please, just turn off your light and call Rudy."

Maggie didn't move. "What for? What's going on?"

"Just do it. Stay calm and ask him to come. Quickly, please."

"Oh, my God. Is it the murderer, Frankie?" For Maggie, the penny finally dropped. She swallowed with an audible click. "How do you know?"

"I don't know. It's just—there's someone outside sneaking around. I—call Rudy."

Flattened against the wall, Frankie threw the bolt, a flimsy thing left from when the building had been a grange hall and checked the lock again. Like in any good horror movie, as she tried the doorknob, it turned beneath her hand with a series of soft clicks.

Her heart gave a hard bump. Whoever was on the other side rapped softly several times.

Relief poured through her. It must be one of the volunteers, she thought, on foot instead of driving. Any moment now, she assured herself, he'd call out, identify himself, and ask her to open the door.

She reached for the lock, ready to twist it open.

Except whoever was there didn't call out. And it occurred to her that no self-respecting volunteer would come at this time of night.

Instead, the door shook hard a few times. She heard footsteps as the visitor shuffled away.

The silence grew more ominous.

In the other room, Maggie sat frozen, watching Frankie with her mouth half open.

Frankie waited, listening. Had he gone? She didn't think so. Not for a minute. She sensed him out there laying low, trying to lure her out. Fear surged through her veins with every heartbeat. Coward. What was she afraid of? Nothing had happened to make her feel this way.

Yet.

The fact remained that she was terrified. A vision of Howie as she'd last seen him flashed across her retinas, then a blinding light and a stab of pain.

No, no. I don't have time for this.

She blanked for a moment.

"Maggie, get down on the floor. Did you call Rudy?" Frankie hadn't heard whether Maggie had or hadn't followed orders, but at least she'd finally turned off the lamp above her desk.

"I can't reach him." Maggie's voice shook, infected by Frankie's tension. "He must be circling Hawkesford Mountain about now. Reception is awful out there."

"Damn."

"What do you want me to do?" Now, at last, Maggie squatted down, pushing her fully-rounded body into the undersized kneehole space of her desk.

"Keep quiet and stay out of sight."

From the truck garage, Marc's snore thundered against Frankie's eardrums. Oh, Lord. Was the garage door down and locked? It was supposed to be in the evening after the firemen went home, but it was hot out tonight. Had Marc followed procedure? Why hadn't she checked?

After a dragging minute that felt more like an hour, she edged toward the desk where her cell beckoned. They couldn't wait for Rudy. As much as she hated waking him, she'd call Gabe.

Her hand was on the phone when a bullet whizzed through the window. Glass shattered. A chunk of the desk flew into the air.

Frankie clutched the phone and leaped back. Blood welled along her forearm. Fiery pain blossomed. Another shot followed, maybe two.

"Frankie!" Maggie's shriek rose to a high C.

Marc's snores faltered, stopped. "Hey!" His boots thumped as they hit the floor. "What was that?"

Caught in the middle of the room, for a moment,

Frankie didn't know what to do. She couldn't think, wits scattering, until her training took over.

Stay low. Return fire.

Except, of course, she had no weapon.

"I'm okay. Stay put, Maggie. Marc, don't move."

Gripping the phone, she dropped to the floor and crawled toward the break room, scrabbling on hands and knees through stabbing shards of broken glass. A thin trail of blood marked her path.

Another shot, the bullet blasting through the station wall a scant inch over her head. Whoever was doing the shooting knew to aim low.

"Shit!" She dove into the lee of the old-fashioned steel cupboard housing the sink.

"What the hell's going on?" Marc yelled. He'd ignored her advice to remain in the garage and stood in the doorway between there and the main station.

Maggie answered, telling him to get down, hide behind something.

Panting as though she'd run a hundred-meter sprint, Frankie squatted. Punched in Gabe's personal number, trying to ignore the pain in her cut fingertips. The keypad turned slippery. Her arm dripped blood. The palms of her hands and her knees stung. Her ears rang with shock.

She held the phone to her ear, plastic bouncing against her head in time with her trembling.

On the other end, the telephone rang what seemed an unholy number of times, but which her brain counted as five.

"'lo," Gabe mumbled at last.

Her whisper sounded thick as if she were winded. "Gabe. Wake up. It's Frankie. I'm at the station. Someone is shooting at us. My arm—"

"Shooting?" Suddenly, he sounded wide awake. "Frankie? Get down and stay there. Don't move. I'm on my way."

"Hurry," she begged.

Hah! She'd known he'd say to stay down—low—whatever.

The phone line remained open and, for a few moments, she continued to hear sounds. Then, after perhaps fifteen seconds, it went dead, and the automated operator came on, telling her to hang up and try her call again.

Gabe was on his way.

Meanwhile, not six feet from where she cowered, the back door shook violently on its hinges as fists drum-rolled against it. Old and weather-beaten, it clattered loosely in its heat-shrunken frame as if ready to fall down.

Another shot rang out, and a bullet thrummed into the wood as if the attacker was trying to shoot out the lock. On the inside, the heavy coat of paint starred.

Frankie shook right along with the door as if to rattle her bones.

In the main room, Maggie cried out, sobbing. Marc was asking over and over, "Maggie, Frankie, you okay?"

Frankie answered him, earning another shot pinging into the siding above her head. "We're all right, Marc. Stay where you are. Gabe will be here in a second."

But they weren't really all right.

Oh, God! Gabe will never make it in time. Someone is going to be killed.

Me, she thought. My turn.

Quickly, before the shooter succeeded in breaking through the door, she reached up and dragged open the drawer next to the sink. Her blood-sticky fingers closed on the handle of a steak knife. So dull it would hardly cut hamburger, she well knew, but if the worst happened—

Nobody was going to catch Frankie McGill

cowering in the corner. No way.

Hidden by the bulk of the sink cabinet, she rose to a crouch, prepared to spring to her own, to the others, defense.

In the distance, the wail of a siren split the night. The disturbance at the door ceased. She heard a muttered imprecation before their attacker took off running, footsteps fading across the parking lot into the yard of the building behind the station.

"Stay where you are," she yelled to Marc and Maggie, wisely adhering to her own advice. Another shot slammed into the building and, as though to vent his rage, the shooter sent a final round into one of the parked vehicles. She heard the bullet clang through sheet metal.

It brought her to her feet.

Outside, brakes squealing, Gabe's SUV pulled up only inches from the station entrance. The headlights threw weird, dancing shadows into the room. She watched through a broken window as he jumped out, clutching his Glock.

"Frankie!" he called

Drawn by the sound of shots and the wailing siren, three men and the bartender from Patterson's Bar down the street raced up to join him.

"What the hell's going on?" one yelled. "Who's doing all the shooting?" The others started talking at once, most of them at the top of their lungs.

"Get back," Gabe hollered.

They flinched away from his gun.

He tried the door. "Frankie, you okay? Open up."

"I'm coming," she called back, her voice without force. Her shoes crunched broken glass as she tottered across the room on unsteady legs. The computer monitor, she saw now, was dark. Funny she hadn't noticed before. The shooter had managed a hit and shorted it out. Lucky Maggie, under the desk. But too, too close.

The dispatcher fought her way from the knee-hole, gazing at the carnage with horrified eyes, her mouth working wordlessly. Marc poked his ghost-white face around the corner.

"I'm coming," Frankie said again, louder this time, and surer. "I'm all right. We're all okay."

She threw back the lock and flung herself into Gabe's arms.

CHAPTER 20

Clasping her against his chest for what struck Frankie as way too brief a time, Gabe thrust her aside. He paced a track around the station, looking at everything and seeing nothing—as far as she could tell. Shirtless, barefoot, and carrying his pistol in his hand, he was in a towering rage.

He managed to yell through clenched teeth—a trick Frankie viewed in utter fascination.

"Goddamn maniac shoots up the station, then gets away free as a bird," he gritted. "But do we know who did it? Hell no. Not us. Somebody tell me why don't we have security cameras around here. Damn all cheap county commissioner bastards."

Oh, yeah. The deputy was definitely on a rant.

Marc jumped into action, binding the wound

on Frankie's forearm and cleaning blood and glass splinters from her hands. He winced as the deputy's anger flowed around them.

For a moment, hoping to take her mind off Marc's ministrations, Frankie considered hosting a contest featuring Gabe and Russ Pettigrew to see who could out-curse the other. She'd sell tickets. Probably make enough for the first month's rent on a new place to live. If she ever worked up enough nerve to look for a place, anyway. Cocooning at her grandmother's old house with Gabe was a lot more reassuring. Except she really didn't want to be on the receiving end of his blistering tongue.

"Ouch!"

"Sorry," Marc muttered as he dug a small, glittering shard of glass from her palm. His hands shook, the tweezers gouging the wound deeper, beyond the glass.

Frankie pulled her hand away. She'd recovered from the trauma of being under gunfire a whole lot more quickly than Marc or Maggie, the latter still sitting at the break room table and periodically emitting a heavy sob.

"Leave it," she told Marc. "I'll take care of the glass later. It's not going anywhere, and you're a wreck."

"Sorry," Marc apologized again.

"Don't you be sorry. None of this is your fault. I'm just glad we all came out okay."

Maggie choked out another sob. "I'm not okay!"

Marc, at least, found a weak smile for the dispatcher.

Yeah, on the surface, Frankie had recovered her equilibrium. Inside she was having a more difficult time wrapping her head around the idea that someone wanted to kill her. Someone other than a nameless foreign enemy, I mean. Someone she probably even knew. This was his, or her, second try.

Fortunately, Lew, along with Tom and the rest of day crew entered the station just then, summoned to finish out the night shift. Their clamor and questions helped take her mind off her dismal thoughts—and fears.

Lew touched Marc's shoulder. "I got this, Marc. Give Gabe your statement, then go on home. Get some sleep. But damn well don't be late tomorrow night."

The normalcy of Lew's gruffness seemed to reassure Marc. "Thanks," he said and gave Frankie a twitchy smile. "I don't know how you service people handle the stress, Frankie. You're the one hurt, but I'm shaking, and you're steady as a rock."

"Practice." She answered his smile with a small one of her own. "People can get used to anything. Loud noises like gunfire is the least of it." Besides, they always said you never heard the shot that killed you. A stupid statement if she ever heard one. How would anybody know?

Marc nodded and, flinching a little, went to face Gabe's wrath. Frankie felt sorry for him. She'd already served her term at answering Gabe's rapid-fire questions. Her answers hadn't pleased him. Marc's probably wouldn't either since he'd been asleep when the affair started.

Maggie, having spent most of the shoot-out under the desk, had only stuttered replies.

Picking up the tweezers Marc had dropped, Lew sat down in his place and grasped Frankie's hand. "How you doing?" he asked.

"Doing great. Living the dream. Just another night in paradise."

The joke, if that's what it was, fell flat.

"Do I detect a little sarcasm? Gabe must've talked to you already." Adjusting the desk lamp, he bent over her hand, plucking yet another glass sliver from the base of her thumb.

"Yes. First thing." Frankie shied away from remembering how she'd thrown herself into his arms like some 1950s suburban TV housewife. Yuk. "I couldn't tell him much. The shooter didn't say a word, didn't show himself, and knew just the right time to break off the engagement before help came."

Lew frowned, much as Gabe had when she'd told him the same thing. And like Gabe, he asked, "A professional?"

Frankie put bloody fingertips to her temple, trying to still the blaze of pain. "I don't know. I don't know anything, Lew, including why this person is still after me. He must know by now that I don't have whatever he's looking for. He completely destroyed the duplex and all my stuff."

"Maybe so." Gabe, already finished with Marc, came over to stand beside her. "But it appears he thinks you do either have or know something to connect him to these murders."

"I know." Guilt gnawed. "I know he does. Honestly, you'd think he'd have figured out that if I could identify him, I would've done so by now."

"You'd think," he agreed.

"And now, the twisted idiot put Maggie and Marc in danger tonight. Or I did."

"Not you. It's all on him." Lines crinkled at the corners of Gabe's eyes. "Marc says he slept through most of the excitement. Didn't wake up until it sank in those were gunshots he heard."

Lew snorted. He yanked a tiny bit of glass from her hand and, on a note of satisfaction, said, "There. I think that's it. Rinse this blood off, Frankie, and let's see how it looks. Marc is a heavy sleeper," he added to Gabe. "I've noticed it before. Never knew Chris to sleep through a call, though. Or any of the others." He twisted around and called over to the dispatch station, "Benton? You reach Chris yet?"

"Not yet. I hope he's all right."

"If he doesn't show up in the next five minutes, I'll send Rudy over to check," Gabe said.

Into the chaos of Gabe questioning everyone, including the bar patrons who'd followed the sound of his siren, Chris walked into the station, his hair mussed with a serious case of bed-head. Eyes wide, he took in the carnage.

"Hey," he said. "What's up?"

A regular chorus answered.

Knees creaking, Frankie got up and headed for the sink. Hot water and soap stung the small wounds, but she knew no single cut was serious.

She allowed Lew to disinfect and apply bandages to her palms, wondering how she was even supposed to wash her face at this rate.

Her temper, as details of the attack came back to her, climbed into the red zone. "I can tell you one thing," she announced at large. "After this, I'll be carrying. No more ambushes for me. Enough is enough."

Gabe's gaze locked with hers. Civilian with a gun? She could almost see the question rolling through his mind. Undeserved self-reproach showed in his face, and then he gave a short nod. Acknowledgment of her army training, perhaps. No argument, although, for a moment, he looked like he wanted to protest.

Loose cannon? Not her.

"You got a gun, Frankie?" Lew asked.

"No," she said. "But I know where I can get one."

***

The clock dial turned over to six-thirty. Frankie gave up on trying to sleep and threw back the lone sheet covering her. Slumbering at her side, the two dogs awoke as she moved, Banner jumping to floor to stretch out his hind legs one by one. Shine waited for help down.

Frankie staggered out of bed, lifting the small dog with her. It had not been a restful night, what with her hands and knees hurting like hell and her worrying about the murderer taking another pot shot at her. It seemed inevitable that one of these days he wouldn't miss.

She teetered into the bathroom, clumsy, using just the heel of her partial foot. Gads! Talk about "rode hard and put up wet." Unable to splash water over her gritty eyes, with a grunt of exasperation, she ripped the bandages Lew had applied with such care from her hands and eyed the cuts. Kind of a mess, the deepest still seeped pinkish blood.

Ignoring the pain, she washed her face and struggled to don prosthesis and clothing without leaving bloodstains all over everything. Just what she needed, to ruin a brand new wardrobe.

"C'mon," she told the dogs who sat waiting for her to finish. The three of them pattered down the stairs, Shine taking the steep steps with care. The bichon was nearly recovered. Still got her meds, though.

Unlike other days, no note informing her

either of progress in catching the shooter or inviting her to help herself to whatever was in the refrigerator waited on the kitchen table.

"Kids," she announced to the dogs who were taking turns lapping water from the bowl, "I do believe we may have worn out our welcome." Pausing long enough to see to Shine's needs, Frankie checked her key ring and continued outside.

Someone had been around earlier because her Ranger had been returned after being examined for any evidence following the shooting last night. Frankie's anger swelled again at the sight of a bullet hole boring through the driver's side front fender. Grandpa would roll over in his grave for sure if he knew.

Gabe had locked the overhead garage door, as expected, up tight. Ditto the side door, with a padlock veiled over by cobwebs and a nest of yellow jackets glued between the steel clasp and the brass knob. The nest teemed with insects crawling in and out. As a deterrent against any would-be burglars, it probably served better than the padlock.

"Huh," she said to the dogs. "You guys better take up a different corner of the yard, just in case this goes wrong."

As though guessing what she had in mind,

Banner grinned at her and headed into the shade on the other side of the wide back porch. Shine, the Samoyed's constant shadow, followed.

Frankie poked around an ancient lilac bush until she found some dead wood. With a strong wrench, she broke off a switch about three feet long.

Switch firmly in hand, she slashed at the nest. Breaking away, it fell to the concrete pad in front of the door. Yellowjackets swarmed through octagonal openings, but before they could rise, Frankie stomped down with her sturdy work shoes. Shuddering, she pulverized the nest.

Selecting one of the keys on her ring, she slid it into the slot and turned. Stiffly, the padlock tumblers clicked over. She removed the lock from the hasp and turned the doorknob.

It was going to feel odd—sad, really—walking into the garage. The last time, she'd been here was with her grandpa, before she joined the service.

Last time in the garage, last time she saw Grandpa. He'd died of a massive stroke not long after that, during her first tour of duty.

She opened the door and slipped inside.

Her curiosity got answered on one level. Gabe did have a personal vehicle. A slightly dusty, as if it hadn't been driven in a while, Jeep Wrangler soft-top in a dark green color. It sat squarely in the middle of the garage, leaving room on either side for a lawn mower, rototiller, and an ancient snowblower. Shovels and garden hand implements hung from hooks on the walls. A workbench still resplendent with Grandpa's well-kept tools was in front of the Jeep.

Frankie flipped on the overhead light, a fixture with three fluorescent tubes, and headed straight for the bench, where an electrical outlet extended from the wall on each side. Taking up a screwdriver, she removed the cover from the one on the left—the one located in the darkest part of the garage. The cover gone, she reached into the aperture and pushed down on a metal latch out of sight beneath the electrical box.

There was a click, and the wood panel covering the space between three studs slid aside. Grandpa's gun safe. So safe—Frankie smiled a little—even Grandma, who had no interest in guns or shooting, hadn't been quite sure of its location. But Frankie knew. It'd been hers and her grandfather's secret.

She studied the collection, finally selecting an Airweight .38 caliber pocket pistol. Small enough to be easy to conceal on her person, enough fire-power to provide decent protection.

"Thanks, Grandpa," she whispered.

For a second, it was as if her grandfather's ghost stood next to her, then she moved, and the momentary apparition faded.

In reversal of the opening procedure, Frankie slid the safe door shut, then left the garage. She didn't even worry about Gabe noticing the yellow jacket nest she'd squashed on the way in. Didn't everybody destroy them at the first opportunity?

With the pocket pistol secured in a quick re-lease ankle-holster concealed by her boot-cut jeans, Frankie set off with Banner and Shine for Spokane to search out a new apartment.

A useless trip, as it happened. Nobody wanted one dog, let alone two.

At five-fifteen, tired and angry, she got back to Hawkesford, barely in time to change into her uniform before work and settle the dogs inside the house.

What was she going to do if Gabe told her to pack up her dogs and leave? No one in Spokane that she could discover rented property to people with dogs. She'd never go back to Mrs. Lane's overpriced and under-maintained hovel, for sure. Which reminded her—she'd never gotten her deposit back. No surprise on that score.

Tomorrow, if she lived through the night, she'd try for a place in Coeur d'Alene. One, going by the balance in her checkbook, that didn't require both a first and a last deposit.

***

A middle-aged man she hadn't yet met sat at the dispatch board with the headphones over his ears when Frankie got to the station.

"I'm Al," the guy said.

"Hi. I'm Frankie."

He gave her a small salute, so she guessed he recognized her. Probably famous for the way trouble follows me, she thought.

Lew and Chris were at the scene of a rollover down by the lake, or so Karl Mager, who emerged from his office, informed her. Marc had yet to arrive.

"He's leaving it to the last minute. He was pretty shook up last night." Karl's chuckle seemed forced to Frankie.

"He's not the only one."

"I may assign Darryl to help you cover EMT if

Marc can't handle his shift. Darryl says he's had a bit of training. At least he's some muscle to lend you a hand."

Boarded over windows—a result of last night's attack—made the station unbearably hot and close. Frankie broke into a sweat at the simple act of stowing her purse in the locker. When Karl looked away to answer the phone, she surreptitiously adjusted the ankle holster. Wearing it was going to take some getting used to, especially in this doggone summer heat. She'd be lucky if the nylon holster didn't rub a raw spot on her leg. But she'd checked in the mirror before coming to work. Her stiff cotton uniform hid the small bulk well.

Another mental note. Next time she was in Coeur d'Alene, she needed to stop at headquarters and request an enhanced concealed carry permit. For now, she refused to worry. Legal or not, she was damned if she'd go unarmed.

With a few minutes to spare, she went into Karl's office as soon as he hung up the phone.

"Heard from Deputy Zantos?" she asked, oh so casually.

"You mean, you haven't?"

She shook her head.

"Huh." He tilted his swivel chair almost to the break-off point. "Well, the crime scene guys were here early this morning, pulling bullets out of the wall and your truck, and looking around outside." Karl's face crunched into wrinkles. "Far as I could tell, they didn't find anything, not even any brass casings. Your shooter is a careful guy."

My shooter? "So no arrest pending." Frankie hunched her shoulders, thinking of the long night ahead. But surely the guy wouldn't be so bold as to try and strike twice in the same way. Or would that be the smart thing to do?

"No arrest that I know of," Karl said. "Although along about seven this morning Gabe took off like a bat out of hell. Said he had a couple people to talk to right away. Hope he comes back with some good news."

"Me, too." Nobody wished it more than she did.

Marc arrived for the shift he shared with Frankie, to her relief. Darryl made her a little uncomfortable, and she didn't want to work with him. Though, when she thought about it, she had no discernible reason.

Lew and Chris finished their run, returning the ambulance to the garage with replenished stores rattling around on the gurney. Which was fine with Frankie. Putting supplies in their proper place gave her something to do in the slack time.

Lew insisted on looking at Frankie's hands before clearing her to work, adding a stern admonishment to "bandage those open sores and wear gloves." Nothing she didn't already know.

Chris wandered around bugging Marc and her for their take on last night's shooting. What he didn't ask, Darryl—hanging around the EMTs, as usual—did.

Frankie decided he was a bit of a ghoul.

To everyone's surprise, Maggie tootled in while both shifts were still there, although Karl was digging car keys out of his pocket.

"Gonna be a party," she announced, determinedly cheerful and acting as though last night had never happened. "Saturday night at the Grange Hall. We can take turns covering the shift for a few hours, so everybody has a chance to show up."

Karl groaned. "I don't like parties, Maggie. What's up with this one? Middle of harvest, nobody will come. You better wait until fall."

"Can't wait." Maggie used her dispatching

voice, cool, crisp, and efficient. "This community is holding an emergency fundraiser."

"Who for?" That was Chris, standing over by the lockers.

"You mean 'for whom,'" Maggie corrected, making Frankie smile at the look on Chris's face. "And it's for one of our own. Hasn't it occurred to any of you except Gabe Zantos that Frankie Mc-Gill lost everything but her dog and her pickup in the explosion the other day? And her pickup just got used for target practice."

"Oh, no, Maggie." Hot blood scalded into Frankie's cheeks. "Really. It's not necessary. I'm fine."

"Fine my foot. Oh, don't worry. This isn't going to be any big thing that'll make you obliged to us for the rest of your life. But I think we'll raise enough to get you going again."

"Please, no," Frankie said.

"This your bright idea, Maggie?" Darryl asked. Every one of the crew—except Frankie—turned a hard stare at him. He backtracked. "I mean, it's a good idea. I just thought maybe we should kick in some extra for the guy burned in the fire out at Hayes's place. What do you think?"

Maggie's eyebrows took on a surprised arch.

"Wow! I think it's a great idea, Darryl. Good on you for thinking about him."

Nobody wanted to listen to Frankie's protests to leave her out. Good lord, what a fraud. Her co-workers insisted on treating her like a charity case when she had a job and money coming in. Once Grandma's house and estate got through probate, which should be in the next couple of months, she'd be well-off, comparatively speaking. Financially, things were just a little tight at the moment.

Frankie's phone jangled. Dr. Kelly was on the other end.

"Hello, Ms. McGill—Frankie. I thought you might like to know I met your policeman today. He showed up at my clinic first thing this morning before I got the overnighters checked and fed. He wanted to discuss the Smoke Signals spreadsheet."

Frankie couldn't tell if the veterinarian found this good or bad. "Did he agree with our summation?"

"Couldn't tell, but he asked good questions. And there was something else—"

"What?"

"Something he saw on the list, I think," Dr.

Kelly said. "I don't know what and didn't have the nerve to ask. Can you? Ask him, I mean."

Frankie didn't have to think. "I can try."

"And let me know what he says."

"Will do. If he says anything. I'm not exactly in the loop around here."

"Well, whatever you can discover."

One thing still puzzled Frankie when they hung up. Why were so many people calling Gabe Zantos hers, when the man was only being polite?

CHAPTER 21

After a fairly uneventful night, Frankie staggered out of bed around noon, feeling heavy and thick—like an overstuffed rag doll, if that made any sense. Heat in the upstairs bedroom had already built to a sweat-inducing degree. Sunlight poured in through the blinds. Perfect weather for cutting wheat or recreation on the lake, but not for daytime sleeping. She and the dogs beat it downstairs where a window AC blew cooler air.

As though she were peeking in the window waiting for the right moment, Jesselyn called just as Frankie poured her first cup of coffee, a liquid so stale and bitter she almost spit the first mouthful into the sink.

"Hiya, Jesselyn." She ran some tap water into the coffee to dilute it from pure mud to slurry.

"What's up?"

"Don't ask me what's up," Jesselyn screeched, almost deafening Frankie. "That's the question I'm asking you."

Frankie held the phone away from her ear. "Does this mean you heard about the excitement at the station the other night."

"Excitement! Is that what you call it?"

"I guess I could call it an attack by an armed man intent on killing someone—most likely me. Although by the way he was throwing bullets around, he didn't appear to care who got in the way."

Jesselyn gasped. "I must say you sound awfully calm about it. My God, Frankie, you could've been killed."

"I've been under fire before." Frankie couldn't quite keep the dryness out of her voice. "And this time no one got hurt. Well, glass cuts, but that's nothing. So I'm not going into hysterics." Besides, she had her little pocket pistol handy now. She didn't plan on going anywhere without it after this.

"Did anybody see the guy?" Jesselyn asked. "Can't any of you identify him?"

Frankie glugged a swig of coffee. "Not that I

know of, but I just got up. Maybe Maggie or Marc has thought of something. I hope so. Actually, I'm hoping the whole case has been solved by now. If so, nobody told has me."

What's more, the idea seemed doubtful. She stared out the window at Banner, cavorting in the yard with a ball in his mouth she figured Gabe had given him. Shine ran after him, yapping. At least someone is carefree, she thought sourly.

"One thing for sure," Jesselyn said, "nobody can point a finger at Matt this time. He was with me—all night."

To Frankie's ears, the all night part sounded a bit defensive. Hmm. Or maybe gloating. Not that she could blame Jesselyn. Who wants a boyfriend with the cops eagle-eyeing him every moment?

"Do tell. Speaking of which, are you ready to introduce me to Matt?" Frankie was trying to change the subject and lighten the moment. Thankfully, the ploy worked.

"You're going to meet him, all right." Jesselyn sounded resigned. "At the party the fire department is throwing for you on Friday night. He wants to meet you too, and says to save him a dance."

Frankie's eyes bugged. "He does? He did?"

"Yep. And Russ will just have to bite me."

"Good for you!"

Another thought struck Frankie, and she groaned. Dance? With her foot?

"You mean Maggie is going forward with the party? I thought I talked her out of it last night. Or at least persuaded her that the guy... um... the burned guy with the broken leg is in more need than I am." Dammit! Her memory let her down again. She couldn't remember the injured man's name.

"It's a nice gesture, you must admit."

"I guess. Embarrassing, though." Frankie was silent a moment, watching through the kitchen window as Shine followed Banner on a trip around the yard, both marking their territory.

"What does one wear to such a party? All I've got is jeans."

"Maybe Victoria could lend you a dress," Jesselyn offered on her sister's behalf. "You're about the same size."

Frankie recoiled. "No dresses. I don't wear dresses anymore."

"You don't?' Jesselyn sounded puzzled.

"Most dresses don't go well with sneakers or hiking boots." Frankie tried for deadpan.

She heard her friend's breath snag before Jesselyn said, "Oh, right. Gotcha. I'm sorry. I forgot your—" She started over. "Then jeans it is. And the royal blue top you bought is pretty enough for a party. Wear that."

"Okay." Frankie waited, certain Jess had more on her mind than what Frankie planned on wearing to a pity party.

She wasn't mistaken because Jesselyn sniffed and said, "So, is there any progress in finding the 'Hawkesford Murderer'?"

"Hawkesford Murderer?"

"That's what the local rag is calling him in a headline blazoned across the front page. Nice, huh?"

"Not to notice."

A second later, Jesselyn exploded. "What is Gabe Zantos doing, anyway? Sitting on his thumb? Hiding behind a billboard in his car with his eyes closed? Slinging mud at the wall to see what sticks?"

"No... I don't know." Wow. Frankie had been under the impression Jesselyn liked Gabe. She must really be upset.

"First, he gives Russ the third degree," Jess went on in a semi-shout, "dragging him in from the field and causing all the neighbors to look at him with their eyes crossed. Then, when Russ turns out to have a definite alibi for when the duplex was wired, Gabe calls Matt in. Matt has plenty of people to give him an alibi for Howie's murder, so that pretty much lets him off, but still. What's up with that? And I think the cops are still looking at Russ. This is ridiculous!"

"I'm glad Russ has an alibi for the explosion and Matt for the other. Honestly, Jesselyn, I think the police are looking at a single person guilty of all events. If Russ—and Matt—is clear for one, it stands to reason he's clear for everything." But I don't know that for a fact. Frankie took another sip of the wretched coffee, curiosity getting the better of her. "What is Russ's alibi?"

"The fire marshal figured out the duplex was rigged at the time of the field fire, and Russ was the guy on the tractor plowing a firebreak."

"Then he's being hailed as a hero." Frankie gave a sigh of relief on Jesselyn's behalf. "People are going to remember that a lot longer than they will hearing Gabe had a talk with him. Plowing that firebreak took a lot of courage."

"I know. And he was on the fire line for hours." For a moment, Jesselyn warmed—a break between meltdowns. "So what does Gabe have to say? Who else is on his list of suspects? And what put them there? What's the connection? C'mon, Frankie. Spill. You've gotta know what's going on."

"I don't. Honestly. I'm a paramedic, not a cop. And they—" She meant Gabe, of course. "—don't discuss cop stuff with me—with any of us fire department people. Not even after the station was targeted. I'm sorry." Moreover, she wasn't about to talk about anything with anybody without Gabe's say so. He'd made that abundantly clear.

"Sorry, sorry. You're living with the guy in charge, for Pete's sake. Don't you two talk?"

What was Jesselyn insinuating? Frankie frowned and came out whining. "I almost never see him, Jess. He's been working non-stop at finding the murderer, and when he's here, I'm not."

Usually. A breakfast and a certain wake-up from a nightmare surfaced in her memory.

"Well, corner him and ask," Jesselyn snapped, and hung up.

A lot of people had acquired a nasty habit of hanging up on her lately. She didn't much care for it.

***

As though bent on proving her a liar, Gabe drove up within ten minutes of Frankie telling Jesselyn she never saw him. He backed into the driveway and got out of the SUV. Even from a vantage point at the window, Frankie thought he looked positively hollow, his shirt rumpled, and his jaw stubbled.

Not enough sleep and too much stress. The kind of face she'd seen soldiers wear after too long on duty in Afghanistan. Hell, she'd worn that look herself. Nothing she could do about his weariness, but she doubted he'd been eating either. Rushing to the refrigerator, she dragged items to the counter. Tomatoes and lettuce grown in Gabe's own garden, bacon, cheese. Nothing like a nice thick BLT on rustic sourdough bread to fill a man up—and maybe soothe the savage beast.

Bacon sizzled in the microwave by the time he finished tossing the ball for Banner a half-dozen times. He stroked an ecstatically wiggling Shine and entered the house, his nose twitching as he caught the scent of bacon. Just like Banner and Shine's as they crowded in behind him.

"Breakfast or lunch?" he asked.

"Both." Frankie dealt bread onto the clean counter and sliced a huge purple-hued tomato, one being plenty for them both. "Are you a mayonnaise man or a salad dressing-er?"

His grin flashed. "A salad dressing-er, through and through."

"Me, too."

The microwave beeped. Frankie assembled several sandwiches under Gabe's watchful eye. He leaned against the counter out of her way while the dogs gamboled under her feet.

"Dr. Kelly called yesterday evening," she said. "She says you two talked. Did our ideas help?" Might as well ask flat out, she decided. Nothing to be gained by pussyfooting around.

"They did. Looks like you two have opened up a possible motive. I don't think it'll take long to trace where the list came from."

Frankie looked up from her sandwich building. "Oh?"

"Yeah. Those names you recognized? They belong to elderly people who've recently passed on. Not—" he hastened to assure her as, eyes widening, she gave a little jump. "—because of foul play, but from disease and old age. From there, it's pretty easy to track their caregivers. I've got someone on that now."

"So this is about blackmail, like Dr. Kelly and I suggested?"

"Seems likely, underlaid by insurance fraud, Medicare being the most predominant. All too common nowadays." He reached into the cupboard behind his head and got out a couple plates. "Those sandwiches look good."

He wanted to change the subject.

Frankie took the plates, but not the hint. "Dr. Kelly said you got something else from the list. Another tip-off. Care to share?"

"Your Dr. Kelly is pretty sharp. No. I don't think I do care to share. Not right now. But I can tell you this much. Our investigation is going to break wide open in the next few hours. Does that relieve your mind?"

"It does."

Or it did until he added, "But until that happens, don't go anywhere alone. And I want you to stay alert until I say different."

Frankie groaned. "Oh, great. Give with one hand and take away with the other."

"Just until the killer is actually arrested. Which will be soon. I'm sure of it."

"So who—"

His hand rose in a stop motion. "Don't ask. I can't say, just yet. But I mean it, Frankie. You take care."

He came across as dead serious, which did nothing to relieve her mind. "Bet on it."

Appetite destroyed, she put lunch on the table, and they sat down, Frankie with a dog on each side of her chair.

Gabe shook his head at the sight of her sharing out tiny bits of bacon from her sandwich. "Have you found a place to live that'll take Banner and Shine?"

Was Gabe hinting or what? He obviously wanted her and her menagerie out of the house and his life as soon as possible. And who could blame him? Guilt rolled over her like a heavy dark cloud. She oughta be searching for a house right this minute instead of sitting in her grandma's—make that Gabe's kitchen since he was the one paying the rent—eating lunch made from the food he'd paid for.

Stricken with embarrassment, she jumped up; her barely touched BLT forgotten. "Sorry. I'm on it. I'm sure I'll find something soon."

Gabe stared at her, his eyes dark. "I'm not

trying to throw you out, Frankie. It was just a question. Part of a conversation."

He'd read her reaction correctly.

"Sit down," he said. "Eat your lunch."

"You're sure?"

"I'm sure."

Slowly, she sat. Beside her, Banner laid his head on her knee. Her hand came up to pet him. "You must be sick of us being here."

"No, I'm not." He crunched bacon. "It's not like we're living in each other's pocket. When you're on shift, I'm off. For the most part, anyway. It works out. Take your time."

Frankie cocked her head. "You're serious?"

He sent another of those dark looks like maybe he was fighting against an eye roll. "If I change my mind, you'll be the first to know. Got it?"

"Got it. Thank you," she said, so overwhelmed by his consideration she could barely speak, let alone eat her lunch. "Thanks, Gabe."

Later, as she stood at the sink washing their few dishes and he, having worked the last twenty-four hours straight, toddled off to bed, his generosity kept playing through her mind. She couldn't help thinking altruism might not be his main focus, and there was one main reason why.

Even with her hands submerged in hot dishwater, a shiver of apprehension traveled up her spine.

Gabe doesn't really think the murders are sewed up. He wanted her where he could keep an eye on her. Why else warn her to remain on alert? To stick with other people?

He probably thought another murder would look bad on his record.

And one thing more.

"I'm a doof," she told Banner who lay on the kitchen rug with his head on his paws, watching her. "Yes, I am. Slow, slow, sloooow on the uptake." She had an urge to pound her head on the edge of the counter, see if it would knock some sense into it.

Gabe might have another reason for having her in his home beyond just keeping her out of the line of fire. He might be using her as a lure to draw the murderer out of hiding.

A lure?

Or a sacrificial goat?

Would he really do something like that without telling her? She didn't know him well enough to say. And what would she do if he did?

***

Maggie, waiting to get off shift, began talking the moment Frankie walked into the station at her habitual fifteen minutes until six. She hadn't been kidding when she told Lew she was never late. That first interview already seemed far away.

"The party is all set, Ms. Guest of Honor," Maggie announced, grinning. "I talked the local country music band into playing for the dance. High school kids, but they're pretty good, especially Karl's daughter who is the lead singer."

The garage door rising on its track interrupted them as the ambulance returned from a run. Frankie drew breath to speak, frowning as Lew and Chris stepped out.

Maggie smoothly cut her off. "The community center agreed to rent the hall for half the regular fee, and some of the fire auxiliary people are baking cookies and making punch and coffee. Starts at eight o'clock on Friday night. We're only going from eight until eleven since it's the middle of harvest," Maggie explained as if this were a fault, "but I figured what the heck. Even farmers need a little break at the end of the week. It's going to be fun. We haven't had a party since Lulu Wells's one hundred year birthday celebration in April. There'll be a good turn-out, you'll see."

If the force of Maggie's will had anything to do with it, Frankie figured that was true. She held up a stilling hand as Lew and Chris came to join them.

"Do not call me the guest of honor," Frankie said. "I refuse. The only way I'll support this fundraiser is if the burn victim is the recipient. The only recipient."

Maggie looked disappointed. "But we wanted to honor you, Frankie. Hawkesford's own returning war veteran and all."

Yeah. Wounded war veteran. Frankie's skin actually quivered with resentment. "I am not a victim." The denial came out a hiss, earning herself a sharp stare from Lew. Immediately regretting the attention, she softened her voice. "I mean it, Maggie. I have resources, you know. Truly, things may be tight until payday, but I'm not hurting. I don't need charity. Mr. Burn Victim does."

"He sure does," Chris said, coming to her rescue. "Hayes doesn't carry insurance on his guys, you know, and Larry Biggs hasn't been working for him long."

Maggie sagged, then she straightened and smiled. "I think you're just being stubborn, but oh, well, I can live with it. At least we're still having a party."

"For a good cause," Lew added. Half-turned from Maggie, he winked at Frankie.

Still disgruntled, she could only shake her head as she headed over to the lockers to stow her purse.

As usual, when he had a couple minutes before quitting time, Chris was already there, poking around at the back of his locker, clearing out before going home.

As she walked up, Frankie caught the flash of light on the blued barrel of a small semi-automatic weapon as he palmed it and stuck it in his pocket. Looked like Chris had begun carrying, too. She couldn't blame him. Surreptitiously, she touched a toe to the slight bulge of her own pocket pistol hidden beneath her loose uniform trousers.

How many others here were going armed after the attack the other night? Aside from Karl, that was, who had an old six-shooter in his desk drawer? Who in their right mind ever would've thought such a thing necessary in Hawkesford, of all places?

CHAPTER 22

Wednesday night into Thursday turned into a boring graveyard shift. Frankie's most strenuous effort consisted of talking to both Jesselyn and Susie Ray on the phone—one at a time, of course—and turning the pages of her book. Marc played games on a little old Nintendo-DS unit. Benton typed messages on his Facebook page from his laptop, keeping one eye on the dispatch monitor. Even he had only two calls between midnight and four o'clock, both of which he swiftly passed on to the State Police. Finally, just as dawn spread its first milky rays over the fields west of town, an EMS summons appeared on his board.

Benton hit their alert. Frankie, already watching the dispatcher, placed her bookmark between pages and jumped up. Only a couple seconds slower Marc dropped his game machine.

"I'm driving," he yelled.

"I am," Frankie replied.

They raced each other for the truck, Frankie, putting on a surprising turn of speed and amazing herself, gained the driver's seat first.

She grinned at Marc, who laughed back.

"No fair. You took a short cut. I'll get you next time."

Settling onto the rock-hard seat, it occurred to Frankie she not only hadn't stumbled with her foot in the hustle, she hadn't even thought about it. Progress.

As the garage door opened, Benton's voice came over the radio. "Destination—south of town on Leiderman Road, third farm on the left after the crossroad. Patient—Arne Birch, probable heart attack."

Marc settled into the passenger seat. "Old fella's on borrowed time. This isn't his first rodeo."

Frankie avoided waking the town to the sound of the siren, although as they neared the farm, she flipped it on.

Marc reached to shut the noise off. "What the heck?"

Frankie stopped him. "No. Leave it on. Victims often find the sound reassuring, knowing help is on the way," she explained. "It gives them a reason to hang on just a couple of minutes more."

Marc blinked as he absorbed the fact. "Huh."

Frankie smiled. For her part, she was relieved the location had come to her without conscious thought. No need to struggle remembering where to find the address. Yet another sign of progress.

Lights shone from the windows of a 1920s two-story farmhouse sadly in need of paint. A heavy-set woman in a faded bathrobe met them, hustling them and the gurney stacked with their equipment down a narrow, dark hall.

"This way." Only a trace of panic showed in her raspy voice.

Frankie, following her, caught a strong smell of cigarette smoke. No wonder she rasped.

"Are you Mrs. Birch?" Something about the name struck her, an elusive memory, but there wasn't time to dwell on it now.

The woman snorted. "How old do you think I am?"

Wisely, Frankie remained silent, rolling her eyes as she caught Marc's wink.

"Well, I can tell you I ain't that old," the woman said over her shoulder. "My name's Chloe Schimmer. I'm Arne's caretaker. I live here with him."

The little cavalcade ended up at the door of a grossly crowded bedroom. An oxygen tank stood beside the bed, a crank-up hospital type with the rental store's sticker on the foot-rail. A sit-down portable potty sat mere inches from the bed. A wizened old man lay propped against some pillows staring toward them out of rheumy, faded blue eyes. One shaking hand clutched at his chest.

"When did you notice Mr. Birch having trouble?" Frankie motioned Marc around to the other side of the bed. It left the near side with the oxygen tank to her.

Mrs. Schimmer leaned anxiously against the foot of the bed. "I heard him thrashing around about fifteen minutes ago and came to see if he needed help. He said not, but his color is bad, and he's having trouble breathing."

"I can talk for myself, Chloe," the old man said.

They leaned forward, into his whisper. Frankie got out her stethoscope, warmed it a second, and put it against his chest.

Damn.

"Like hell, Arne. You ain't got the strength God gave a mouse." Despite Chloe's rude words, Frankie had an idea the woman truly cared for the old man.

Ignoring her, he looked up at Frankie. "My chest hurts. Feels like Chloe is sitting on it."

Chloe ignored the implied slur on her weight. "You're having a heart attack, you old fool. You need to go to the hospital and have the doctors take a look at you."

Frankie agreed with the caregiver. Sweat rolled down Mr. Birch's face; his skin grayed like old fireplace ash.

While Marc took vitals and started the IV, she made certain air was coming through the tube into his nose, cranking it up a bit to increase the flow. Frankie got on the radio to the medical center and reported, receiving instructions to bring the patient in STAT.

Chloe smirked, as though vindicated. "Told you so."

"Will you follow us to the hospital?" Frankie asked. Mrs. Schimmer had her back turned as she rummaged in a messy closet.

"Not me." The woman handed over a packed duffle bag. "Here's Arne's stuff. There's an envelope right on top. It tells you all the medications he's taking along with his medical history and his directive. I'll call his son. He lives in Coeur d'Alene. I expect he'll meet you at the hospital."

The woman's preparation impressed Frankie.

"This ain't the first time Arne and me been through this. Got 'er down pat." Echoing Marc's earlier diagnosis, Chloe made as if to glare at the old man, but her eyes swam with unshed tears.

Frankie and Marc loaded Mr. Birch onto the gurney. The poor old fellow couldn't have weighed more than one twenty-five.

"Don't you worry none," he quavered to his caregiver. "You won't be out of a job. I'll be back before you know it."

"I know you will." Appearing rather lost, Mrs. Schimmer nodded as Frankie and Marc wheeled their patient out.

Marc drove. Frankie sat with the patient in the back of the ambulance, monitoring equipment. The old man seemed more comfortable now, his clenched hands relaxing.

She smiled down at him. "All right, Mr. Birch?"

"Fine." Of course, he wasn't.

Frankie got out the envelope with his medical history and list of pharmaceutical needs, scanning it quickly. The meds were all familiar, no surprise for a man with a history of heart disease. A long history, as it happened. Arne'd already had two previous emergency runs to the hospital this year. Chloe's list included a roster of his physicians. His regular seemed to be Doctor Cloudet, a Spokane internist with a specialty in geriatric heart patients. The only other mentioned was Dr. Muncie.

Given the nudge, as she slipped the notes back in the envelope, her patient's name finally penetrated the fogs of her memory. Arne Birch was one of the names on the Smoke Signals list. Only while most of the other people whose names she'd recognized were all dead, this one was still alive. So far.

She glanced at Mr. Birch, whose eyes were closed. He seemed to be asleep, his chest rising with a breath, then shuddering its way back down.

Retreating to the back of the ambulance, she got out her cell phone. After three rings, Gabe picked up.

" 'Lo."

"Smoke Signals, have you found out who the list belongs to yet?"

A pause. She heard the bed frame squeak as if he were sitting up. "Frankie? Is that you? What are you doing calling me at five o'clock in the morning."

Her shoulders hunched. Oopsie. He sounded a little crotchety—No, He sounded a lot crotchety. "I'm sorry to wake you. It's just that we got called out a while ago to an elderly gentleman named Arne Birch. His name ring any bells with you?"

The bed frame, at least, she assumed it was the bed frame, squeaked again. "It does," he said slowly. "You mean he's still alive?"

Was that surprise she heard?

She glanced at her patient. "So far, yes. But…" She left it there, unwilling to say more for fear the old man would overhear.

Gabe seemed fully awake now. "What does this have to do with Smoke Signals."

"I have in my hand a list of Mr. Birch's physicians. All two of them."

Oh, yes. Gabe was definitely awake. "And?"

"A Dr. Phillip Cloudet and Dr. Ned Muncie."

She heard his breath go out.

"I'm on it," he said and hung up.

Frankie blinked down at her phone. One of these days, she was going to hang up on somebody—anybody—just to see how it felt.

***

As promised, Gabe was up and gone when Frankie got home. The house sat silent and a little lonely, except for Banner and Shine who came to greet her with tails wagging like windshield wipers in a cloudburst. The kitchen smelled of coffee, and when she felt of the carafe, she found it still warm to the touch. A note scrawled in Gabe's strong handwriting lay on the table.

Did I remember to tell you, Good Work?

No. He hadn't.

The note said something else. Save me a slow dance.

Frankie smiled. Then frowned. Save him a dance? She didn't dance. With her clumsy foot?

But as she washed her face and donned shorts and a T-shirt before bed, she remembered the physical therapy tech saying she could do anything while wearing the prosthesis that she'd done before. Run, hike, climb—dance. She just needed the confidence to try these things, and enough practice to master the activity.

She dreamed of waltzing in a princess-like setting and racing down the dance floor with the intricate footwork of a quick step. In the dream, both feet were perfect. She wore high-heeled sandals and a short, twirly green skirt made of gossamer lace. Her partner, matching her step-for-step, wore Gabe's face.

Fat chance.

She'd never danced a quick step in her life.

***

Maggie's benefit party for Larry Biggs was in full swing. The high school kids and their country rock band sounded pretty darn good, belting out a mixture of new stuff and old standards. Karl's daughter stood a chance of making a career choice in music if tonight's performance was any indication. Americas Got Talent or The Voice was mentioned more than once.

Frankie, wearing fancy jeans, the blue blouse Jesselyn had chosen, and an ordinary pair of shoes, heard a low-voiced argument break out between two farm wives over which program found the superior talent.

Somebody—more of Maggie's doing, no doubt—had decorated the community center with paper streamers and colorful tablecloths. Platters of home-baked cookies, a never-empty coffee urn, and a clear plastic bowlful of bilious green punch furnished refreshment. Only the younger kids had enough nerve to try the punch. Anyone over the age of ten gave it a wide berth, preferring to bring in their own cans of soft drinks. Frankie suspected a few were spiked with something a little stronger than Pepsi or Mountain Dew. A clear jar stuffed to the point of overflowing with currency, fives, tens, twenties, sat at the end of the table. The burned man was going to be very relieved.

So far, Frankie had managed to maneuver around the hardwood floor at least a dozen times without stumbling. Maybe because, just for tonight, she left off the ankle holster. One of those dances was with Matt Chavez, whom Jesselyn introduced to her at last. Matt, blue-eyed but with a dark Hispanic complexion to match his ebony hair, was lean and lanky and totally not what she expected. He started their conversation with intelligent questions about Afghanistan culture and edged in a mention of the murders—in a general sort of way.

"Jesselyn tells me you moved into Denise Rider's duplex at her instigation." Matt guided her to the right, barely avoiding a couple involved in a slow dance. "She feels bad about what's happened."

"Me too. Believe me, I've rued the day I ever saw that place, especially when it blew up around me."

He gave a snort. "I can imagine."

"You knew her—Denise—didn't you?" Frankie watched his face.

Matt nodded. "I went out with her for a while—a lady with expensive tastes. I got lucky. She dumped me," he admitted with no apparent rancor.

"Did you know Howie St. James, too?"

"Sure. Everybody knew Howie. It's hard to believe anyone considered him a threat. He always struck me as an innocent."

"An innocent?"

Matt gave her an easy twirl. "Yeah. Not too smart, but always his own worst enemy."

His opinion exactly matched Frankie's. Dropping the subject, Matt ended up raving about Jesselyn. Frankie decided she liked him.

She danced the next couple of tunes with Lake people who'd turned out in number to support the cause. To Frankie's own surprise, she was having fun.

The only disappointing aspect of the evening was the promised slow dance with Gabe. Apparently, it wasn't going to happen since he hadn't as yet put in an appearance. With most of the EMS group rotating attendance, so no one entirely missed the party, she knew there'd been no new emergency to demand his presence. Today was his scheduled day off—so where was he? One thing for damn sure. She didn't plan on calling him to ask. No, siree.

Jesselyn, perched at Frankie's side on one of the folding chairs lining the curved Quonset hut walls, sipped from a Pepsi can that emitted a strong odor of bourbon. Her eyes followed Matt, circumspectly two-stepping with one of his co-workers.

"He's nice, your Matt Chavez." Frankie nudged Jesselyn in the ribs. "Why didn't you want to introduce us before?"

"I don't know. I guess I was afraid you'd think he was another of my loser boyfriends." Jesselyn sighed. "I have a kind of reputation for picking bad boys. But he's not a bad boy, regardless of his jail time. And he's not a loser."

"I can tell." Frankie didn't even try to prevent the little smirk curling up the corners of her mouth.

Jesselyn wiggled in her seat. "Talk about me,

what about the way you keep watching the door? Expecting someone?"

Frankie hoped the room was dark enough to hide the tell-tale flush she felt burning over her cheekbones. "Who me? No. What makes you think I'm expecting anyone?" Bad enough getting stood up. No need to let everybody know.

Jesselyn rolled her eyes in a "gimme a break" look. "Pretty obvious. And unless you've met someone I don't know about, it must be either Gabe Zantos, Chris What's-His-Name, or Lenny Ludiker."

"Lenny who?"

"Guess it's not him." Jesselyn grinned. "Bet it's not Chris What's-His-Name, either."

Jesselyn saw too much.

"Atkins," Frankie said as if she hadn't caught any of the other names. "Chris Atkins."

Of course, Gabe chose that moment to put in an appearance. Jesselyn leered. "As if you even care what his name is."

"Right." Frankie watched as Gabe surveyed the room from the doorway before heading toward her. She barely heard Jesselyn's laugh, was unaware as her friend got up and moved away.

A trill of excitement touched her as Gabe approached. He looked tired and a little worn, but something more, too, like a weight had been taken off his shoulders. His smile down at her was easy.

He stopped in front of her. "Ready for that dance?"

Frankie peered up at him, tuning out everything else going on around them. Music, motion, too many people talking at once—it all evaporated.

"If you don't mind having your toes stepped on. Literally, I mean."

He laughed and held his hand out to her. Taking a deep breath, she rose, aware of Karl's daughter crooning a love song perfect for the promised slow dance.

"I've got some good news," Gabe said as she moved into his arms. "We arrested Dr. Muncie early this evening. It's taken this long to get him booked into the county jail."

They glided smoothly over the dance floor, steps melding, fitting together like sugar and spice. It should've been romantic. Should've.

"The charges?"

"Fraud, to begin with. Your Mr. Birch provided critical information. A search warrant allowed access to Muncie's records. We also found a second set of books. We got him."

Fraud was good, but it wasn't foremost on Frankie's mind. "What about the murders? What about the explosion and the attack at the station? Those too?"

"He's been charged." Gabe hesitated. "Evidence is not so cut and dried there, but we're still looking. Turns out Denise worked for him at one time. They had an affair, but then the doc got tired of her. He found another babe and fired Denise. Evidently, she'd seen the handwriting on the wall and guessed the split was coming. She managed to get the goods on the doc and tried a spot of blackmail. His motive is solid."

Frankie sensed something lacking. "But?"

They'd almost managed a full circuit of the floor without Frankie stumbling even once, or having been guilty of stepping on his toes. Gabe was a good leader.

He shrugged. "A few loose ends. We still need to find the gun. Check an alibi. That sort of thing. Don't worry. We've got the right man."

As they neared the door leading to the parking lot, a commotion stirred through a small group of smokers standing outside puffing on cigarettes. Frankie peered over the top of Gabe's shoulder and saw a woman push another woman aside as if batting at flies. The yard light glinted off a flash of diamonds.

"Look out," she breathed. "Incoming."

Before Gabe could ask what she meant, Mrs. Ned Muncie—No, make that Alexis Barwick—strode into the hall, her eyes like a pair of heat-seeking missiles boring down on Gabe.

"You," the woman hissed. She grabbed Gabe's arm and, ignoring Frankie as though she were invisible, wrenched him around. "You miserable, stupid son-of-a-bitch. What do you think you're doing? You won't get away with arresting my husband. He's an important man. I'm telling you."

The couples nearest them halted mid-step, their attention riveted on Alexis. As though on cue, the music died. Those talking hushed in mid-sentence.

Frankie, her hand still on Gabe's shoulder, felt his muscles tighten into clumps like frozen earth. Still, he answered coolly enough. "Your husband's arrest is based on the available evidence, Ms. Barwick. Just doing my job."

"Your job." It sounded more like a mama wolf's growl than actual words. "Your freaking job! We'll see what kind of job you can get after I'm done with you."

"Are you threatening me, ma'am?"

"You bet I am," Ms. Barwick snarled.

"I'd like to point out there are a good many witnesses," Frankie cut in, even though she knew better.

Alexis Barwick ignored her, a mere gnat on the bug screen. Actually, Gabe did the same, his focus all on Dr. Muncie's famous wife.

"I'll have my husband out of your filthy jail tonight. I'm warning you, keep your hands off him. I won't tolerate it." The woman's heavily made-up eyes bulged. It was eerie as if no one but she and Gabe were there.

"Or?" It seemed to Frankie that Gabe almost smiled.

"You'll see." Alexis took a breath. Her apparent case of tunnel vision lifted and she fixed on Frankie. "Or maybe this slut will see."

Frankie's eyes narrowed. Her heartbeat revved up a notch.

"I think you'd better leave, Ms. Barwick." Gabe moved in front of Frankie. "Before you say something you'll regret. Your husband will be arraigned Monday. You can say your piece to the judge."

Alexis's nose pinched with the breath she took. "Oh, you can bet I will." She whirled, tilting a little on her stiletto heels, and rushed out of the hall as swiftly as she'd entered.

"Wow," Frankie said.

So much for her slow dance.

CHAPTER 23

Gabe was still absent the next morning when Frankie climbed out of bed, fumbling her way from between two dogs. Gabe had left immediately after the confrontation with Ms. Barwick at the dance, going back to work collating facts and evidence against Dr. Muncie. Frankie hadn't heard a word from him since.

She understood. He didn't want any loose ends fouling the investigation at this late date. She didn't want any either. The sooner the case was cleared up, the sooner she could resume a normal life.

All of which, home alone after the party last night, caused her to wander the house for an hour, speculating on whether he showed up at the benefit just to dance with her. Nah, she decided finally. Couldn't be. But then why—

This was a new day. Putting coffee on to brew, Frankie took the dogs out for their morning pee and territorial marking. While they cavorted on the grass, darting from sunlight into shade, she watched two hummingbirds fluttering in a fragrant purple butterfly bush. She noticed her grandma's roses had a new flush of blooms—and she spied three bullet holes in the big old dog house located beneath the spreading branches of a massive spruce tree.

Bullet holes that hadn't been there yesterday.

"Crap." It came out a squeak.

Standing back, she walked a cautious circuit around the doghouse. No tracks, no sign of boo-by-traps, no brass spun out from the potshots. Just the holes. The angle of fire suggested the person had stood at the street—or maybe sat in a car—and shot toward the property at random. The bullets had passed through the wood, gone who knows where.

Since no one called into EMS with gunshot wounds, it appeared the doghouse was the only victim.

If this was Alexis Barwick's idea of following through on her threat to the "slut," she hadn't done her homework. She must not know Frankie kept her dogs inside.

Which is, Frankie huffed to herself, where they'll stay until this is over.

Her temper boiled with rage, even as her heart jumped with apprehension. Yet she couldn't help feeling a bit of scorn along with everything else. This had been a stupid move, vindictive and childish. Odd behavior, she couldn't help thinking, for a woman with Alexis Barwick's reputation of sophisticated shrewdness. The attorney's actions last night must be an aberration.

Once the thought got in her mind, Frankie couldn't get it out. Dr. Muncie's fraudulent billing of insurance companies made sense. Well, it didn't, but it was a so-called non-violent, supposedly victimless crime. Of course, with Denise blackmailing him, she may have pushed him too far. But all the way into murder?

Frankie's thoughts ran like a gerbil on a treadmill. What about Howie? Would a man like Dr. Muncie go after a semi-alcoholic like Howie just because he happened to live next to Denise? Maybe even run Howie down? Why attack me, when I moved into the place? I never even met Denise.

A sensation of cold shook through her even though the sun beat down on her head. The day promised to be another scorcher in a whole string of scorchers.

"Banner, Shine, come." Calling the dogs into the house, Frankie poured herself a cup of coffee and stood staring out the kitchen window into the glorious summer day. One thing for sure, whoever shot the doghouse full of holes, it hadn't been Dr. Muncie.

Was Gabe positive he had the right man? Because Frankie couldn't get the memory of those size twelve hiking boots prints out of her head. Boots that didn't fit with Dr. Muncie, neither his size nor his style—just one inconsistency among several. Here was another: how could Dr. Muncie know where she was living now, or even that she had dogs? For that matter, how could his wife? Because it was a lead pipe cinch, he hadn't been doing any shooting last night.

"Oh, lord," she told Banner, who pricked his ears and came to stand at her side. "He's going to hate me for sure." She sat the coffee cup down with a clink.

Banner cocked his head, his almond-shaped eyes wide with questions. Like maybe, what did she mean. There could be only one.

Picking up the phone, she dialed.

Spoke.

Got hung up on.

Again.

She no more than clicked off from speaking with Gabe when, ears still burning, her phone rang again. It was Maggie.

"Hey, girl!" Maggie burbled. "Was that one heck of a party or what?"

Frankie couldn't help it. She laughed. Which after Gabe's cool reception, felt warming. "That may depend on which part you're talking about."

Maggie laughed too, not even pretending to misunderstand. "Both. Number one, we raised $1208.00 for our recipient, so as a fundraiser I consider it a rousing success. Then at the end, well, there were some pretty entertaining elements with Alexis Barwick's meltdown. Poor Gabe, though. Has he recovered?"

Safe where Maggie couldn't see her, Frankie made a face at the phone. If that wasn't a leading question, she'd never heard one.

"I don't know." She chose her words carefully. "I haven't seen him since he followed Ms. Barwick out. I think he probably worked through the night."

Think? She knew he had, and as far as being poor Gabe, when she talked to him a few minutes ago, he appeared to have taken a page out of Barwick's book. Fact of the matter is, he'd gone off like an IED when she told him about the dog house. And the reminder of those size twelve boots definitely went unappreciated.

"Really?" Maggie said. "I thought when he showed up just before the dance was over that you two, well, maybe you...um—"

"No."

"No? Well, I guess he has been pretty busy. Now he's caught Howie and Denise's killer, maybe he can slow down. You must be relieved, too. It's hard to believe Dr. Muncie would deliberately kill anyone, isn't it? I mean, a totally respected, big-wheel physician like him? He's taken an oath to save lives. And he never came across as a violent person."

"Do you know him?" Frankie asked.

"Not exactly. Met him, not to say know him. I expect I'm no more than a voice on the phone, not that he thinks of me as a real person. He's quite the hand with women, though, or so I hear. His preference seems to be the young married ones—or is when he comes to our parties at the community center. I don't know if you noticed last night, but a bunch of people who live down at the lake attended. They always do."

"Like hobnobbing with the great unwashed, do they?"

Maggie snorted. "The great unwashed, my foot! What drivel have you been reading?"

In truth, Frankie had noticed the summer people during Alexis's diatribe against Gabe. She'd heard one women whisper, "Ned seems to have been a bad boy," to which another replied, "Can you blame him, married to Alexis? Serves her right if he's in trouble."

Evidently, the attorney was not a popular figure with anybody. Not even her neighbors. Maybe everybody came in for the edge of her tongue upon occasion.

"Anyway," Maggie said, "I wanted to let you know about the party." She paused. "Wait a sec."

Frankie was pretty sure the purpose of this call was to see what she could find out about Gabe and the murders. A report of the dollars donated was an excuse.

Mixed up in the background noise coming over the phone, she listened to Maggie speaking to someone. Soon a siren began wailing, an emergency in progress.

Her phone went dead, although the wail went on. Even from the distance of her post inside the house, Frankie heard the heavy fire truck's rumble as it gained speed, heading south on the highway.

Banner accompanied the noise by lifting his snout and yodeling along with it. Shine stared at him in wonder, all of which cracked Frankie up. Her laugh of the day.

***

Gabe drove up shortly before noon, backed his SUV into its accustomed spot in the driveway, and got out, slamming the door. His feet clumped across the porch.

Banner and Shine ran to greet him, but even their cheerful attention couldn't pierce his gloom.

"Stay down," he told Shine brusquely when she set a foot on his shin. Tail tucked, she backed away.

Frankie, anxious to learn the latest and following right on the dogs' heels, winced and retreated right along with the dogs. Gabe's bad mood meant only one thing. His case was falling apart.

And he positively drooped with exhaustion, like guys in the unit used to when they came in off a long, dangerous patrol.

"You look like you could use a beer," she said. "Or a shot of Maker's Mark. Unless it's too early for alcohol."

"Not as far as I'm concerned. I'll take a beer if you're offering. I'm dry." Unbuckling his gun belt, he placed it, along with his Glock, inside her grandma's old wooden sewing box and closed the lid. The box, with a rack for spools of thread and cubbies for scissors and the like, had sat beside her grandmother's TV-watching chair for as long as Frankie could remember. Now it served as an end table to Gabe's leather recliner and a repository for his weapon. Gran would laugh at the use he made of it.

Seeing Frankie's amused expression, he huffed. "What? It's a good spot. Out of sight, but handy. Not too many people expect to find a gun in a sewing basket."

"True." Snickering to herself, she went into the kitchen to fetch his beer. When she came out again, he was fussing over the dogs. Apologizing.

"You're not drinking?" Gabe took the icy bottle and chugged a couple large gulps.

She waved her glass, ice cubes rattling. "Peach ice tea. I'm working tonight."

Gabe looked at his bottle, magically more than half-gone. "Me too. But not for a while. I'm gonna need another of these."

Hint, hint. Like a good soldier, she retraced her steps to the kitchen. When she returned, the room was empty. Hearing him stirring around in the bedroom just off the parlor, she disposed of the now-empty beer bottle and sat the fresh one in its place. Then, quietly, she took a seat on the couch and waited. A few seconds later he was back, clad now in Levis and a T-shirt, twin to the one she'd stolen to sleep in a few days earlier.

He sat in the recliner, popped up the footrest, and leaned back. Shine leaped onto his lap and Banner pressed against his knees. All forgiven.

"Is there any point in me going out to look at holes in an old doghouse?" he asked wearily.

"Probably not. The bullets passed through and ended up somewhere in the field out back. And I suspect whoever did the shooting was in a car, so there's no brass left behind."

Gabe reached for his beer. His mouth opened in a yawn wide enough to break most people's jaw. "Mind telling me how you deduced this?"

Deduced. He sounded like a minor league Sherlock Holmes.

"I've seen bullet holes before. Quite often." An understatement. Frankie sipped her tea. "Being able to judge the angle of fire helps evade snipers. As for the brass, I looked. Didn't find anything."

"Lacking the manpower for a full-out search for bullets, I expect you've done as well as any other investigator." His eyes closed.

He wasn't going to sleep on her, was he?

"Did you have to turn him loose?" She meant Dr. Muncie, of course.

Gabe's eyes opened. "Not yet. We're not charging him with murder, though. So far. You were right about the footprints and the shoes. He wears a size nine. More importantly, he's got an alibi for two of the charges against him, including one for setting the booby trap at the duplex. The fire marshal figured that must've taken place while people were at the field fire."

She already knew that. "Was the fire deliberately set?"

"Yes. The sabotaged combine started it going. The whole scenario was probably caused, so somebody could wire the duplex to blow. Good thinking, since the fire drew almost everybody out to the field to watch. But Muncie was in the operating room at the time of the fire and had been for three hours. Plus, on the night the station was shot up, he was at a Rotary Club meeting giving a speech. He went on late, and he stayed the night in Spokane. Lots of witnesses."

"I'm not surprised. Anyway, what happened at the station or at the duplex doesn't strike me as being his kind of thing."

His lips twitched. "But murder does?"

"Oh, yes. Could be." Frankie twirled her glass, condensation making it slippery. "Doctors see a lot of death and dying. After a while, it doesn't scare them much."

Gabe's dark eyes bored into hers. "Does it scare you, Frankie?"

"Some. Probably not like it does Jesselyn or Maggie—or even you." She didn't look away. "But murder does. The cruelty of it. The waste."

He nodded.

"So—" She sat up very straight. "—you're letting the doctor go?"

"Not a chance. He may not be a murderer, but he's sure in hell guilty of insurance fraud."

"Have you told him you're dropping the murder charge?"

He shook his head. "We're keeping the news quiet as long as we can. Gives us time to look into other possibilities. Makes it a little easier for people to talk if they think the case is wrapped up."

"Easier?"

"Careless might be a better word. Makes them careless. Anyway, we're holding him for arraignment on multiple charges. They just don't include murder."

"Won't Ms. Barwick post bail? I'm surprised she hasn't managed to have him released before now, what with all the judges and important people she keeps telling us about. You know, the ones standing in line to do her bidding?" Frankie failed to hide her dislike of the attorney. "I don't think it would matter to her if her husband had murdered two people. She'd be right in there, covering up for him. And meanwhile, who did murder them?"

Gabe's grin faded. He sat, as if frozen, his hand buried in Shine's soft, curly hair. A minute ticked past. Suddenly, he released the recliner's footrest handle and stood up, barely saving the bichon from being dumped on the floor. Sweeping his half-empty beer aside, he opened the sewing box, rooted out his holstered Glock and buckled it on.

Frankie set her glass on the table with a snap. "Was it something I said?"

"It does make you wonder, doesn't it?" Bending over, he kissed her hard on the lips.

She spared a moment to savor his kiss. Regaining her senses, though still bewildered, she asked, "What does?"

Already halfway to the front door, he paused, looking at her over his shoulder. "If Alexis is willing to overlook her husband's affairs with other women, it makes me, for one, wonder what else she'll overlook." His eyes narrowed. "And what she won't."

CHAPTER 24

If someone—anyone—had called and volunteered to pay her a dollar to stay home from work, Frankie would've taken it and flopped right down on her bed. Tired to the bone, she'd been in Hawkesford only a little over two weeks and already endured more excitement than her poor wounded brain cared to process. Murder, explosions, ambushes. War on the home front. Who'd ever think of this kind of crap going on in a little burg like her own hometown? And now, here they were back to square one, or so it appeared.

But of course, nobody volunteered the dollar, so Frankie parked her Ranger in back of the station, at exactly five-forty-five p.m., ready for work. Her blue uniform shirt was crisply ironed, her britches smartly creased, her shoes, one hiding the prosthesis, clean and polished.

Ditto the Smith and Wesson Airweight revolver hidden beneath her pant leg. Clean and polished, that is. Also loaded. Given Gabe's reaction, he must be on to something new. He hadn't told her, but she wasn't about to go unarmed. Not with shots wantonly fired into the station. Not to mention the doghouse at home.

Maggie, on duty for another fifteen minutes, greeted her cheerfully. Karl, sitting in his office, looked up from the stack of paperwork spread on his desk and waved. Darryl and another volunteer fireman who sat hunched over a hand of cards in the corner nodded. Lew, busy washing dust and wheat chaff from the ambulance headlights, saluted a greeting, and Chris, knowing quitting time was nigh, headed for his locker.

"Another farm accident?" Frankie asked Lew, gesturing to the dirty rag he used to scrub the bug-splattered headlights. Chaff glued to the dead bodies made the insects look like they'd sprouted hair.

He shook out his cloth. "Not an accident. Just a case of heat exhaustion, dehydration. The victim is a fellow the unemployment office sent over to drive a truck for Herb Maher. The idiot forgot to bring water out to the field. Somebody should've told him farmers don't stop for regular breaks, no matter if it is nearly a hundred degrees in the shade. His own damn fault."

Frankie remembered being a newbie in the desert. "The boss should've told him. That's part of a leader's responsibility."

"This ain't the frickin' army."

Obviously, Lew wasn't in the best of moods. Made her glad Marc was her partner now.

Mouth compressed to silence a sharp reply, Frankie headed toward the lockers to stow her purse. Chris chose that moment to slam his locker door shut, giving it one last metal-bending blow with his fist. He turned his back on her, a sure sign of his state of mind.

"Damn Lew," he muttered under his breath, but loud enough for her to hear. He shook his hand out.

"What did Lew do?"

"Chewed my ass 'cause I missed inserting an IV port. Twice. Not my fault the guy's vein collapsed."

"Awkward," she muttered back.

She beat a hasty retreat, having no desire to

mix in a quarrel between Lew and Chris, especially one in which she'd no doubt end up siding with Lew. Not that he'd care, one way or another.

Besides, going by the vigorous head motions and screwy faces Maggie was making she had news, and from the way she acted, it was for Frankie's ears alone. Trying to be inconspicuous, Frankie ambled over to Maggie's desk.

"Did you know Gabe is calling in everyone who might've had a reason to kill Denise? You know, the guys she dumped?" Her whisper would've penetrated a steel bank vault. "He wants to question them all again."

Frankie shook her head. "News to me," she lied. "Does this mean Dr. Muncie didn't murder Denise or Howie?" She was interested to hear what the others thought about this development.

Maggie's whisper dropped lower. "I think it might. Dr. Muncie is still in jail, though. Ms. Barwick has called here five times this afternoon, and if I weren't so tactful, my butt would be gnawed plumb off by now."

"Ouch."

"You can say that again. But Gabe is in Coeur d'Alene, and he's got Rudy Swallowtail gathering our local guys. Russ Pettigrew, Matt Chavez, even Marc and Chris have summons."

Frankie shook her head. "I guess that explains why Chris is so surly." She'd be willing to bet Jesselyn was fit to be tied, too. Brother and boyfriend. Double whammy. As for Marc, well, the new call explained why it was six o'clock, and he hadn't shown up for work.

"Dang." Her heart sank. "So the investigation is right back where it started."

"Looks like."

Ashley Harcourt arrived just then to take over dispatch duty from Maggie. Frankie hadn't met her before and wasn't impressed. Maggie informed her, sotto voce, the girl was putting in time before her sophomore year at the University of Idaho, earning brownie points for some sorority she wanted to join. Ashley sat in Maggie's chair and, pulling a bottle of sparkly green Kermit the Frog nail polish from her bag, began painting her fingernails, basically ignoring everyone but Karl.

Maybe, Frankie decided, the girl was shy. But she doubted it.

The question of overtime came up as day shift ended, two EMTs being required on duty at a time. Chris slumped out the door to his meeting with Gabe like a revolutionary to the guillotine, still muttering about Lew. Darryl gave him a 'thumbs up' as he, too, left.

Maggie called, "Don't worry, Chris. It'll be okay."

Chris didn't reply.

"Sour grapes," Maggie said knowingly. "He doesn't like being chewed out. He'd better put on a cheerier face for the detectives, or they'll throw him in the slammer just because."

"I'll stay until Marc shows up." Lew lounged in his chair and fiddled with a pen. "Looks like it's a good thing I never dated this Denise character. Looks like everybody else in town has."

The assistant fire chief and two new volunteers took over for Karl and his group. An hour into the shift, Marc arrived, lacking his usual good cheer. His closed expression warned anyone who wanted to ask questions they'd better lay off. Frankie couldn't blame him.

Soon after he arrived, the team was called out for a kitchen fire—a farmer in late from the field and his supper left cooking on the stove.

Frankie thought the "accident" might've been deliberate. Could be the Mrs. was just sick of the boring summer routine. At any rate, there was no damage to speak of except for a smoked wall and ceiling, and nobody inhaled any toxic fumes. The crew pulled back into the station within a half-hour.

Nobody called while they were gone, Ashley reported. From crew's raised eyebrows, no one was sure what she would've done if there had been an emergency.

At ten o'clock, the fire crew went home, on call in case of trouble, and the big garage doors came down. Which made the station's interior even more stifling. Marc's continued moroseness, and the way the self-absorbed Ashley ignored everyone else got on Frankie's nerves. She stepped outside.

"Hot tonight," Marc roused himself to say as she went out. "Why don't you leave the front door open?" He seemed to have forgotten the station being shot up only a few days ago, and the standing order to lock up after dark.

"Looks like another storm is brewing." With a view to keeping him happy, she propped the door with a cow-plop sized rock left there for the purpose. Staying away from the lighted windows, she moved into the shadows at the side of the building.

A rising wind stirred her short hair. She

pointed her nose into it, clearing the fumes of diesel-laden air from her head. The stench was always present in a building where motor vehicles idled.

The wind smelled of dust, of wheat, and of the lone old giant pine tree standing sentinel over the hardware store across the street. And it smelled of rain. Looking north, Frankie saw a semi's headlights break over the hill as it followed the highway into town. A streak of lightning lit the sky behind it. She felt no premonition of danger like she'd sometimes had in Afghanistan.

Her peace shattered as the alarm went off. Ashley, either ignoring or forgetting procedure, yelled for the EMTS. Frankie ran to join Marc.

"Radio us the location," Marc yelled to Ashley over his shoulder. He strode toward the ambulance. Hitting the button to run up the overhead garage door, he climbed into the driver's seat.

His decision suited Frankie fine. Somewhat to her surprise, Ashley calmed right down and was already on the radio, repeating information as they pulled out.

"Car reportedly hit a tree head-on three and a half miles north of Hawkesford. The caller says a woman is slumped over the steering wheel and isn't moving. He says he thinks she's badly hurt."

Light's flashing, Marc hit the gas, skidding out onto the road. Soon they were speeding along the dark road. He didn't slow down until they reached the three and a quarter mile mark. Wind blew a tumbleweed across the road in front of them, then another. Animal eyes gleamed iridescent as their headlights touched them. A deer. Two, their shadowed forms leaping high.

"There." Frankie pointed off to the right.

"I see it." Marc swerved to the side of the highway and stopped. A few feet off the road, an old Chevy Cavalier nosed up against a tree. Under the swirling flash of their overheads,

Frankie spied a form draped over the steering wheel. Just as reported. No one else was present. Whoever called the accident in hadn't waited for them to arrive. Odd.

While Marc set flares on either end of the bus, Frankie sped around to the back and retrieved the medical bag. Scrambling up a slight slope, they crashed through weeds and some low bushes to approach the car from the rear.

Frankie's headache flared. She stopped suddenly. "Wait." She reached out, catching Marc's arm and drawing him back.

"What?"

"Something's wrong. Look. The car isn't touching that tree. This isn't a wreck." She glanced around. "And where's the person who called it in? He should be here."

"Are you crazy?" Marc pulled against her. "Listen. You can hear the wind whistling through the broken windows."

"But there's no glass on the ground. This scene has been staged." Frankie's heart raced. She knew a set-up when she saw one. "Let's get out of here."

"But the patient—"

Frankie spun, searching the night for an enemy she sensed beyond the lights, watching them argue. "There is no patient, Marc. Just an old coat thrown over the steering wheel. C'mon."

Squinted toward the wreck, Marc didn't budge. "Shit." He turned around and stared at her. "You're right. Not very damn funny if you ask m—"

A sharp crack sounded from behind the car.

Frankie jerked, spotting a muzzle flash from some bushes. But it was Marc who fell to the ground. His sentence collapsed with him.

Illuminated by the ambulance's perimeter lights, Frankie became the target for the next shot. It came while the report of the first still echoed off the rolling hills.

Her military training took over. Frankie no longer stood in the same place. In fact, she no longer stood at all. Flinging herself to the ground almost in tandem with Marc's fall, she let go of the equipment box, rolling into a patch of overgrown weeds at the road's verge.

"Marc," she whispered. "Marc?"

He lay without moving. Maybe dead. Maybe just unconscious. But bleeding. A dark stain spread, soaking the area beneath him.

Frankie fumbled the Airweight out of its holster. She tried to still her breathing, both blessing the wind stirring the weeds around her—and therefore covering her careful movements—and cursing it for hiding any sounds the shooter may have made.

There! The crunch as a dry stick broke over by the car. A small ping of metal on metal, perhaps the gunman using the car for a shooting platform.

She risked a look, raising her head bare inches and spreading weed stalks apart. Yes. She saw him. The hulking form a man, almost hidden in the shadows, and he was pointing a pistol at Marc. Going for a kill shot in case the first hadn't done the trick.

Shit.

He was too far away for the Airweight to be effective. And she couldn't waste a single one of the pistol's five rounds.

Frankie's fingers closed on a clod of dirt. Now. While the guy was busy getting a bead on Marc.

She gave the clod a toss. Threw it well, the dirt flying apart as it hit the car, startling enough to spoil the man's aim. The shot went off, landing halfway between Marc and her. Or where she had been when she threw it.

Taking advantage of the shooter's momentary distraction, she rolled again, farther into the ditch. The small embankment gave her some protection. Not enough. And he heard the rustling of the weeds. A bullet passed an inch overhead, digging into the side of the ambulance with a metallic smack.

The passenger door of the bus gaped open. From where she lay, Frankie heard words coming over the radio. Ashley's voice, repeating a message twice as Frankie listened.

"Number six, the report of an accident on Highway 27 is a false alarm. Repeat, a false alarm. Return to station immediately. Acknowledge, number six. Please acknowledge."

She'd just love to do as Ashley begged and acknowledge the message—if only she could. Or better yet, get to the radio and call for assistance. It was odd, though. Something must've warned the guys at the station the situation was a set-up. Why couldn't they have reached the conclusion five minutes earlier? That's what she wanted to know.

As if the message were on an automatic loop, Ashley repeated the litany again. But that wasn't all Frankie heard.

She choked on a breath. Her brain felt as though it had frozen in a leap of fear.

Marc had just moaned. Softly, almost inaudibly, but a moan nonetheless. And created a small stirring as he tried to move.

Oh, God, Marc. Lie still. Don't give the gunman a reason to shoot you again.

She tried to will him into heeding her unspoken message. She knew he was probably in shock and bleeding badly. How long before he bled out?

Meanwhile, the shooter had her pinned down in a freaking ditch, and he held all the cards. What she wouldn't give for one of Grandpa's 1911 Colt .45s with a full magazine right now, instead of this puny five-shot .38.

Stalemate. Something had to give.

"Frankie McGill."

The harsh whisper blew eerily toward her, backed up by the noise of tree limbs brushing against the cold metal of the old car. The car and the tree were a distraction, one her brain had to separate from the job at hand.

Involuntarily, Frankie tried to burrow farther into the earth.

Ignore all things extraneous. Concentrate on the voice. On the man.

"She found out it was you."

He'd moved closer—and she hadn't heard him.

"Jeez," he said in his hoarse stage voice, "was she ever pissed when Zantos came around asking questions!"

Her? Her who? What she does he mean? What is he talking about?

And now he forgot to whisper.

"She's pissed at me, too," he admitted ruefully, "for not finding the disc. Not even after I took care of Howie St. James. I told her it was de-stroyed in the explosion, but I guess I lied. I kind of thought so when I saw the DVD you found."

The hairs on the back of Frankie's neck raised. Unbelievably, she knew that voice. But why? Why would he—

Frankie risked a peek over the top of the embankment. His shadow had changed from ethereal to solid form, an entity creeping toward her with a pistol in his hand.

"You might as well come out, Frankie. What do you say? A war hero like you, with medals and all? Don't want people to find your body hiding in a ditch, do you?" His chuckle struck her as oily, maybe a bit hysterical. "Makes a damn big difference, doesn't it? No machine gun here to blast me away. Oops. No weapon at all. Guess you won't be earning any more medals."

Hah! Did he have a surprise coming, or what?

But she was surprised, too. Why hadn't she guessed it was him? He was a big guy. Big feet wore hiking boots most of the time. Maggie put him on the list of guys panting after Denise, too. Not the main list. Even worse, on the also-ran list. What a fool she was.

Darryl Holland chuckled again. "Of course, by the time we're through here, you won't have a chest to pin a medal on. I'll make sure."

Bastard.

"She oughta be pleased then," he added.

She who? Frankie barely kept the words in her

mouth. He was almost close enough for the Airweight to be effective. And then it was a matter of beating him to the draw like they were two gunslingers dueling in front of the saloon.

Marc stirred, moaning like an extension of the wind blowing around him. Darryl glanced at him and shrugged. Frankie eyed the glisten of fresh blood.

When she looked up again, Darryl stood right in front of her. One more step and the weeds would no longer provide any cover. It was now or never.

An icy flood embalmed her. Now or never.

She raised the Airweight, poked the short barrel through a break in the weeds.

But as quietly as she moved, Darryl heard her. He looked down, spied her crouched form, and smiled. His Colt lifted. Orange flame spat from its muzzle. Two sharp reports split the night and echoed over the hills.

The single shot from Frankie's Airweight sounded like a cap gun in comparison.

CHAPTER 25

Darryl screamed like a girl as Frankie's shot struck home. A piercing cry that stabbed through the dark, causing small animals to seek cover. Dark forms Frankie assumed were deer bounced away over the hill.

After what seemed an age, he clamped down on the yelling.

Too late. His noise roused Marc, who stirred and opened his eyes. "Frankie," he croaked. "Need help."

Frankie couldn't afford to look at Marc. Didn't dare. Because just as soon as Darryl figured out all she'd done was shoot the pistol out of his hand, and that although it hurt and he was bleeding, he wasn't actually crippled, she figured he'd try to jump her.

"One of those medals you mentioned?" she said to him, more of a reminder she was the one in control than anything else. "One of them is for sharpshooting. I don't miss what I aim at—ever. I could just as well have put that bullet between your eyes. Which is where I'll put the next one if you provoke me. Step back, lie down on the ground, and link your hands behind your head."

He cradled his wounded hand in the other and glared into the weeds where she lay. "You won't shoot me, Frankie."

"I just did. And believe me, I won't have any problem doing it again. Now get on the ground." Her voice rose to a shout. To tell the truth, Frankie was trying hard to damp down the urge to pull the trigger one more time, cap him good, just to make sure he had no fight left. The only safe enemy is a dead one. It was a creed she'd learned the hard way along a dry road leading to a mountain village in Afghanistan.

Darryl shuffled backward in incremental millimeters, body tense, face black with anger, barely leaving room enough for her to scramble from the ditch without putting herself in his reach.

Gaze locked on him, she shuffled closer to Marc whose face was screwed into a grimace of pain.

Darryl watched her every bit as carefully as she watched him. His head lifted, cocked toward Hawkesford in a listening attitude. Yeah. She heard it too. A siren—maybe two sirens—blaring away, becoming louder every second. Gabe, riding to the rescue. She'd bet on it.

She'd also bet on Darryl making one last try for her.

"Why'd you kill Denise?" She hoped to distract him, to delay the inevitable. "Why Howie? Why come after me?"

Hurry, Gabe. Please hurry.

He ignored her order to lie down. Not much of a surprise. What did she need to do, shoot him again? Maybe in the leg this time?

Frankie gestured sharply. Slowly, glaring like a madman, he put his hands behind his head and sank to his knees. Not quite good enough, but better than nothing. She sure as hell couldn't physically take him down.

Good shooting from her little pop gun was all she had. Surreptitiously, she kicked the Colt he'd dropped into the ditch.

Breath, angry as a bull snorting, came from his nose in deep, harsh puffs.

"Well?" she urged.

"Money, of course," he said. "Damn good pay-off. And after that bitch swatted me down like a fly, it was a real pleasure."

Frankie assumed he was talking about Denise. Maggie had said...something. Frankie didn't quite remember what.

"Who paid you?"

"Why should I tell you? What's in it for me? Unless you let me go afterward." His fingers twitched, dripping a splatter of blood.

Trying to shake off the numbness, she figured, getting ready to make his move.

"Not hardly, Bozo." She didn't see any point in kidding him along.

"Then I guess you don't want to know." His body tensed as he prepared to jump her. She knew the signs.

"Why Howie, then? I can't imagine he ever hurt you any." She skipped another foot closer to Marc, out of Darryl's reach.

What was taking Gabe so long? Why couldn't she see the lights of his SUV barreling over the hill yet? Sweat trickled into her hairline. The old scar of her head injury itched like it hadn't done in months.

Darryl shrugged, rocking on his knees as

though to gain momentum. "What can I say? He was stupid. He got in her way, and she's got a hell of a temper. Then you moved into the duplex and complicated matters. She didn't like that." He grinned. "Me, either. Her and me, we work well together."

"Got in whose way, Darryl? He got in whose way?"

At last, at last, Frankie spied the whirl of lights atop Gabe's SUV, cresting the hill. The siren's noise racketed up a notch as the car broke over. A minute—sixty seconds max—and Gabe would be here. Then she could relax.

Trouble was, Darryl had been watching for the police, too. Waiting for them. In the millisecond of her distraction, he lunged forward, slashing with the forearm of his injured hand like a martial arts expert, knocking the Airweight downward. A haymaker from his uninjured fist slammed into her shoulder.

Helplessly, she stumbled and almost fell even as he regained his feet.

Frankie's pistol hung uselessly in numbed fingers. Her stumble averted his punch from delivering a solid hit, but her reflexes were slowed, too. Then, as she lurched aside, she slipped in

Marc's blood. Darryl's second blow glanced off the side of her head, and she dropped like a rock. Blood gushed. A size twelve foot hammered her hip like the thud of a pile driver.

Darryl grabbed for her Airweight, but she managed to turn, protecting the pistol with her body. He kicked her in the stomach instead.

She lay there, forcing away the agony until she could breathe again in the precious seconds he fumbled in the weeds trying to find his pistol. He came up with it in his uninjured hand, waving it in triumph and grinning down at her.

"Time to finish the job," he said. As if he were some kind of outlaw in a movie, he towered over her, drawing a careful bead on her head. The pistol barrel wavered as he concentrated. Excitement lit up his face.

Frankie had warned him. A couple times, in fact. Not her fault if some people never learned.

Darryl fired as Frankie rolled. The shot went wide, giving her just enough time to bring up the Airweight. And she, as promised, didn't miss. Or not entirely. The bullet slammed into his shoulder.

Dammit. She'd been aiming at his heart.

He didn't drop the pistol or fall, but his eyes widened like he couldn't believe what had just happened.

The rise and fall of Gabe's siren became louder, then very loud.

Backing away, Darryl gave Frankie a last hate-filled glare. Finally, he turned and took off in a shambling run. He disappeared behind the decoy car, his tread heavy as he charged through a narrow strip of wheat stubble between him and the trees.

Then, at last, Gabe arrived with the cavalry.

He pulled up behind the ambulance, tires skidding on the gravel verge. Rudy Swallowtail drew in after him, his cruiser's bumper almost touching the SUV's. Frankie's Airweight dropped to the ground as she turned toward Marc.

"Frankie," Gabe yelled as he got out of the SUV. He crossed the ditch toward her like a broad jumper, Rudy taking it only a little slower. The men skidded to a stop beside her.

Gabe knelt, gripping her shoulder. "Frankie, you all right?"

"I'm okay." It must've been obvious from the way she winced away that she wasn't. A bright flow of blood ran down the side of her face. Damn Darryl and his boxer's fists and his crappy gold nugget ring. Another scar to add to her collection.

Service weapon in hand, Gabe scanned the area before coming back to shake his head over Marc. "Marc?"

Frankie didn't think it was worth her while making the effort to stand and then having to bend down to check Marc. Her hip felt like it was on fire and she wasn't even sure the leg would support her.

Taking the easy way, she crawled to her partner, pulling the dropped medical box with her. Once at his side, she rose to her knees. "Darryl is your killer." Frankie found her voice at last. "He shot Marc—and Denise and Howie. He confessed to me. Bragged, actually."

"Darryl? Darryl Holland?" Gabe sank down beside her, his fingers seeking out Marc's pulse as Frankie opened the box and drew on latex gloves. "Darryl Holland, the volunteer fireman, is our shooter?"

"Yes." She tore open Marc's shirt. "Go after him, you and Rudy. He ran off that way." A vague wave indicated direction.

"Not until you get in the car," Gabe said. "Your safety comes first."

"Marc comes first," she corrected, yanking a cuff from the med-kit and starting on Marc's vitals. "You just get Darryl. But don't shoot him dead until you make him talk. He's not the brains behind these murders."

"He isn't?" Gabe stared at her. "Then who is?"

"A woman."

Gabe's impatience showed in his exasperated question. "A woman? What makes you think so?"

Neither expected Marc's entry into the discussion. "'Cuz he told Frankie after she shot him," he rasped before his voice died away.

Maybe he wasn't hurt as badly as Frankie first thought if he'd been awake enough to know what she'd done—and tell about it.

Pulling a pack with an IV line out of the box, she started a saline drip, ignoring her patient's wince as the needle went in. Not, perhaps, her smoothest work, poor guy.

Marc's remark brought a frown to Gabe's face. "Frankie shot him?"

"War hero," Rudy said as if it were the most commonplace thing in the world.

In the distance, a car roared awake, its Cherry Bomb glass pack muffler making them all jump.

"That's Darryl's car." She'd know it anywhere after hearing the old Chevy's rat-trap motor and exhaust system in the parking lot these last couple weeks. Worried and angry, Frankie turned toward the sound. "He's escaping."

"We'll get him." Gabe touched his shoulder mic.

Marc pushed Frankie and her stethoscope aside, struggling onto his elbow. "No," he told Gabe. "Darryl has a scanner in his car. He'll hear everything you tell dispatch."

Gabe gave him a long look. "Okay, we'll do it this way." He whipped out his phone, punched in some numbers, and held it to his ear. Connection made, he called for aid from the state police. A second call warned the Washington people across the state border to be on the lookout.

Wincing, his face nearly as white as Banner's fur, Marc collapsed again, finally allowing Frankie to get to work.

She put a sterile pad over his wound and turned him enough to see if the bullet had exited. It had, having gone through the soft part of his side. Another pad went over the larger exit wound, along with layers of gauze to hold it in place. With the IV in place and fentanyl administered, Marc's blood pressure stabilized.

"Feeling any better?" she asked him.

Eyelids drooping, Marc's face relaxed. "These

drugs ain't too shabby, Frankie," he muttered. "You oughta try some."

She laughed. "Pass. I've already had more than my fair share." If he only knew.

Lew and the volunteer on-call showed up just as Frankie finished prepping Marc for transport. Lew, being Lew, had plenty to say about rescuing the rescuers. Frankie knew him pretty well by now and didn't quite buy into the off-hand dress-down. The acerbic part of his speech where he yakked about taking unnecessary chances was belied by the almost-tender way he wiped blood from Frankie's cheek and pressed a butterfly bandage over the cut. He finished with a lecture on dripping body fluids all over a patient—but he smiled as he said it.

A little woozy, her hip and stomach both aching desperately, Frankie tuned Lew out and concentrated on her own misery. She was glad to collapse on the sidelines and leave the volunteer to care for Marc. The minute she sat down, the shakes started—belly deep, adrenaline coursing through her veins like pure grain alcohol.

She put her hands under her thighs to hold them still.

Gabe, thank God, wasn't around to hear Lew

chewing her butt because the moment he saw Frankie and Marc into the paramedic's capable hands, he climbed in his SUV and hurried off in pursuit of Darryl. From the look on his face, she wouldn't want to be in Darryl's shoes when Gabe found him.

Wounded, his identity finally known, she couldn't imagine Darryl escaping clean. Not with a cop as determined as Gabe on his trail.

Even so, this thing wasn't over yet. Not by a long shot. She knew it like she knew her own name.

Rudy, bless him, elected to stay with the extra ambulance until it could be retrieved from the side of the road. All EMS needed was to have someone raid an unguarded ambulance for drugs. All their ducks were in a row, and thank God, events were out of her hands.

Frankie sat in the passenger seat as Lew sped, top lights flashing, toward Coeur d'Alene. The truck motor droned, and the background noise faded as Frankie's mind drifted.

She. A mysterious she with a bad temper. That's what Darryl said. Who was the woman who'd hired him and turned him loose to murder at will? The puzzle was enough to give Frankie a headache. Or... wait. She already had one of those from Darryl's blow to her head.

When the headlights of an oncoming car blared into her eyes, Frankie's vision blacked out. So did everything else, until she woke up to find Lew and a hospital orderly unloading her from a gurney onto a bed. Crap!

***

Morning, after a short follow-up by a brusque on-call physician, found Frankie released into Jesselyn's tender care.

Jesselyn strode into the lobby like a plump elf, her soft strawberry blonde hair flying every which way. She stopped, did an exaggerated double take. "Holy crap, girl, you look like hell!"

"Thank you." Sourly, Frankie acknowledged the hit. "You mean, I look exactly how I feel?"

Jesselyn, hands on hips, studied her, not without sympathy. "Like you've been whupped with an ugly stick and, believe me, I'm being kind."

Frankie's wry smile indicated she knew what Jesselyn meant. The mirror in her hospital room had been all too revealing. A black eye with a row of bright blue stitches above the arch of her eyebrow. Check. Cheekbone swollen and with a purple tinge. Check. And that was the easy stuff.

What Jesselyn didn't see was the deep bone bruise on her hip, resulting in a limp on her "good" side. The only reason the doc turned her loose this morning was because an ultrasound determined her spleen wasn't ruptured after all. Double check.

An encounter with Darryl's size twelves was pretty much like being on the wrong end of a big ugly stick.

"Do you need a wheelchair? I'll get you one," Jesselyn offered after further study of Frankie's face.

"No, thanks." Grunting with effort, Frankie pushed herself out of the chair, where she'd been waiting for her ride, and rose to her feet. Holy crap! "I'm good as long as you're not parked at the far end of the parking lot."

And if she wasn't all that good, she'd act the part until she convinced herself.

"No problem. I'm right out front." Jesselyn positioned herself, so Frankie could hang onto her if necessary.

Frankie, determined not to hang on anybody, stumbled along leading the way through the revolving doors to Jesselyn's Liberty. She even managed to hoist herself in. Small blessing. At least her friend didn't drive a subcompact or a sports car requiring one to fold in half.

"Is there any news about Darryl?" she asked once they were underway. Having had to wait until the pain in her hip ebbed, she was still a bit breathless.

Jesselyn glanced over at her and flipped on the radio. A local news station was broadcasting, a woman's deep voice murmuring in the background. "Let's give a listen. Last I heard was the same old stuff. I can't believe this guy found a place to disappear so fast—or one so well hidden the cops can't find him. Scuttlebutt going around says every law enforcement officer in the county is on this one."

"Whole state, more likely. And Washington and Montana besides."

"I didn't know Darryl more than to say hi to him. He always seemed like a nonentity to me."

"I hate to admit it, but to me, too. A rough-edged nonentity. I think the whole department thought so."

Flicking her turn signal, Jesselyn whipped around a slow-moving car from Vermont. "And now, apparently, the cops are looking in all the wrong places."

"I'll bet he's with the person who hired him," Frankie said, earning herself a long stare. "Watch it," she urged, beginning to wonder if Jesselyn was about run off the road.

Inches away from the ditch, Jess steered back into her lane. "Somebody hired him? Really? You mean this isn't a grudge killing?"

Me and my big mouth, Frankie thought. The police are probably keeping the killer for hire aspect of the investigation under wraps. Well, too late to worry now.

"Doubtful. I'm pretty sure this situation is more complicated—and serious—than a simple grudge."

Jesselyn, to the detriment of her driving, was staring at her again. "I hope that means my brother is off the hook. Does it?"

"Umm...probably."

"And Matt?" This time Jess managed to keep the car on the road.

"I doubt the police are looking for anyone but Darryl at this point." He'd been definite about his boss being a woman, too, so unless either Russ or Matt could work a cross-dressing disguise better than she imagined, they were in the clear.

Jesselyn's wide grin equaled the sunny day in its brilliance. "Wow! This is great. Do you mind if I call Russ and Matt with the good news? They'll be so relieved."

What could it hurt? According to the news media, everyone knew Darryl was the subject of an all-out manhunt. Anyone involved in the search for Denise and Howie's murderer would figure it out anyway.

Frankie gestured toward the radio where an announcer was giving an update on the latest crime statistics. "Might as well. Doesn't seem to be any big secret."

She closed her eyes as Jesselyn multi-tasked with her phone calls and driving—causing some hairy moments.

No. No secret about Darryl's guilt. But what about the woman who'd hired him?

CHAPTER 26

Dreams of fire and bombs awakened Frankie. Gasping for air as though an imaginary IED had sucked all the breath from her lungs, she flung herself to the side of the bed, almost tossing Shine, who'd been sleeping beside her, over the edge.

Instead of protesting this rough treatment, the bichon scrambled to her feet, eyes glowing in the moonlight purling through an uncovered window. But then Frankie noticed Shine wasn't looking at her. The dog had her gaze fixed on the door.

Banner's gaze, too. His lips coiled into a silent snarl. On his feet beside the bed, his plumy tail, normally spun in a tight curl over his back, hung halfway down his hocks. Frankie, fighting the dream's spell, put her hand on his head, feeling a deep vibration rumble through him.

"What?" she asked, the question soundless. But she knew what. Danger.

Swinging her feet onto a rag rug still warm from where the Samoyed had been sleeping, she came slowly to her feet, hoping to ease the old floor's natural creak. From the hall outside her room came a whisper of incremental movement.

Head cocked toward the sound, she heard a small snick as someone opened the door to the other bedroom then left without closing it again. Ditto the bathroom, the linen closet, the attic stairs. Until her own was the only door left.

Not Gabe. Definitely not Gabe.

Old-fashioned fear stopped her for a moment. The bogeyman is coming to get me. Adrenaline pumped. Tension took fear's place.

"Sit," she breathed, waved Banner down, and flipped the blankets over Shine, silencing the small dog who stood rigid on the bed, a growl or a bark building in her throat.

Damn Rudy for confiscating her .38 after the shooting last night. And damn her for giving in to her aches and pains today and neglecting to choose another from her grandpa's stash in the garage. But she wasn't entirely unprepared. This had been her room as a teenager, and she'd had the best batting average of any girl on the slow-pitch team. Her favorite aluminum bat stood propped against the nightstand, just as it had for years.

Frankie picked it up and inched into a crouched stance on the far side of the dresser—the best she could do in the way of shelter—along the same wall as the door.

Stay. Her hand motion kept Banner still, out of the bat's likely reach.

Seconds ticked past. Five…ten.

The door inched open. Now she heard breathing—quick, harsh panting.

Over on the bed, Shine thrashed, fighting the blanket holding her down.

The man—and Frankie clearly saw it was a man—crept into the room. He held a gun in front of him, and it rose as he zeroed in on Shine's movement on the bed.

Frankie cocked the bat, ready to swing.

One step more. C'mon, you sonofabitch.

But Banner couldn't stand the wait. He broke 'stay,' bounding forward, his bark, deep and angry, echoing through the silent house. The man's gun hand swung toward the dog, sighting in on Banner as he leaped at the intruder.

No time for Frankie to wait. Her bat arced around with every one of her one hundred and ten pounds behind it.

The first hit broke his arm in at least two places with an audible crack. The pistol dropped from his hand and skittered away, discharging as it hit the floor, the bullet going God knows where.

Frankie's follow through strike slammed into the man's shoulder. He screamed—a high-pitched noise silenced by her third hit, this one, with only marginally less force, aimed at his head.

He crumpled to the floor like a sack of old clothes and lay unmoving in a pool of moonlight.

Darryl. No surprise there.

Banner jumped on top of the body, stuck his nose in Darryl's ear, and sniffed, then sneezed as though disgusted by the odor. Darryl remained dead to the world.

Or maybe just dead.

Which was fine with Frankie. Right this moment she didn't care if she'd killed him. All she felt was relief—and pain where she'd tweaked her bruised hip. Pain she owed to him.

Shaking in the aftermath, she scrambled under

the rocking chair where the pistol had landed and picked it up. Shine burrowed her way free of the blankets at last and barked peremptorily. Frankie collapsed onto the bed beside her.

"We got him," she said.

But the explanation didn't satisfy Shine. The bichon jumped down and ran past her, past Banner, past Darryl, and out into the hall to the top of the stairs. Bouncing on all fours, she set up such a caterwauling the walls seemed to shrink.

"What the hell?"

Frankie limped after the little dog. Banner, distracted from examining the unmoving Darryl, caught Shine's distress, and rushed to join her, growling low in his throat.

"Hey, guys, ease up. What is the matter with—" Her question cut off.

She stopped at the top of the stairs. From this vantage point, she had a line of sight all the way outside and across the porch. The front door hung wide open, swaying a little as though someone had just passed through. Even from inside the house, she smelled what the dogs already had scented—a strong odor of gasoline.

Her heart clenched.

Furtive movement stirred around the lilac

bushes bracketing the porch steps.

Darryl hadn't come alone. Someone else lurked in the shrubbery. Someone equally as dangerous as he. The dogs knew.

Fear struck Frankie. Without pausing to think, she scooped the bichon up under her arm, called to Banner, and dashed down the stairs as though she not only had two full feet but as though she was graceful as a dancer and as fast and sure as a high-wire gymnast.

Frankie and the dogs fled outside just as an explosive thump fractured the night. Flames shot from under the porch steps the exact moment they cleared the bottom riser. Banner, thrown by the concussion, yelped and rolled. Frankie lost her footing and fell, still holding Shine.

Thirty yards down the street, she spotted the figure of a person racing away. A person fleet of foot and inches smaller than Darryl who lay unconscious upstairs. Almost certainly his mysterious boss. A woman. But who?

"Banner."

The dog looked at her.

"Get 'er."

She pointed at the person, even now disappearing into the night. And Banner, although

Frankie wasn't at all certain what he'd do with the woman if he caught up with her, bounded forward, hot on the trail. Shine struggled for release from Frankie's arms. Gaining her freedom, the bichon dashed after the bigger dog, barking her head off.

Next door, a porch light came on, and a man stepped outside.

Oh, Lord. What should she do? Save her house or follow the dogs?

Aware of the fire already igniting the rough old porch boards, Frankie ran for the garden hose. Attached to the spigot, the garden hose lay in a neat, tight coil. She flipped on the tap and, dragging the hose, began spraying down the porch as the flames caught hold.

"Call the police," she hollered at the neighbor, choking on a puff of accelerant-laden smoke. "Call the fire department."

He ran over to lend a hand. "On their way."

It seemed forever before she heard approaching sirens. Even as she fought to save her house, her legacy, uppermost on her mind were the dogs.

"Please, please," she chanted, unable to voice the rest of it—the part about not letting them be hurt. Not be killed. "Please."

***

Karl Mager was first on the scene, driving his pickup. He took the hose from Frankie and told her to get out of the way.

"Good Lord, girl, you don't have any shoes on. You can't fight a fire in bare feet."

Frankie couldn't think of how ugly her amputation was, or that people were going to see the stump. That Karl was seeing it now didn't make any difference. The dogs—they were what mattered. And her house. It mattered, too. Gladly, she released the garden hose into Karl's capable hands even as the pumper truck roared up and three men and a woman, garbed in their breakouts, jumped down and set to tearing away the front steps and the parts of the porch on fire.

The neighbor was there, too, staring into the flames. With the fire in good hands, Frankie ran over to him.

"Did you see her?" She gripped old Mr. Furnough's arm tightly enough to leave a bruise. "Did you see my dogs?"

He splayed his fingers as if they were going numb under her pressure. "Saw somebody running away. Saw your big white dog. Only the one."

Shine was little. Maybe he just hadn't noticed her, what with everything else going on.

"Which way did they go?"

Mr. Furnough wrenched his arm free, shook it out, and pointed. "That way. Toward the lake road. Looked like the dog was about to catch up."

Without another word, Frankie tore off down the road, running. With her pickup blocked in by the fire truck and Karl's rig, it was on foot or nothing. And she was damned if she'd leave the dogs to the woman. What if she had a gun?

What if she…

It'd been a mistake to drop Darryl's pistol at the faucet when she turned on the water. Another mistake not to go back for it.

Well, it couldn't be helped now. She had to catch up before the woman got away. Hell, she'd use rocks for weapons if that's what it took.

Panting, she raced down the middle of the road, oblivious to the stones rolling beneath her feet.

Headlights shone on the road from behind Frankie, throwing her shadow out in front. A car horn beeped.

Beeped again. Frankie pretended not to hear. About a block ahead, the sound of dogs barking shattered any peace the night might have held. She knew Banner's gruff bark like she knew her own voice. Shine's, in keeping with her small dog status, rose over the Samoyed's, higher and sharper. Blended together as they were, Frankie was certain they had their quarry treed—so to speak.

The horn blared again. Huffing and puffing like an old granny, Frankie slowed to a jog and moved to the side of the road. The rig pulled up beside her.

"What the hell do you think you're doing?" the driver yelled. Gabe.

Irritated? Oh, yeah. Carefully, she avoided looking at him.

"I'm playing dogcatcher. Banner and Shine are chasing the woman who started the fire."

"Playing? Jesus, woman, get in the car."

"No time." She spoke between breaths. "They're on the next street over. I'll cut across yards. Don't want her getting away." Frankie felt every single one of her aches from last night—did she ever!—but she kept going. Gabe wasn't going to stop her from finally finishing this.

Speeding up, he passed her, then turned the SUV, so it blocked the road.

No avoiding him now.

"Get in the goddam car," he said.

Can a man whisper, yet shout at the same time? Apparently.

Frankie got in the car.

Tires churned as he goosed the accelerator. Gabe stuck his head out the window, following the dogs by sound. They weren't hard to track. Shine had a good set of lungs on her and so, Frankie discovered, did Banner when he got aroused. A deep, satisfying strong tone.

The SUV swept around the next corner.

Gabe stomped hard on the brakes, jerking Frankie forward. Only his out-flung arm stopped her collision with the windshield. She hardly noticed because there, caught in the beam of the SUV's headlights, a woman stood pressed against the side of a sleek black car, trying to get the door open.

Banner led the charge against her, although as far as Frankie could tell, he never set tooth on the woman. Every time she reached for the handle, he pounced, so she never quite succeeded in sliding inside. The woman shrieked curses at him, which only intensified the Samoyed's efforts.

Shine did her part by keeping the woman

flustered, jumping, barking, and running circles around the woman's feet. The woman kicked repeatedly at the bichon, Shine mostly avoiding the size-eight ballet flats. Only once did one catch her under the belly, sending her tumbling.

Undeterred, the bichon bounced up and went back to work.

Ballet flats, hah. Call them sneaking-around shoes. Home-invasion shoes. Quite different from stilettos, for sure. Frankie almost laughed at the spectacle. Almost.

Porch lights flipped on along the street. Front doors opened a crack, then widened, and heads appeared. A couple men started down their walk. One woman, braver, or more foolhardy than the rest, came out carrying a shotgun in the crook of her arm. It appeared she knew quite well how to use it.

Frankie squinted as the woman stood under a yard light. Hah! She knew how to shoot, all right. It was old Mrs. Breeden, famous for once shooting a burglar breaking into the family grocery store. Killed him and never expressed a word of regret.

Gabe turned his spotlight onto Banner's prisoner. He got out.

"Stay here," he ordered Frankie.

Stay here? Was he crazy?

Before he finished speaking Frankie was ahead of him, racing toward the dogs and Alexis Barwick. She'd seen what Gabe either hadn't or had chosen to ignore. The attorney somehow had managed to evade Banner long enough to reach through her car's open window and retrieve an automatic pistol.

For some reason, she didn't shoot. Maybe because of the spectators gawking at her and the dogs. Maybe the safety was on, and she forgot how to release it.

But she did bring the pistol barrel down on Banner, missing his skull and striking his withers. Banner howled his fear and pain, but he kept coming.

And so did Frankie.

The last six feet she went completely airborne. A flying tackle brought her close enough to grab the taller woman around the waist.

The wind went out of Alexis Barwick as Frankie dragged her to the ground. Frankie landed on top, taking great pleasure in wallowing the attorney and her designer suit into the grit of the road. Skirt above her thighs, Barwick beat at Frankie's back with the pistol.

Frankie grunted under the blows, but the tackle served to blunt some of the larger woman's force. The blows lacked momentum.

Barwick shrieked her rage, which is when Frankie slammed a righteous fist into the side of her face.

Damn! That was fun. She did it again.

The woman folded like a hand of throwaway cards. The pistol sagged in her hand before someone—Gabe—snatched it away.

Frankie, a trickle of blood running into her left eye where the cut had been reopened, looked up to find him standing over them, his own weapon drawn, a slight smile on his face.

"Bet that felt good," he said softly, so she was the only one to hear. "I got this. You can let go now."

Frankie grinned. "It did feel good."

But then Gabe had to help Frankie up, the fury running through her so hot and wild she was trembling with it as she stepped away.

Hawkesfordians gawked like spectators watching gladiators in an old Roman arena. Mrs. Breeden remained by the gate into her yard, head cocked like an aged eagle, her shotgun ready for action.

Holstering his weapon, Gabe stilled Shine

with a quiet word. Frankie's soft whistle brought Banner, unhurt after all, prancing to her, and of course, the bichon followed along. Frankie knelt, put her arms around the Samoyed's neck, and hugged him. "Good brave boy," she whispered and gathered Shine into the circle. "Good girl."

Alexis Barwick lunged to her feet, awkward and cursing a blue streak. Reaching behind her, she fumbled with the Mercedes' door as if she thought Gabe would let her flee.

Not so. "You stay where you are." Gabe held the car door closed. "Turn around and put your hands on the fender."

Ms. Barwick turned around all right, but it was into Gabe's face. "I won't. This is harassment. I'll have those damn vicious dogs killed. I'll have this woman jailed. I'll have your badge. You have no right—"

Gabe interrupted the tirade, his voice as soothing as cocoa. "Ms. Barwick, you are under arrest for the murders of Howie St. James and Denise Rider. Also for the attempted murder of Marc Schillinger and Frankie McGill, as well as a double count of arson. I wouldn't be surprised if a few more charges come to light before this night is over."

The woman clawed at his hand where it pressed against the door.

He launched into the Miranda rights spiel. "You have the right to remain silent. If—"

"I never touched any of those people," Alexis screamed as Gabe caught one diamond-laden hand an instant before it struck him. With a smooth, practiced motion, he wrenched her arms back and clipped plastic cuffs around her wrists.

"That wasn't me. You know it wasn't," Ms. Barwick yelled, twisting and fighting the cuffs like a demented thing. "This is all a lie. It was Darryl Holland. He did it. He killed those people. You're hurting me. This is police brutality. You're nothing but a small town errand boy. I own the judges in this state. You'll never convict me, understand? Never. Nobody will believe you, do you hear me?"

Frankie rather thought everyone heard her as she pretty much drowned out Gabe's reading of her rights. No big deal. She was quite sure Ms. Barwick knew the statement by heart anyway.

And Ms. Barwick was badly mistaken if she really thought she'd get out of this free as the wind. Gabe was a good policeman. He'd have evidence tying up all the loose ends, whatever they might be.

And Frankie's own eye witness account would count for something.

Gabe practically had to carry Ms. Barwick to his SUV. Practically had to lift her into the back seat. The woman never ceased her clamor the whole time.

He smiled at Frankie, who still squatted beside her dogs. "Got 'er."

"Sure do."

"Can you walk home from here?"

She glanced around, finally becoming aware that she was in her jammies and barefoot. And her feet damn well hurt from running over gravel she hadn't felt in the jazzed adrenaline rush of rage and fear. Was that blood oozing from the stump where toes used to be? Jeez! What a trip.

Well, she was used to pain. "Sure. But you'd better stop by the house anyway."

"No need. Karl will have the fire out by now. I don't think it got much of a start."

"I hope you're right. The thing is, the last time I saw Darryl, he was laid out unconscious on my bedroom floor. You might want to do something with him after EMS gets done treating his wounds."

"On your bedroom—Darryl's—" Gabe's jaw

dropped the least little bit. "What's wrong with him?"

Frankie couldn't help preening. "Broken arm, a little lump on the head. Nothing much."

Gabe opened the passenger door for her. "Guess you don't have to walk after all."

He was laughing as she and the dogs piled in, laughing as they started off. He hadn't quit by the time they pulled up beside the pumper truck parked in front of her—their—house.

They found one of the volunteer firemen in charge of the garden hose, dousing the charred porch while another man leaned on a shovel and watched.

Oh, yeah. And there was Karl, standing guard over a dazed-looking Darryl who lay strapped to a stretcher with Lew kneeling beside him.

"Hey, Gabe," Karl yelled, coming to meet them. "Look what I found."

CHAPTER 27

Frankie opened her eyes to find Gabe sitting on the edge of the bed. He had Shine on his lap and was rubbing Banner's back with a barefoot. The dogs basked in satisfaction under his attention.

Outside, the sun blazed a path through the sky, shone through the bedroom window, and bathed the room in morning light. And she wasn't afraid. Nervous to find Gabe so close, but not afraid. And not screaming. In fact, she enjoyed looking at him.

"How are your feet?" he asked when he saw she was awake.

Wiggling them under the covers, she found they still moved. "Guess I'll know when they hit the floor."

He smiled, his hazel eyes warm. "Guess you will."

The window, open to let the smell of smoke from the burned porch—which called for a total replacement—dissipate overnight, allowed in the cheerful singing of some kind of bird.

Frankie had never been good at distinguishing varieties of birds, but she liked this one's song.

Scooted herself up against the headboard, she made sure the sheet demurely covered her lap. Kind of wasted effort, considering she'd been running up and down the street during the night wearing these self-same pajamas. Or T-shirt and shorts. Whatever you wanted to call them. It was just that the top was a little big and showed a little more than she normally exposed.

"Got everything sewed up?" she asked Gabe brightly, adjusting the top since he didn't seem adverse to peeking.

"Enough to hold our two suspects in jail. Darryl is talking his head off, hoping to catch a break, and Ms. Barwick is still protesting her innocence."

Frankie couldn't help worrying. "Do you think her muckety-muck friends will get the charges dropped?"

"Not a chance. The evidence, along with Darryl's testimony, has her pretty well sewed up. She may find those friends prefer to disassociate themselves from her." He gave Shine another pat and set her on the floor. "And I've got a confession to make."

She stared at him, noting the tired lines around his eyes, the grim set to his mouth, the slight slump of his shoulders. He must not have been up for long—if he'd even been to bed—because his hair was still damp from the shower. He wore one of his ubiquitous T-shirts and Levis.

"What is it?" She tried a smile. "Should I 'gird my loins' so to speak?"

He looked away. "Not you, but maybe I should."

A sudden fear gnawed at her subconscious. "Marc... Is he all right? He's not—"

"No, no," he hushed her. "Marc's okay. I checked with the hospital this morning. Pending his physician's check-up, he'll probably be released this afternoon."

"Thank God." Frankie closed her eyes and went limp for a moment. "One thing off my mind. So what's your confession?"

He inhaled like a mammoth sea creature before a deep dive and, abruptly standing, headed for the door. "On the other hand, I think you'd better get dressed and meet me downstairs for coffee."

With Gabe so grim, alarm replaced any relief

Frankie previously felt. She swung her feet out from under the sheet, uncaring of their bruised and admittedly filthy condition. "All right. Give me five minutes."

The minutes edged nearer to fifteen before she found herself ready to face whatever had Gabe all hot and bothered. The warm water from her shower felt too good to cut short, and then there was her hair to dry, her makeup to put on. And Frankie really did feel she needed the makeup. Something to bolster her self-image and cover a bit of the damage done to her face.

After donning a pair of her new jeans and a bright, aqua-colored tank that went well with her dark hair and eyes, she made her way to the kitchen. Still barefoot, because every cut and bruise on her feet rose up in protest. But she was done hiding her foot. It was part of her. Deal with it.

Anyway, she didn't own a pair of shoes her feet would fit into in their present condition.

A cup of coffee already marked her place at the table, fragrant steam rising from its depths. Gabe leaned against the kitchen counter, sipping from his cup as if it needed all his concentration.

Or maybe not quite all.

"I see you can walk," he said.

"Sure. Hurts, though."

"I imagine."

What in the world was the matter with him? In every conversation, they'd ever had he'd been decisive. Upbeat. Grim, sometimes, but never so damned inconsequential.

Sitting at the table as much to take a load off her tortured feet as for any other reason, Frankie picked up her coffee and drank. A mellow roast, it tasted just as good as it smelled.

"Confession about what?" she asked as though the last quarter hour had never occurred.

Gabe seemed uncomfortable as if he didn't like where this conversation would lead. "First, you should know Ms. Barwick's involvement, in this case, came as no surprise. Not after we learned, thanks to you and Dr. Kelly, about Dr. Muncie's scheme of billing insurance companies and the federal government for services he never rendered. Denise Rider worked for the doctor for a couple years. She kept the books for his practice. Both sets of books. She also had an affair with him. When the affair ended, so did her employment. That's when she started blackmailing him."

Frankie nodded. "I thought it might be something like that."

He nodded too. "When you found the Smoke Signals disc, it helped shorten the investigation. Motive became clear. Apparently, she was cleaning him out, taking too much of his profit. Denise had bank accounts in sums that amounted to almost half of what Dr. Muncie took in with his fraudulent billing these last three years."

"Wow. Sounds like she got a bit greedy."

"Yeah." Gabe finally abandoned his post by the counter and came to sit across from her. "But that's only part of the picture."

"It is?"

"We hauled the doc in and got a confession out of him. He told us this business model was nothing new. Apparently, he's been bilking various insurance programs for years. First time he had anybody, meaning Denise, catch him at it, though. First time he had to pay anybody off. But when he said he didn't kill her, we believed him." He spun his cup around in his hands.

Frankie, having no doubts about who killed and who didn't, cocked an eyebrow. "You did? Why?"

"His ironclad alibi for the time Howie was killed, among other things. For another, he seemed genuinely concerned when we showed him the murders stemmed directly from his fraud scheme. Then, after he thought about it a while, he was terrified. He called me back for a meeting."

Frankie's eyebrow arched higher. "How endearing of him. Just an old sweetie pie, huh? I imagine this is where Ms. Barwick takes a hand, right?"

"Nice deduction." Actually, he seemed surprised. "Accurate, too. Turns out his wife had bailed him out of sticky situations with his cast-off mistresses before when one of his many affairs went wrong. He couldn't give us any details of how she accomplished the bailouts. I don't think he cared. He just knew the women stopped 'pestering' him. His word. Then he discovered a couple of them had received calls from Ms. Barwick. Threatening calls. One, a little more emotional than the others, had a midnight visitor who left her alive, but with scars."

Frankie shuddered. She knew all about midnight visitors. And scars. "Jeez. Why didn't she go after him, instead of the women?"

Gabe shrugged. "Don't know. Apparently, the lack of fidelity in their marriage wasn't of great concern to her. Reputation, prestige, those were what she cared about, according to Muncie. At least it didn't matter until Denise got warned off and perforce, broke with the doc.

"The thing is, Denise took copies of the cooked books with her. Not only that, she camped right on the doc's doorstep, her presence a reminder to him that he'd better pay up. All of which did concern Ms. Barwick. She was afraid Denise would let word leak, maybe to one of her boyfriends. And if the story got out, her husband was done, his reputation ruined, and, along with it, hers. Not to mention all that money, which left them a little short."

"How sad."

Gabe finally smiled. "Isn't it?"

"So how does Darryl enter into all this?"

Gabe flinched at her question. At last, they were getting down and dirty, to the crux of the matter. She was about to hear Gabe's confession.

"Darryl was one of Ms. Barwick's pro bono cases several years ago when he was a juvenile in Seattle."

"Pro bono? Her?" Frankie couldn't keep from showing her surprise.

"Most attorneys set aside a certain portion of their time for indigent people. Enhances their reputations. Makes them look good among their peers, especially if they intend on running for public office." He shrugged. "Anyway, she managed to keep him under juvenile court auspices instead of charged as an adult on a couple of bad assault cases. After he served his detention, she hired him to watch her husband.

"When Denise moved to Hawkesford to keep tabs on Dr. Muncie and continue her blackmail scheme, Darryl was Johnny-on-the-spot," he continued. "He got a job where he could spy on Denise and Dr. Muncie while he waited for orders from Ms. Barwick."

Frankie shuddered. "Working up their nerve for murder."

Gabe firmed his mouth. "That's right."

They were finally reaching the confession part, Frankie judged. She waited.

"It came to the point where Denise had gotten too greedy, too pushy. Ms. Barwick took a hand, and, by hand, I mean she sent Darryl after Denise with orders to get rid of her by whatever means necessary. And destroy the evidence of her husband's malfeasance."

"The Smoke Signals disc."

He nodded. "Right. And when Darryl couldn't

find the disc, everything escalated. Ms. Barwick became more strident, more desperate. And she sent her hired killer after you when you moved into the duplex right after they kidnapped and killed Denise."

"And shot Shine and Howie."

"Yes."

They fell silent. The refrigerator clicked on with a loud hum. They both jumped when Banner, Shine hard on his heels, bounded in through the flapping doggie door. The dogs lay close to Frankie, panting from a run in the yard. Probably trampling Gabe's small garden.

Frankie met Gabe's eyes. "Are we to the confession part yet?"

"Almost there." But still, he hesitated. "You may have noticed last night that Rudy was nowhere in sight."

"Now you mention it, yes." Missing Rudy hadn't been on her list, but the seeming non-sequitur must have a point.

"We found Darryl's car abandoned yesterday morning along one of the lakeshore roads. Lot of blood on the seats, but no sign of him. We got Boyd Holliday and Freak out. The hound followed the scent into the lake and lost it." Gabe grimaced. "To tell the truth, we thought maybe he got in deeper than he meant—there's a hell of a drop-off there—and couldn't get out. The dogs didn't find any sign of egress."

"But—"

"Yeah. I know. We—I—thought wrong." He jumped up and refilled their coffee cups, taking his time.

Frankie recognized a delaying tactic when she saw one. What had he done next? Whatever it was, it embarrassed him in retrospect. She could tell by the way his tanned face darkened even more.

"So," he continued, "I asked for a warrant to search Muncie's house. While we waited for a judge willing to sign it, we put a watch out for Ms. Barwick's Mercedes. Picked it up yesterday evening, finally, when she showed up outside Hawkesford. But instead of pulling her over right away, I had Rudy follow her. Sometime, between here and there, she spied the tail. Instead of making a run for it, she stopped and confronted him. You know she can be a little...um..."

"Strident? No. Scary?"

"That's one way of putting it."

Amazing herself, Frankie laughed and sipped

hot coffee. "Don't forget, I've seen her in action. So what happened?"

"She argued with him. Called him out. Made threats."

"The usual."

"Yeah, until she suddenly ran for her car and took off again. Her Mercedes left Rudy's beat-up old cruiser in a cloud of dust. He lost her. And meanwhile..." He fell silent again until Frankie felt like giving him a good shake.

"Meanwhile?" With Banner curled at her feet and Shine asking to sit on her lap, Frankie got the hunch she might need the dogs' comfort. She lifted Shine and stroked the bichon's silky ears. The unwounded one, anyway, although the other with its bullet-hole no longer seemed to bother her.

"Meanwhile, it turns out Darryl, whom Ms. Barwick picked up in the doc's boat after he waded into the lake, slipped out of the car and made his way here. Ms. Barwick joined him once she had Rudy all turned around and discombobulated. Then, while Darryl went after you—killing you, or so she believed—she set the fire to cover up the crime. And maybe take Darryl out at the same time." Gabe fell silent and stared into the depths of his cup as though reading tea leaves— or coffee grounds. What did he think he'd find in there?

"Don't tell me she admitted to all this." Frankie's eyes widened in surprise.

Gabe spun his coffee cup, swirling a splash of liquid over the side. "Lord, no. Not her, but Darryl is talking plenty. He's going down, and he knows it. He doesn't plan on going alone. See, he figured her plan called for him being the next to die."

"Wow. Makes sense, I suppose." Somehow, Frankie wasn't terribly shocked by the revelation.

At last, Gabe set the cup aside, braced his hands on the table edge, and stared at her with a hang-dog expression. "What you don't know, Frankie, is that I almost got you killed. Me."

Her mouth opened. She closed it again. "You did?"

He nodded. "I should've been prepared for the two of them working together," he said slowly. "I shouldn't've believed Darryl was out of the picture just because the dog trailed him into the lake. No body? No drowning. Most of all, I should've been keeping watch on you, alone here at the house. "

Frankie kind of thought so too. She heaved

one of those big sighs people always use in times of relieving stress. "Easier to think of that stuff in retrospect, isn't it? Maybe I should've shot him dead in the first place. Used a heavier gun. Taken better aim." She thought a moment. "I don't know what I could've done about Ms. Barwick. The way it all played out means we have proof enough to put her jail right alongside Darryl, though, right?"

Grimacing, he ran a hand through his hair. "Ever heard of juries?"

Frankie'd had enough. "Hell with it." She jumped up, wincing at the pain in her feet and almost knocking over her chair. The dogs scrambled to get out of the way. "They're both in jail, and I don't want to think about them anymore. I want to live my life, do my job, play with my dogs, and—and—"

Gabe leaped to his feet, steadying the chair before it fell. "And?" he asked when she broke off.

What she wanted to say was "get to know you better" or maybe "get laid" or something along those lines. A possibility, now the artificial way they'd been thrown together was ending. But maybe it was too soon. Or too late.

"And find a place to live," she ended.

He glanced around the kitchen, at the dogs, at her, shook his head, looking back at her with a question in his eyes. "Lots of room right here."

Did he mean... He did.

Not too late.

"That was a crappy confession." Her accusation came out soft and a little breathless.

A smile lit his whole face. "You're right. Let me try again. And I'll apologize, this time."

A LOOK AT LOST GIRL LAKE
BY C.K. CRIGGER

The day Truth Diamond and her dog, Razz, find a woman's charred hand at one the Golden West Resort's campsites, is the day her busy life spins out of control. A search for a body turns up nothing. Truth believes her resort on Lost Girl Lake is in the clear, but when the rest of the body comes to light, the situation goes from bad to worse. She receives one of those "offers you can't refuse" for the resort, her flirty young employee, Becca Keene, vanishes, and a camper is murdered. Why? That's what Truth wants to know.

Finding whoever is doing the killing should be quick and simple. Plenty of law enforcement is around. There's Pratt, the quiet and appealing undercover FBI agent; Hunter, the dishy Fish and Wildlife officer; the Sheriff's department detective and his hardworking deputy. Can't anyone find Becca before she ends up gone forever? It's beginning to look like Truth has to do everything herself, unless she becomes the next victim

.

AVAILABLE NOW ON AMAZON

ABOUT THE AUTHOR

C.K. Crigger was born and raised in North Idaho on the Coeur d'Alene Indian Reservation, and currently lives with her husband, three feisty little dogs and an uppity Persian cat in Spokane Valley, Washington.

Imbued with an abiding love of western traditions and wide-open spaces, Crigger writes of free-spirited people who break from their standard roles.

Her short story, Aldy Neal's Ghost, was a 2007 Spur finalist. Black Crossing, won the 2008 EPIC Award in the historical/western category. Letter of the Law was a 2009 Spur finalist in the audio category. The Woman Who Built a Bridge was the 2019 Spur Award winner for best western romance.